YOU COULD BE HOME BY NOW

TRACY MANASTER

TYRUS
BOOKS

For Marc Alifanz

Published by
TYRUS BOOKS
an imprint of F+W Media, Inc.
10151 Carver Road, Suite 200
Blue Ash, OH 45242. U.S.A.
www.tyrusbooks.com

ISBN 10: 1-4405-8312-9
ISBN 13: 978-1-4405-8312-4
eISBN 10: 1-4405-8313-7
eISBN 13: 978-1-4405-8313-1

Printed in the United States of America.

10 9 8 7 6 5 4 3 2 1

**Library of Congress Cataloging-in-
Publication Data**

Manaster, Tracy.
  You could be home by now / Tracy
Manaster.
    pages cm
  ISBN 978-1-4405-8312-4 (hc) -- ISBN
1-4405-8312-9 (hc) -- ISBN 978-1-4405-
8313-1 (ebook) -- ISBN 1-4405-8313-7
(ebook)

1. Married people--Fiction. 2. Grand-
parent and child--Fiction. 3. Retirement
communities--Fiction. 4. Interpersonal
conflict--Fiction. 5. Psychological fiction.
I. Title.
  PS3613.A527Y68 2014
  813'.6--dc23

2014021993

Cover design by Frank Rivera.
Cover image © Anna-Mari West/123RF.

*This book is available at quantity dis-
counts for bulk purchases.
For information, please call
1-800-289-0963.*

ACKNOWLEDGMENTS

There simply aren't thanks enough for my agent, Ayesha Pande, for her faith in this venture and in its author; I'd accomplish very little without her patience, perceptiveness, warmth, and wit. The same can be said for "Team Truck" at Tyrus Books, Ben LeRoy and Ashley Myers, for their enthusiasm, humor, and keen editorial eyes; this book wound up so much *better* than the one I thought I'd written, and so much of that is due to them.

There would've been no book at all without the extraordinary generosity of my many talented teachers: Kiana Davenport and Anne Greene at Wesleyan University, and Ethan Canin, Edward Carey, Adam Haslett, James Hynes, Marilynne Robinson, and Jennifer Vanderbes at the Iowa Writers' Workshop. Copious thanks. Prodigious thanks. I'd list more adjectives, every one of them true, but they also taught me the value of restraint.

Probably the best thing about being a writer is that you get to make writer friends. I am deeply indebted to V.V. Ganeshananthan and Robert James Hicks for their support, both literary and moral, their friendship, and for the way they put up with my intermittent bouts of whining. I'm fueled, as a writer and a social being, by the Wednesday night wisdom of The Guttery, a thriving writers' group that has lasted longer than the average American marriage (at least if Wikipedia's statistics are to be believed). This work owes a particular debt to longstanding and emeritus members David Cooke, Bruce L. Greene, Jennifer Lesh Fleck, Beth Marshea, Lara Messersmith-Glavin, A. Molotkov, Brian Reeves, Kip Silverman, Cameron McPherson Smith, Carrie-Ann Tkaczyk, and Robin Troche.

Thanks also to Sigrid Brunet, who looked at this book earlier and oftener than any friend of the author should be obliged to; Lily's voice especially owes her an *uber*debt. To Rachel Jagoda Brunette, for the constant general support and the occasional specific word. To Cristina Cavazos, who converted me (kind of) to running; I got a subplot out of it and also a really great friend. To the denizens of 40 Fountain, Ben Paradise, Emily Archibald, and Nicky Pessaroff, who have been waiting a long while. To Sophie Bird, who always *gets it*, and then helps me say it better.

To my parents, Steve and B.J. Manaster, for telling me my first stories, and to my sister, Katy Strand, whose willingness to listen encouraged the nascent storyteller in me. Thanks is far too small a word. To my in-laws, Jeff and Susie Alifanz, for their many years of cheerleading.

To my astonishing daughters, Adeline and Elodie, with absolute love. Next book, I'll try to put in the witch and the cheetah that you asked for.

And to my husband, Marc Alifanz. It sounds glib to say thanks for everything, but it's exactly what I need to do here. For your support. For your patience. Your humor. Your taking out the compost and talking me off metaphorical ledges. For your insight and your honesty. For everything. Everything.

THE HENRY QUESTION

IN THE FACE OF CALAMITY, the Colliers' first impulse was to over-spend at the bookstore. Seth and Alison were thirty-one and twenty-nine, respectively. They taught journalism (him) and history (her) at North Chettenford High. They were approaching their fourth wedding anniversary and meant to do as the grief books said: Be gentle with each other. Maintain open communication. Treat mourning as a sacred process. Put off major decisions for at least a year.

Only.

A Tupperware of coleslaw sent Alison retching from a lunch-time staff meeting. Principal Shipley—who hadn't offered a word of condolence—winked and punched Seth's shoulder. "Again?" The implication being, well done, you dog you, the grin better suited to the locker room.

That close, cabbagy smell. Seth wanted to hurl, too. One of Alison's nurses had said crushed cabbage in the bra would ease things when her milk came in. He'd left his wife's bedside to get it, driving out from the hospital in concentric circles until he found an open grocery store. He'd bought two heads. The nurse hadn't stipulated purple or green.

The lunch meeting dragged. The vat of coleslaw returned half-empty to the fridge. That night, Seth told Ali what Shipley'd said.

"Principal *Shit-ley*," was her only response. Alison, who never went for the cheap joke. She just sat there on the horrible hound-stooth couch they'd had since college. She adjusted the cushions and turned on the TV. It was Friday night. They were looking at two whole days alone together.

Alison changed the channel.

Seth went to bed and whispered Timothy, Timothy, until it no longer made sense as a word.

The front door slammed early the next morning. Ali, off on her run. Seth sat at the kitchen table with a cup of coffee. There were papers in neat stacks; Alison must've been up all night grading. AP European History. He picked up a test and thumbed to the back.

- Discuss the role of clergy in fifteenth-century Italian governance, economics, and art.
- Which Lutheran critique was most essential to the Reformation? Justify your response.
- How would the world today be different if Henry, Duke of Cornwall, had survived to maturity?

Seth scanned the essay. *Henry, Duke of Cornwall, was what Henry VIII called both his sons with Catherine of Aragon who died at birth. If they'd lived then England would be different.* Alison had underlined the word *different* three times. *How?* she wrote. *Your thesis statement must be specific.*

Alison turned away whenever guys got whacked on *The Sopranos*.

Alison turned away when guys got their *knees* bashed on *The Sopranos*.

Sixteen students had answered the Henry question. Alison had read all sixteen essays and awarded five of them full marks. She's been so strong, people said, that's one hell of a wife you've got. And they were right. Ali was strong, Ali was the one who boxed up

Timothy's things: the crib, the car seat, the Special Edition onesie they'd meant him to wear home.

Seth topped off his coffee and watched his wife stop at the end of their driveway, a finger at her wrist to take her pulse. She ran every day. What soft hints remained of Timothy were waning fast. Her key clicked in the lock. She splashed her face at the kitchen sink.

"You got a lot of grading done," he said.

"Yeah." She shrugged. "Nothing good on after midnight."

"You've got the Ambien."

"I'm okay." Her skin was damp, her bangs flat against her forehead. Her face and limbs and neck (and, he knew, breasts and all the rest of her) were freckled. I'm a leopard, she'd joked when they first got together, so you know I'm going to be wild in the sack.

"Good run?"

"Good enough." Ali rubbed her arms, their skin pinked over with cold. He'd joined her once, maybe a month ago. A blunt, clear morning, glittery with snow. Less than thirty degrees out and even so there'd been four fucking strollers. An Orbit, two Chiccos, and one of those Joovy doubles. Alison hadn't said a word.

"See anything interesting?" Seth set down his mug. They'd done more research on Timothy's Maclaren than they had on their car.

"Nada." Above the V of her T-shirt, Alison's collarbones were very prominent. Seth understood Henry VIII. The divorces, the beheadings, the faith of his boyhood in ashes. She hadn't said their son's name in weeks. The Maclaren was with the rest of his boxes in the basement quadrant they paid their landlady extra to use, separated from her tool bench and Christmas lights by a duct-tape line of demarcation. Their landlady had sent a card. She had told them that they were young, that they could always try again. Everyone seemed to think it was nursery-rhyme simple.

Alison drew an arm across her chest and leaned into the stretch. "Any coffee left?" She reached up toward the ceiling. Her shirt gapped, exposing a pale ribbon of stomach. Seth remembered the old wives' tale: Don't raise your hands above your head. It'll loop the cord and choke the baby.

"We have to leave," he said.

"Leave what?" There *was* coffee still. Alison helped herself.

"All this. Vermont. New England. Maybe even the country."

"The hemisphere. The planet. The universe." Ali gestured broadly with her mug. Coffee sloshed.

"I'm serious. If we don't leave here together, we're going to wind up leaving each other."

I'm going to wind up leaving you. It almost came out that way.

Alison was meant to say *No, no, we're in this together, I love you, Seth, everything will be fine.* What she said was, "Okay, sure. We'll leave."

It felt like the essential part of her had left already. Ali loved Chettenford. As a girl, she'd been sent to a nearby summer camp and had been bused in for the Fourth of July fireworks; she'd bought penny candies at a general store that was now a CVS. Ali'd wanted to live here and so had made it happen, selling Seth on Chettenford's cost of living, equidistance from their respective families, miles of bike paths, independent bookshops per capita, and abundant greasy spoons.

"I'm serious," Seth said.

"Then we should go." And just like that, they could. There was a lot they could do just like that. Stay up. Sleep late. Loiter in bars till last call. Jaunt off to Paris on a whim.

"I'm serious," he said again.

"It's fine, Seth. I said I'm game."

They sat side by side with laptops, touching up the resumes they hadn't glanced at in years. Alison deleted her maiden name one glowing letter at a time. Seth had misspelled *proficient* and that idiot Shipley had hired him anyhow.

How was this for a waste of miracles? They got interviews, despite an economy that skewed ever more toward crap. Seth lied. To Shipley, their colleagues, the subs. A doctor's appointment for Alison, who would need his moral support. Autopsy results. In the staff room, people stood at an unsubtle remove, as if distancing themselves from a bad smell. Counseling, Seth said and only Ross Henry—whose wife was expecting *twins*—offered a hearty "Good, good. I'm glad you're talking to someone."

Alison told him to stop. Alison said he was being awful. Fine. He wanted to be awful. He wanted somebody to actually say something. Those first few weeks, formula samples kept arriving. Seth called the customer hotlines. Take us off your goddamn list. My son is *dead*. He liked the apologetic stammering. He liked that the bald fact of it was as much a shock to the voice on the line as it was to him.

When they flew to Arizona, Ali said she would handle the excuses.

The Arizona jobs weren't teaching jobs, which was fine by him. The bigger the change, the better. The Commons sought an editor for the newly established *Commons Crier* and had a one-year contract open for a town historian. The Commons. Its *the* integral, like The Vatican or The Hague. A luxury retirement community consisting (according to its website) of more than six thousand residences, two golf courses, and three convenient villages for all your shopping, entertainment, and social needs. Everyone was hale and athletic in the photos.

The Colliers paid their own way out. The jobs were a long shot and the last-minute airfare more than they could afford, but what were they scrimping for, a college fund? A uniformed driver met them at the airport. The AC was cranked much too high. Seth shivered in his suit jacket, thinking Ali must be miserable in her thin blouse.

They turned off the highway and up a palm-lined straightaway. The golf courses were a shocking green after the long, dry drive. A red-rock arch, flanked by fountains, marked the official entrance and the car delivered them to a sprawling, hacienda-style building. Here, too, the air conditioner blasted and Seth—whose grandmother had never been without layers of mismatched sweaters—wondered how the aging residents could stand it. The receptionist directed them to wait. Alison flipped through the latest *Golf Digest*. Seth clenched and unclenched his hands so they wouldn't be icy when the time came to shake. The door opened and there stood Hoagland Lobel, president and CEO of The Commons, Inc., whose photo and greetings graced the inner flap of all the brochures. Lobel wore jeans and rolled-up shirt cuffs. He was aggressively tan. "The Colliers," he said, without prompting from the girl at the desk. "Our two-for-one recession special."

Ali rose, hand extended. "I'm afraid you'll have to pay us both, Mr. Lobel."

Lobel had the reedy laugh of a much smaller man. "Call me Hoagie. Either of you tee 'em up?"

"Mini golf only, I'm afraid," said Alison. His wife: her unfussy, vulpine prettiness, her smile that pulled slightly to the left. Most of her friends were men, most of whom had managed to navigate the awkwardness of realizing that it wasn't flirting, it was Alison being Alison, friendlier and more direct than attractive women usually were. Lobel leaned toward her. Some hybrid of defensiveness and desire twisted through Seth, and then awareness. This was the first time he'd thought of her body as her body without that undertow of Timothy.

"Mini golf." Lobel shook his head. "I never saw the point of it, myself."

"At least you can count on us not to tee off on the clock," said Seth.

"True enough." Lobel checked his watch. "Tell you what, let's start you off with the grand tour."

They rode in a golf cart, Ali and Seth in back, Lobel up front. He steered one-handed, an arm slung across the passenger seat. "Everything at The Commons is cart accessible," he explained, looking back at them over his shoulder. Seth knew that; all The Commons materials said as much. Still, he nodded. Though his hair was almost entirely gray, Lobel had the buoyant, vigorous air of a kid cutting class. He pointed at a distant fence, hewn of the same red-brown stone as the entry gate. "There's a road for cars on the other side. Runs round the whole place. Inside it's all carts. Cost of gas these days, it saves folks a bundle and their kids don't wind up worrying about car wrecks and all."

"Like Zion," said Seth.

"Zion?"

"The National Park. Up in Utah? They've closed the whole place to cars to cut down on pollution."

"The green angle. Good call."

Lobel drove them through neighborhoods of sprawling adobes ("Six years ago this was all sagebrush. Used to be a working ranch. Got the old land deed framed in my office. Had a time tracking it down. You'd get a kick out of it, Alison. Man couldn't write so they had him sign his name with an X."). They trundled around a blaring blue lake ("Stocked. Trout. Folks love it. You could make a killing selling gear."). They skirted golf courses and rode through a neatly gridded town ("Centerville Commons. I never was much good with names"). The houses were all flat roofs and projecting beams, sand-colored stucco, corners rounded to benign nubs. They devoured their lots, and the trees were all spindly and new.

"I don't see any For Sale signs," Alison said. "I guess you haven't been hard hit by this real estate mess?"

"HOA doesn't allow them. Messes with the neighbors' heads." Lobel tapped his temple. "But we're doing all right. Had to postpone work on Phase Four, but what's already built . . . well, most folks bought to live here, right? And that's why you're here, see. We're going to add to that whole experience." Lobel drew out the word. "Tough times hit and people like living in a real place. Like to be a *part* of that place. So we'll get our own paper. And you—" He turned to Alison. The cart drifted into the neighboring lane. "You, Miss, you've got to add some authenticity to our town. Some history when there's really none."

"Not to talk myself out of a potential job, but shouldn't you be looking for someone in PR?" The cart had picked up speed. Ali had to shout.

"I want a real historian. You know those little brown signs by the side of the highway?"

"Historical markers, sure."

"I bet you're the kind of folks who always pull over for them."

"Sometimes," said Seth.

"My students get extra credit for reading them," Ali said. "Last week one of my sophomores discovered his grandfather's place was once a hub on the Underground Railroad."

"That's what I'm talking about. History. You'd never guess if it weren't for the brown signs. And even if you don't read them, you see them and you think, good, this place is a part of things. Folks need a dose of that here. My latest brainwave. We've got to stop it from feeling too much like summer camp."

"Summer camp's not so bad," said Seth. Ali hadn't told him about the hub house.

"For vacation, yeah. That was my *first* brainwave. Took off like crazy, let me tell you. First and second phases sold out like that. But now—tougher times, people want to *belong*. I can give them that. Started up a festival last year, food booths and a sidewalk sale, art stuff, live music. Founder's Day. Big hit. Going to repeat it this summer. June the second. Mark your calendars."

"Why the second?" Alison asked.

"My birthday. I know. The ego of it." They jostled along. Lobel showed them where the cart paths burrowed beneath the highway toward the strip malls on the other side ("They set up special golf cart parking for us and everything. Though anything you get there you can get here, and *we've* got award-winning landscaping."). He waved a hand at the employee parking lot, heat shimmering off acres of windshields ("Most neighborhoods in these parts got a free shuttle for Commons employees. We're the biggest show in thirty miles.").

It had been hailing that morning in Vermont. The Camry had taken three tries to start. Arizona was all naked warmth and hallucinogenic colors, and Seth's lungs felt fuller here than they had in ages. He and Ali could rent a place with a patio and a view of distant mesas. They could jog down the streets of a town without strollers. The Commons, where the rules were painless and explicit. All residents must be at least fifty-five years of age. They had six months left on their lease back home, but so what, they'd break it. Two weeks' notice wouldn't be anywhere near the end of the school year, but the books were unanimous and frank: Do what you must to take care of yourselves. Seth wanted this job. He wanted Shipley to gripe about being left in the lurch. He wanted to grasp the man's shoulder, to clasp his hand, to look him straight on, and say, "I am so very sorry for your loss."

BENJI IN ELDERLAND

THE LAYOUT OF THE CART paths made it a huge pain in the rear to shop offsite, so most folks didn't bother. Ben Thales did though. Eggs were fifty cents a dozen cheaper at the Walmart across the way. Chicken breasts, too, almost a dollar less a pound. And it'd been a close eye on his money that had gotten him here in the first place. Golf twice a week, tennis twice a week, a guest suite for Stephen and Anjali with jets in the bathtub and a loft for the kids they'd presumably get around to having someday; not bad for a dumb kid out of Wheelsburg. Truth be told though, it wasn't about the nickels and dimes. It was the way the whole system reeked of coal scrip. It wasn't easy shaking a thought like that, not when your family's two generations out of the mines. He'd been the first Thales to leave the state for college; his father the first to go, period, thanks to Uncle Sam. And even then, Ben hadn't known anything about anything. When Veronica Corbin, his beautiful Phi Beta Ronnie, had said yes, she'd marry him but only after she finished business school, he'd thought she meant secretarial training.

She was the smartest woman, hell, the smartest person he had ever met. Oh, Ronnie, he'd said. I know you can do more than that.

Ben started up the golf cart and backed down the drive. One of The Commons' thousand groundskeepers stood jumpsuited across the way, pruning. Ben waved. Call it the mark of a decent man: to look straight at the people your money meant you could look away from.

The other man kept working. What he must think of the lot of them. Everything you could desire, for sale and self-contained. Ben's son, Stephen, once had an assignment like that, a frog he'd had to keep alive for grade school. Think of its needs and how to keep them in balance. Seal its terrarium and see what happens.

It wouldn't have been grade school though. Nor middle. If it had been he'd have remembered Tara with a frog, too.

Down the street a car approached, breaking through the heat shimmers. An actual car. You didn't see that much; once they got over feeling like fools on a parade float, people here liked zipping around in their carts. Ben slowed to let the car pass. It stopped, its window opening with a brief puff of chilled air.

"Benjamin! Off to practice on the sly?" Sadie Birnam was his standing Thursday golf date. She had a capable, elegant swing, and though she could best him, easily, from the advanced tees, she always set up at the ladies'. When he'd joked—tentatively, because they'd never talked politics—about women's lib, she'd shut him down. She'd been teeing up at the ladies' forever. If she changed her standard at this late date, she would have no proper measure of her lifetime progress.

Ben raised his hands in a show of innocence. "Wouldn't take a swing without you. Just headed across the way. Need anything?" Sadie didn't seem the helpless widow sort, but with Gary gone— last Founder's Day, his heart, no warning, there but for the grace of fruits and veggies—Ben did his best to be solicitous. He'd always been an early riser and had fallen into the habit of walking a mile or so each morning with the Birnams. The morning after Gary's funeral he'd shown up as usual because he reckoned Sadie could use the company.

Sadie shook her head. "I stocked up last week. My granddaughter's out for a visit. We've just come from the airport. Lily, this is

Ben Thales. Best neighbor money can buy." There was weight and glint to that smile, an invitation. Or maybe not. He *had* been handy with jumper cables a month back. He was useless at reading these things. Decades since he'd had to.

"Hi." The girl in the passenger seat raised a hand. Dozens of thin bracelets clattered. Sadie in her prime, perhaps: eyes blue and enormous when she raised her sunglasses, skin clear and smooth, long dark hair, long fine neck, cleavage he should not be looking at. She smiled, and—proof he really, really should not be looking—her teeth were heavy with orthodontia.

"Good to meet you, Lily." Tara should've been Lily's kind of sixteen. The thought hurt.

"Ben used to be a veterinarian," Sadie said. "Lily wants to be one, too." Again, that tone he couldn't quite get a read on. Marvin Baum, one of his Tuesday golf buddies, liked to remind Ben: Men die younger; it's a question of odds. But beat those odds and the odds are in your favor, and you know I'm not talking actuarially. Marvin was right. There were six houses on Daylily Crescent: three couples, two widows, and his solitary self.

"I *used* to want to be a vet," Lily said. "I'm going to do something in fashion now." She gave her grandmother a quick, conciliatory smile. "I still want lots of pets though." There were boys out there, and plenty of them, who were going to wind up with ill-advised lily tattoos thanks to this girl. Her sunglasses slotted back into place, turning the girl inscrutable.

Sadie let the car idle as Ben drove off, and he wondered if she was watching him. He wondered if Veronica had started seeing people, if she'd tell him if she had. He passed the sixth hole and then the fifth, its water hazard glinting like a disco-ball in the sun. He trundled past Main Street, its far end dominated by the achingly pristine Hacienda Central. He crossed a series of artificial creeks, skirted the lap pool and the gym, then turned through a gate and onto the brown and shriveled expanse of nothing that up until the housing freefall had been slated to be The Commons' Phase Four. Then he floored it. Call him a big dumb lug, but you were never too old for a lead-foot love affair with the accelerator. He passed hundreds of surveyors' stakes marking out lots that were no longer for sale. He passed the remains of an adolescent bonfire and a midden of broken bottles and burger wrappers. The path turned sharply and dipped down, tunneling toward the shopping center, and Ben held his breath like a child until he came out on the other side.

He parked on the lot's outer margin, because it never hurt to build a bit more exercise into your day (dogs helped on that front, but Ronnie had kept Musetta). Ben walked each morning and always caddied for himself. He was sixty-eight and trim, firmer in his chest and shoulders than his own son, whose first deskbound years of legal practice were taking their toll. Before the divorce, he hadn't bought pants in decades—new pairs appeared in his closet at whatever intervals Ronnie deemed appropriate—but he'd been pleased to discover the tags were right and that a thirty-inch waistband fit him fine. Ben did the crossword every day and hadn't written a shopping list because he didn't need one; his mind wasn't going anywhere, thanks. Let's see. He wanted eggs and butter spray to cook them with. Bread. Oranges. Orange juice, too, now that he was thinking of it, the fortified kind. Chicken and that Cajun rub if they had any.

It was nice and cool in the store. Say what you like about these big-box places, but this one had a real neighborhood feel. Always someone he knew. See? Mona Rosko—Daylily Crescent's *other* widow—waited in line for customer service, overdressed and holding a red file folder to her chest. Lee and Joanie Stamp waved from an endcap display of bottled salsa. Ben's phone rang, the onscreen letters announcing *V. Corbin*. Though Stephen and Anjali had talked him through it step by step last Thanksgiving, he still hadn't assigned his ex her own ringtone.

"Hello? Veronica?"

"Benji in Elderland!" Ben's father was dead. Ben's mother was dead. Ben's sisters phoned on his birthday and Christmas. Veronica was the only one left who called him Benji. "How's Camp Commons?"

"Not a cloud in the sky. Raining in Portland?"

"Buckets. That's what I get for not running off to live in an amusement park."

"I've been meaning to call you. You know there used to be a ranch here? I read the other day that back in the forties they packed off a hundred crates of dirt to Hollywood. You'll never guess why."

"Probably not."

"They used it for *Gone with the Wind*. On the plantation sets. Actual Georgia clay didn't look right in Technicolor." Ronnie loved that movie. Every time she watched it she made the same guilty joke about getting herself kicked out of the feminist clubhouse.

"The red earth of Tara," she said. They'd been back and forth on Stephen's name until he was three days old but Tara Ruth Thales had always been Tara.

"The red earth of Tara." Ben had seen the movie maybe three times to Veronica's three dozen but he got it, oh man, did he ever get it: Tara the big symbolic heart of it all, Tara for which no sacrifice is too great. "You could come down and see for yourself. I've got room."

"A thousand miles for a bit of dirt?"

He could've quoted something then, something from one of the sweeping romantic scenes. God knew he'd learned the whole film through osmosis. Ronnie would laugh. It would be sweet to make Ronnie laugh, but the silence after—these things were hard enough to read in person. "Not just that. There's tennis and golf and a lake and a brand-new spa."

"Sounds nice."

"You'd like it." He'd met Ronnie their sophomore year at Bucknell. If someone had told that rangy kid this moment was in his future, divorce from Veronica would've been harder to fathom than the existence of the cell phones they were speaking on. "I think you'd like it a lot."

"You sound funny."

"I'm out shopping. It's too damn cold in here." Ben didn't say he was at Walmart. Veronica had read an expose and had opinions, capital O. Not that it mattered now, but still. Over forty years together. A bit like Pavlov saying, Oh never mind about that bell.

"I won't keep you."

"It's fine. Say, do you think I should get the five-alarm spice rub or stick with the three?"

"What happened to four?"

"Doesn't seem to be one."

"Go with the three. You can always add pepper." Every time they introduced him to someone new, his golf buddies insisted he tell the joke. What brings you to The Commons? Well, I'm newly divorced. And without my ex, I need the HOA to tell me what to do.

"Good call." Silence from Veronica. They had phones now that could send photographs and articles from the *New York Times*. You'd think they'd invent one that could interpret those damn silences. "Look, I'll bring you some of that dirt when I'm up next." Ben flew back to Portland every six months or so to touch base with his old life. He slept in the guest room, on the now-sagging queen bed that had been their first furniture purchase, and timed his trips with the Chinook run so that time-with-Ronnie didn't become too-much-time-with-Ronnie. They hadn't had the best marriage—they'd made an absolute mess of things by the end—but that was no reason not to shoot for the best possible divorce.

"That'd be nice," his ex said. "Listen, there's a reason I called."

"I figured."

"Not that I wouldn't just call to—"

"It's fine, Veronica. What's up?"

"Rand needs to reschedule. He's got a lead—"

"A lead, really? Where? What? Should I come home—"

"Another client. No. Shit. Sorry. Ben, I didn't mean to get you thinking—He's heading out of town for a few weeks and I'm set smack in the middle. So I'm seeing him either tomorrow or at the end of the month. If the timing matters to you—"

"I'm sure you've got it under control." Rand Danovic. They had to have paid for his summer home by now, not that he was a summer-home kind of guy. The ex-cop looked more like an ex-hippie and drank from a perpetual thermos of hay-scented tea. They'd considered another guy, innocuous and balding, the detective from Central Casting, but five minutes into the interview he'd known they'd go with Rand.

I'm not going to promise I'll find her. You seem like nice folks and an empty promise is the last thing you need. I can say I'll do my best and that I'm very good at what I do. I can say that, sure. But I'll also say this. I get even a hint she's running from *something in this house instead of just running, the three of us are done.*

Ronnie sighed. That sure as hell was readable over the phone. "I wanted to see if you had anything to contribute. Any questions."

"There's only ever the one question."

They owned a lovely craftsman in the hills off Washington Park; they remodeled the kitchen and hung a calendar on its wall; a housekeeper and landscaper came weekly and Ronnie wrote their names in the appropriate square. E. Mancera, P. Royal. And then, R. Danovic. Their cleaner. Their gardener. The private detective they'd hired to track down their only daughter. Every December 31st, Ronnie chucked the calendar and every January 1st, Ben fished it out of the trash. He squirreled them away, calendars dating back to 1995, R. Danovic appearing every other week, then once a month, every two months, every six. The only proof Ben had that it wasn't their fault. *I get even a hint she's running* from *something in this house instead of just running, the three of us are done.*

"Ben," said Veronica.

"Just—fill me in, okay? If he has any new strategies. Maybe with the Internet—"

"Of course."

"And, you know, tell him hi. Did he ever wind up marrying that girl?"

"Mariah? Yeah, this April. We sent them a beautiful wood salad bowl."

When she left, Tara was sixteen years old. Rand had been in their employ for nearly as long. The last time they'd met, Ben's things had been in boxes. I hate to see you split, the PI had said. And frankly, I hate to keep taking your money.

No, said Ronnie.

No, said Ben.

At least they agreed on that much. You had to think of it as tithing. You had to look upon the bank statements as evidence of faith.

AN OFFICIAL
DELINQUENT

THE LAWS OF CHEESE DICTATED there were three possible ways for this visit to go down. One: Lily was going to fall hard for the scion of the richest family in town; he'd break her heart; she'd cry, then realize she was meant for the impoverished, edgy, and ambiguously ethnic guy who'd warned her off Mr. Daddy's Platinum Card in the first place. Two: Lily was going to discover an obscure shrew whose nesting ground was threatened by development, band together with plucky locals, and expose the developer as a palm-greasing old fraud. Or three: Lily would chafe under her grandmother's curfew; she'd sass and slam doors; she'd wind up learning some old-lady hobby that was an obvious metaphor for life, love, and the passage of time, then call upon her newfound inner strength to see said grandmother through a mild health scare.

Not going to happen. Not in a million years.

She'd *invented* the Laws of Cheese. Last fall, with Sierra, when they were supposed to be studying the laws of physics. Besides, Gran didn't knit or quilt anything like that, Arizona was one hundred percent golf courses already, and everyone knew that Lily liked girls.

She opened the fridge and helped herself to a piece of pineapple. It probably didn't count as a granny hobby, but Gran was really good at cutting fruit. There was a huge bowl full, every slice completely rind-less. Lily popped the pineapple in her mouth, then a piece of mango, then a piece of watermelon, and then something mysterious and yellow that was less tart than she'd expected. She grabbed a bottle of water and shut the refrigerator door. A familiar magnet held Gran's weekly schedule in place: the acorn-topped crest of the Forest Park Day School. Lily sniffed and inverted it so the pair of acorns hung like a dangling set of (not that she would know) testicles.

According to the schedule, Gran was off at yoga. She'd invited Lily to tag along, but a dozen old-lady butts in Downward-Facing Dog? Thanks, but no. So Lily had the house to herself, miracle of miracles. Better warn the National Guard; Cyber-Bully Birnam was momentarily unsupervised. Lily gave the magnet the finger. A tasteful finger, manicured with OPI's Mod About You, since being an official delinquent should in no way eradicate the possibility of elegance. Then she smiled, adjusted her bikini straps, slung her bag over her shoulder, and stepped out into the sunlight.

It felt good. Maybe she'd run away and go nudist, ha ha. Talk about an *actual* scandal. Imagine. An eensy-weensy hint of sarcasm was all it took to turn the collective minds of a rigorous college preparatory program into a wad of chewed up Hubba Bubba. If Lily ever actually *did* anything, so many heads would explode they'd have to hike tuition to cover the janitor's overtime.

Only, she'd last about eight seconds as a nudist. Consider the size of her suitcase. "Seriously?" Mom had said at the airport. "We're going to have to pay to check this. Gran has laundry. Who are you trying to impress, anyhow?"

No one. Everyone. Herself. Mom would never get it. Just because she was into girls didn't mean she had to stop looking like one.

Lily was pretty: petite, even-featured, bulge-less, zit-less.

And it mattered, being pretty. She worked on it.

Which apparently made her Little Miss Vapid.

Even Sierra had thought so, at least a little bit. "You're different than I thought you'd be," she'd said, maybe a month after starting at Day. "I thought you'd be all does-this-mascara-make-my-eyelids-look-fat?"

"Nah. My eyelids are perfect."

"They are. You should do a whole post about how to get eyelids like that."

Sierra had been following *Lipstick Lillian*, Lily's beauty blog, since before she'd even moved to St. Louis. When someone—someone's troll mom, probably—picked a fight, Sierra had fully slaughtered her in the comments.

NRBeautyFly: You are so much more than your looks, girls!

Secanthelpit: f*ck u. we know. im in honors math and my GPA is 3.82 and guess what? i look gooooood doing it. u can be good at math AND makeup and its nobodies business if u r.

Lily liked Secanthelpit. Like Secanthelpit, Lily was equally adept at math and makeup. She began to keep an eye out for Secanthelpit in the comments. And then, let the trumpets sound, there she was, Secanthelpit herself, Sierra, the only other sophomore in AP Calc and a girl who got it: Pretty wasn't everything, but it was enough of a thing to be worth the effort. Lily had thought about using something like that as a new tagline but didn't. The least little change turned her readers rabid.

Or once upon a time it had, back before the All-Powerful Parentals canceled her cell service, confiscated her iPhone and laptop, and made it clear they'd be monitoring *Lipstick* for new content.

They hadn't even let her post a farewell.

Classic case of parental amnesia. Up till the minute Headmistress Brecken phoned them, they'd been going on about how key it was to be conversant in the new media, how pleased they were she was coming out of her shell, and how the blog probably had something to do with her stronger grades in all those classes that required essays.

She was going to flunk them next year on purpose, just to show them.

Well, not flunk. Not considering how important junior year grades were. But she'd fudge a little in her footnotes.

Lily shut the front door with more force than was wholly necessary. Across the street, that guy, the vet, Mr.-Thales-but-you-can-call-me-Ben, came out of his house and waved. He'd come along on her walk with Gran this morning, bringing with him the distinct vibe that it was actually *Lily* coming along on *his* walk with Gran. He'd asked all these weird questions. Where did she go when she wanted to be alone? Had she ever hitchhiked? Did her PE classes cover self-defense? What a creep. You could tell even before he opened his mouth. A veterinarian without pets of his own, enough said. And then Gran had gone and invited him over for barbecue. Lily scowled. He waved again and called her name. She didn't wave back. They'd had a self-defense speaker last semester. Don't feel you have to be nice. That's conditioning. Trust your instincts. Better rude than dead. Pretending he wasn't looking—but she could tell he was, the guy was probably going to wind up in the ER with one of those four-hour Viagra erections, God, penises were *disgusting*—Lily approached the trellis beside her grandmother's front door. The Commons' map showed a pool nearby, but there was no way she was going to walk past and give the vet, no, wait, the *per*-vet, a free show. Lily shook the frame, tested her weight against it, and climbed. When she'd first moved down here, Gran had tried to train wisteria—a cutting from the old St. Louis place—up the trellis, but the vine had shriveled in the Arizona heat. Midascent, Lily kicked away a last, thirsty, brown coil.

The roof was flat and so hot she could hardly touch it, but the towel she'd snagged from the guest bath was spongy and thick. She unrolled it and lay down. Spring had come late in St. Louis and she was pale enough to signal ships at sea. In the interest of avoiding lobster mode, she'd lie out for thirty minutes per side at the absolute max. Or as close to thirty minutes as humanly possible, considering she didn't have a *phone* to keep track of time. Think how bad the parentals would feel if she died of melanoma because they'd thought one little blog post was a back-to-the-Bronze-Age worthy offense.

Lily stretched, relishing the one-hundred-percent-genuine privacy. Gran was Madam Popular here and they must have paused their walk a dozen times to have the same basic conversation. She should've printed out business cards. Lily Elinor Birnam, Visiting Grandchild. In answer to your questions, I am (a) not sure how long I'll be staying, (b) almost sixteen, (c) going to be a junior, which, yes, is unusual but I skipped second grade, (d) not sure where I want to go to college, and (e) having a lovely time, thank you. If any of them sensed that Lily had been sent down so that Gran wouldn't be alone on the anniversary of Grandpa Gary's death, they didn't show it. Gran had to know; Dad and Aunt Manda hadn't been exactly subtle. But she wasn't making a big weepy deal about it. Gran was tough, and it rocked having those genes.

Lily rolled onto her stomach, checked that the per-vet had retreated into his lair, and unhooked her bikini. She surveyed the neighborhood. The house next door had a hot tub in its courtyard. Gran's just had a grill and patio furniture, herbs in terracotta pots. I keep thinking I should set up a pink flamingo there, she'd told Pervet Ben on their walk. Just because the HOA won't be able to see it. They'd laughed and raised an imaginary glass to the Flamingo Police. It was possible, but not probable, that to outsiders her and Sierra's inside jokes were just as dumb.

Sierra. Le sigh. If Sierra were here, she'd probably talk Lily into sneaking next door for a midnight soak, because Sierra always brought the fun. Last year had been twelve times less boring than the sum of the fourteen preceding it, and Sierra pinky-swore that junior year would be even better.

And it would, even though Sierra-like-the-mountains-not-the-truck had gotten together with Rocky-like-the-mountains-not-the-boxer over Winter Break, which, by the way, was an absolute violation of the Laws of Cheese.

"Don't sulk," Sierra'd said. They were studying in her room, which smelled of the incense she lit because it made her stepdad paranoid that she was doing it to mask the smell of pot. "You knew I liked the boys."

"I'm not sulking."

"And if I was going to experiment, I wouldn't with you. You're too good a friend to mess with like that."

"Fine. But Sierra and Rocky? Kill me now."

"Just wait till we find you a nice femme named Rose."

And it *was* fine; it was, though even an amateur cheeseologist could anticipate the insane degree to which Sierra's heart was going to get shredded.

Lily stretched then resettled, contorting to resecure her bikini straps. She took a swig from her water bottle and watched a woman jog along one of the winding cart paths. A woman-woman, not an old woman, with a long ponytail and breasts that jostled about as a single entity. Sierra would have something to say about that. Ponytails were lazy and generally uncute, and Sierra had a thing about proper bra fittage.

Urgh.

Just thinking about it triggered utter depression, because Sierra plus bra issues equaled a surefire candidate for a Fixit. Lily used to post them each Friday—a makeover in three easy steps. They'd been *Lipstick Lillian*'s biggest draw and Sierra could even be relied upon to shut up about Rocky long enough to help draft them.

Down below, the runner veered off the path and ran through the sprinkler. She stopped, resecured her ponytail, then made for a prickly clump of succulents. She'd probably appreciate the Fixit. Everyone did (well, everyone minus one). They were funny, yeah, but they were meant to help. Look better, feel better, be better. It was as simple as that. Like Sierra said: the most noble and magnanimous Headmistress Brecken should have given her community service credit instead of summoning her parents. But no one would listen that day in la Brecken's office. Lily wasn't picking on anyone. She didn't go around looking for Fixits. Girls sent in their *own* pictures. And she was careful. She'd listened to the bajillion assemblies on Internet predators. The policy was right there on her blog. She'd only consider photos with the heads cropped off.

Another Visiting Grandchild, a little-kid version, had appeared in the hot tub courtyard. They should exchange cards. He walked robot style, knees locked. Between the goosesteps and his bowl cut he kind of looked like a mini Hitler. He found a stick and brandished it at his reflection in the sliding glass door. He poked it at something on the ground. He tapped it against the hot tub.

Lily reached for her bag. She still had one airport magazine left.

Down in his courtyard, *Der Führer* stood on a picnic bench and jumped.

Lily flipped through a couple of pages then tossed the stupid thing. It skidded across the roof. Mom had given her a fat stack of magazines when they'd said goodbye at airport security, like what was eating Lily alive was a dearth of articles on how to perfect your cat-eye liner. The beauty tips weren't the point. Her blog could be about the mating cycles of fruit bats. The point was, Lily had friends. Saintblonde lived all the way in Tampa and wanted Lily's opinion on what haircut to get. Fizzimiss was from somewhere in Arizona and if Lily didn't ping her to let her know that she was nearby and eminently visit-worthy then she really would be as snotty and shallow as all of a sudden everyone was convinced she was.

Dad had said they weren't real people. He'd joked about outgrowing imaginary friends.

No. The person who wasn't a real person was her mystery classmate, Anonymous Crybaby VonFragilekins.

This time, *Der Führer* climbed onto the table to jump. He stuck the landing.

Lily hadn't even had the chance to face her accuser.

Headmistress Brecken identified her as a classmate-whose-image-you-appropriated-without-her-knowledge-or-consent. A classmate-who-you-then-held-up-for-public-ridicule. As I'm sure you're aware, Miss Birnam, we expect better of our student citizens.

Lily hadn't even known the girl went to Day.

She hadn't been wearing her uniform or anything, and the image arrived in her inbox pre-cropped.

Der Führer was back on the picnic table. He made a running start.

Lily shifted, chin in her hands.

Three stupid paragraphs and boom. Goodbye, two years of work. *Auf wiedersehen, au revoir,* and *sayonara,* international following. Not to mention two weeks' grounding and total technological confiscation.

She wasn't mean. Ever. She had a rule. Only criticize what a girl can actually change.

And there'd been *compliments* in the Fixit in question.

First things first, chickie-dee: can the lace collar and the cutesy little cap sleeves. You're not ten. Obviously. We can all see the Boob Fairy thought you were a very good girl. If you weren't wearing a blouse like a first grader in the Thanksgiving pageant, everyone here would be dead of envy.

Second, the Boob Fairy was generous but she forgot to leave an instruction manual. Your bra strap is showing. Bonus points for purple though. Is that satin? I wish more readers had your guts.

Third, I'm worried about your necklace. Points for taking on that whole charm and bauble boho thing, but between you and me and the Internet it looks a little bit Etsy.

Lily frowned and watched *Der Führer* jump again, his thin arms flapping. He landed on the hot tub cover, but only barely. He toppled off, stood, wiped his palms on his shorts, and climbed right back up to try again. Talk about easily amused.

She took another swig of water.

Sierra said she was lucky. Anyone else would be suspended for sure, but nothing's going to stick to you for long. Nothing scares the trustees like the prospect of a big fat lesbian lawsuit. Be all angel food cake and they'll let you up again in no time. That sounded a bit optimistic to Lily, but she didn't say so. Sierra probably felt guilty. The Boob Fairy had been her invention. Lily'd balked about posting it but Sierra said no, it was hilarious. She even drew a cartoon Boob Fairy for Lily's locker.

Down in the courtyard, *Der Führer* missed the hot tub. He landed square on his butt. A shocked, solid breath escaped.

Lily stood and checked the back of her legs for color, pressing a finger to the flesh of her calf. The white mark flared then faded. It was a hundred and eighty degrees today and, in the absence of her iPhone, terminally boring to lie out. She'd stay for ten more little Hitler jumps and then head in. The kid positioned himself and ran. He cleared the space between table and hot tub, landed, and let out a small cheer.

The ponytailed runner circled by once more.

Der Führer made another headlong start. Another perfect landing, maybe half a foot beyond the lip of the hot tub cover. She should start holding up cards, awarding points out of ten.

Or not, bearing in mind what happened the last time she made any kind of critique.

Der Führer scrambled back into position. His feet pounded down the length of the table and he hurled himself into the air. His landing was a bit off. He wobbled backward and then overcorrected. He staggered toward the tub's center.

Then he was gone.

The hot tub cover collapsed in a brutal V.

Every hair on Lily's body stood straight. "Hey, kid," she called down. Her hand went by instinct to her hip, but she didn't have pants and didn't have a pocket and she didn't have a goddamn *phone*. The day went wonky. All the colors crisped. She'd taken the Red Cross babysitting class. A little card in her wallet said she knew CPR, but all she could recall was the dummy's plastic lips, their red worn away in patches.

"Kid!" she called again.

She saw a small sneakered foot and pulsed with bright relief.

Then the foot twitched and she worked out the physics. If it was above water then the rest of him was under.

Her bones went hollow. She made it off the roof, and then into her grandmother's kitchen. There was no phone anywhere. She checked the living room. The bedroom. The weird little desk alcove where she spied one beneath a sheaf of papers. That kid. That poor kid. The time she had cost him. She should have had her cell. The landline buttons sank in when she pushed them, nine then one then one. The phone was blue, with a blue tangle of cord. There was an impossible amount of wire involved in getting the signal out.

A KIND OF
TIME TRAVEL

TWO YEARS BACK, IN THE lead up to the presidential election, the Colliers had spent their weekends going door to door. They hosted debate-watching parties and framed the same Shepard Fairey poster that everyone suddenly had on display. They decided to ditch Alison's pills; the stick said yes just before the inauguration and they joked about a fertility bump across liberal America. Optimism babies, a kindergarten crowded with wee Michelles and Baracks.

And now they lived in Arizona, the only place left where John McCain was routinely televised. Every time the senator appeared, Seth felt a brief, fierce dart of relief, like it was 2008 again. It was embarrassing. And it wasn't just the senator. It was the throng of men here made in his image. Anyone with that high, arcing hairline or an off-kilter lump on his cheek. They walked The Commons en masse, geared up for golf. Seth had always gotten a kick out of off-beat collective nouns. He'd hung a list in his old classroom: a congregation of alligators, a convocation of eagles, a phalanx of storks. Quorum would be apt here. A roving quorum of McCains.

Arizona.

They'd leased a condo fifteen minutes from The Commons. Columns at the entry meant to look like stacked stones, sage-colored bathroom tiles, a patio that bordered an electric blue communal pool. The walnut grain of their good furniture looked fusty and wrong in that condo. The blinds in the bedroom were no defense against the morning light. They hadn't unpacked the Shepard Fairey poster yet, and Seth hardly needed his English degree to get a read on that symbolism.

But the grief books said that was okay.

The grief books said they should give themselves time.

At the books' encouragement, they held fast to their routine. They took the free Commons shuttle to work together and they took it home again. On Saturday mornings they made pancakes. On Wednesdays after work they went for burgers at The Homeplate and watched whatever classic baseball game the restaurant decided to screen. The old games ran clean and uncluttered by advertising popups. Seth liked that. It was a kind of time travel. Tonight was Mets versus Braves, July 4th, 1985. Hell of a game.

Ali was waiting for him by the front steps of the Hacienda Central. Nicky Tullbeck, Seth's summer intern, sat beside her, inexpertly flirting. The boy's bike stood, kick-standed, nearby. Alison fiddled with the sunglasses that hung from a chain around her neck. It wasn't a coy gesture; this was Alison, after all. She was only trying to make them sit right. The glasses chain was something new. She'd made a fragile sound that tried to be laughter when she'd first tried it on. A few months at The Commons and I'm already an old lady. She leaned toward Nicky and said something Seth didn't catch. The boy laughed, and Alison smiled like she'd never lost anything more than a poker hand. She spotted him and stood. He was pretty sure she'd worn that dress on their honeymoon. She'd torn the hem hopping the fence to a private beach. She waved him over and kissed his cheek. Seth returned the gesture, wishing he could've watched her with Nicky a while longer. Alison was still Alison if she had an audience. No one would guess that she didn't yet have a local library card, that she hadn't registered to vote.

His wife said, "Nicky's tracking down petroglyphs this week-end." She smiled once more. She had a great smile; everyone said so. "There's supposed to be a bunch of them ten miles down this arroyo." Nicky gestured vaguely toward the horizon. Ali reminded him to carry water. Seth didn't so much think Alison-sounds-like-a-mom as he thought don't-let-yourself-think-Alison-sounds-like-a-mom. Semantics. Either way he felt it, raw and nestled between his ribs. Nicky biked off, hand raised in casual farewell. Ali said, "I wish he'd wear a helmet."

Nicky zoomed down the straightaway. Whatever gunk he wore in his hair made it helmet enough. "He's a good kid."

"That doesn't have anything to do with anything."

"What I mean is, he'll be careful."

"That doesn't mean everyone else will be." Whenever his mother-in-law visited, she fussed about Ali's posture—you're not short, sweetling, don't carry yourself like you are—grabbing her shoulders and wresting them back. Seth wished she was here. Anything to straighten the sorry crescent of his wife's spine.

He changed the subject. These days, that was the best trick he had. "So. Mets versus Braves." He checked the time. They'd make the first pitch if they hurried.

"Yeah," she said. "Mets versus Braves." Alison was the one who'd won him over to ESPN Classic. She TiVoed nearly all the baseball. I need it to get me through the winters, Seth. Spring train-ing doesn't even start till February. He'd given her a hard time when they first moved in together. Why bother when you already know who wins? Especially when there's basketball live. Football. Hockey. Pick your poison. No, this is better, she'd said. Like reread-ing a good book.

It had taken a few years, but he got the draw now.

If you aren't hung up on the ending, it's easier to see the moment-to-moment grace.

"Supposed to be a good one?" he asked. As if he didn't know. Mets take it sixteen-thirteen after ten, count 'em, ten extra innings. Fourth of July, so the game ends with fireworks. By this point, it's four A.M., 1985. The Wall in Berlin will stand for another four years. The good people of Atlanta awake and think *invasion*. Seth was acting like one of those girls in his classes, the ones he'd always wanted to shake, playing dumb so some guy could feel oh so smart. This was Alison. Alison.

"Sure," she said. "It's a great game. They wouldn't rerun it otherwise."

They walked. He couldn't see it but he knew: an inch or so of her hem was hand-stitched in white. It had been the only thread in their hotel sewing kit. Belize. Their honeymoon. Alison's pursed expression as she threaded the needle. She'd wanted to redo it when they got home. He convinced her not to bother. We'll want to look at it and remember, he'd said. Alison had kissed him and called it the saddest, sweetest souvenir in the history of honeymoons.

"Alison?" he asked.

"Yeah?"

"Tell me something about your day. Something I wouldn't be able to guess." Another line from one of those pitiful little girls.

Ali didn't say anything. She was tan now, but their first week out here she'd burned. I look like a strawberry, she complained. Red skin and all these freckles. Seth had said nothing. He'd thought about strawberries, how amazing it was they evolved at all. They were so fragile. They carried their seeds on the outside.

"Alison?" he asked again. Because the thing was, it was an actual question. He didn't know what she did all day. Her office was upstairs from his, on the top floor of the Hacienda Central, two doors down from Hoagland Lobel's. It held a small desk and a large bookcase. The bookcase was genuine wood. Seth had thumped it with his knuckles and listened to the reverberations so he knew that much at least.

"I'm thinking," she said.

"It's not a hard question. How was your day?"

"I may have tracked down a photo of Adah Chalk. You know? The rancher's wife? The first one? She followed Garner Chalk West from Louisiana and—what?"

"Nothing."

"I know you. You had a look."

"It's just—you're going to tell me about this Adah, and I was asking about you."

"And this is what I worked on. What do you want me to say?"

"I was only—" He could say *being romantic*, but romance implied sex and sex implied the question. You're young. You can try again. Ali's OB said there was no reason they couldn't. At first Ali had said that she didn't trust herself yet. Now, more and more, she left out the *yet*. They arrived at The Homeplate. His wife ducked inside before he had a chance to hold the door. Cara, their usual waitress, escorted them to their usual table. Alison unrolled her napkin.

"Please," Seth said. "Tell me about the picture."

"It was a picture, okay? It was old."

"And?"

"And you've basically told me you aren't interested."

"I am."

She shook her head.

"I'm more interested in *you*."

Half a smile.

"C'mon. That's a good line."

"Maybe. But not exactly a get-out-of-jail-free card."

"I just wanted to hear about—"

"How's this? A crazy girl in a bikini told me I should put my hair in a braid when I run."

"And you told me about Adah's picture first?"

"I had to think if I wanted to tell you."

"Because?"

"I'd rather talk about the picture."

"You know your hair looks fine."

"It's not that. Look. I ran on my lunch hour, right?" As usual. Seth could see the firm outline of her calves even when she didn't flex. Her clothing hung loose. Thank God for that seersucker patch of stretch marks beneath her navel. It hadn't been her fault; it hadn't been his; all the doctors said there'd been no way to foresee. But sometimes the thought twisted through him: a criminal, purging the scene of her crime. "There's a loop I like," she said, "out by Daylily Crescent? Sometimes they run the sprinklers."

"Sounds nice." If Alison were still Alison, she'd be drafting petitions about the water waste.

"Usually. Today there were all these sirens. Police, ambulance. I guess you could say I rubbernecked. A whole bunch of people were standing around. Bikini girl was there. She walked up to me and said I shouldn't wear a ponytail."

"Weird."

"A pony is a horse. You don't want to look like a horse, do you? She said it like that, completely calm."

"Strange kid."

"I think she might have been in shock. She was the one who called the police." With Timothy, Alison hadn't gone into shock, not for an instant. Instead the noises that had come from her throat, the fluorescent clarity of the delivery room.

"Let me guess," he said. "Someone had a stroke." It was an awful thing to say, but so be it. *These* were the people who were supposed to be dying.

"It was a kid." Alison opened her menu then shut it again. "You get why I'd rather talk about Adah Chalk? They brought a kid out on the stretcher. Six years old? Five? I can't tell. A little boy."

"Fuck. Ali."

"Don't say anything nice to me. They were taking him to the hospital. One of the neighbors rode along."

"A neighbor? Where were his—"

"He was alone in the house. And there I was, jogging along—"

"You couldn't have known."

"I said, don't say anything nice to me."

Cara arrived with their usual, unasked. Alison's 7 and 7, a cold pint for Seth. From the next booth a pair of the countless McCains debated the specials in excruciating detail. "Hey," he said. "Tell me about the photograph."

"She had a dark dress with a white lace collar. Kind of like a Puritan. Glasses. Little round ones. That's all. Your turn."

"What?" Seth was zonked and they had nineteen innings ahead of them. That was more than twice a normal game.

Ali echoed him. "Tell me about your day. Something I'd never guess."

He'd had to run five fucking birth announcements. Adair Lewis-Stamp, Molly Flemming, Zachary Bierbaum, Brandon Wilcox, Riley-Claire Stouser, and happy birthday to them. There'd been pictures, too: Adair swaddled, burrito-style, Zachary with wide unfocused eyes. "I was jealous of Nicky," said Seth. "Just now."

"Oh, ha."

"He was flirting."

"He was practicing. For all those girls this fall at Rice."

They paged through their menus. Seth had already tried everything that sounded remotely interesting. When she brought out his sandwich, Cara had swapped rings for fries without his having to ask. The Homeplate only showed the latter half of the game. Someone had cued it to start at the top of the eighth. It made sense, logistically, but what a slap in the face. They should've done something to acknowledge those first seven innings of outs.

The next morning, Jeffrey Stouser called to complain that his granddaughter's name was spelled Riley-Clare, not Riley-Claire. The weekly public safety report landed on Seth's desk. Police had tended to victims of a golf cart collision at the corner of Buckthorn and Ratany Streets. They were investigating the disappearance of a charm bracelet from the ladies' locker room at The Sun Wren Pool and Spa. They'd been called to the scene of a purported home invasion that turned out to be raccoons and rendered assistance to a minor resident of 16 Daylily Crescent.

Seth could have simply run the report. He almost did. But there were questions: What was the child's current condition? Where were his parents? Why had he been left helpless and unsupervised, and shouldn't Child Protective Services be involved? There were rules about children at The Commons—why was he here at all?

Seth opened a blank document.

There were questions, yes, and also: He hadn't moved them to Arizona for this. Ali, brittle at The Homeplate, then up most of the night with that photo of Adah Chalk. Ali, tossing a handful of blueberries into her morning yogurt. Their life here was meant to deliver a certain kind of mindless peace. But those berries. All Seth saw was the chart in the book they'd bought with such giddy anticipation. At eight weeks Baby is the size of a blueberry. At thirteen the size of a peach. The first time she saw it, Alison crossed her legs and said, please God let it stop before watermelon.

THE ANGEL OF
THE COMMONS

DER FÜHRER LIVED.

The hot tub had been empty. He spent two nights at the hospital and came home wearing a cast. A heavyset woman—by the power of deductive reasoning, his grandmother—accompanied him, toting an enormous stuffed rabbit. She had the posture of someone who knew she was in trouble but wasn't letting on. And she *was* in trouble. Big trouble. Because the papers—first the rinky-dink Commons one and then the *Daily Star*—all said that *Der Führer* wasn't allowed to be here. The Commons had a covenant. All residents agreed upon it. No full-time resident shall be under fifty-five years of age.

Gran spied them right away. Of course. She'd become a twenty-four-hour Rosko channel. All Lily and her heroic rescue, all the time. She'd begun introducing Lily to her friends here as—*gag*—The Angel of The Commons.

Some angel.

Lily was freaking literate. She read the news. Mona Rosko had been hiding her grandson in her home for half a year. Now that *someone* had blown their secret, the pair were facing eviction. The papers all wanted to know where the grandmother had been when the kid fell. A social worker was involved. Clearly Lily was in the running for neighbor of the year.

"We should bring them a dish," Gran said. She had a second freezer in the garage, packed solid with foil-wrapped trays. "These days, it's easier to freeze the extra than to scale back my recipes for one. I'm not a math whiz like *some* people." Gran winked, like a dose of cute would cancel out the fact that she was cooking for one because Grandpa was dead. Gran ran her index finger from tray to tray. "Something with pasta. Kids like noodles." She handed Lily a stack of three. They walked over, Lily's fingers going icy at the tips. Gran rang the bell.

Nothing.

"We could leave the trays," Lily said. "Write a little note."

Gran rang again, leaning on the bell. As if that would make a difference.

"Let's go. Please."

"Why, Lily, I've never known you to be shy." Gran's words came out hyperdramatic and bizarrely accented, Deep South by way of Dublin with an inexplicable hint of Jamaican, mon.

"The kid's grandma's in trouble. I saw it in the papers. He's not supposed to be living there and—what?"

"Half my friends' grandkids don't even read the news."

They probably did online. Grandparents were required by law to be proud of things, but really. "He's not supposed to be living there," she said again, shifting the stack of frozen dinners. "No one would know if I hadn't called nine-one-one."

"He'd be dead if it weren't for you. He wouldn't be living anywhere."

"That's what my friend Sierra said." They'd actually gotten to talk last night. The Angel of The Commons, availing herself of her techno-ban's landline loophole. Sierra'd said Gran's dead-if-not-for-you thing verbatim, which was kind of creepy. She and Gran were a Venn diagram Lily'd never expected to overlap.

"She sounds like a smart girl. Have I met her?" Gran rang the doorbell once more, then did that deliberately casual thing with her eyes that marked her as the ten thousandth person to assume that Sierra was Lily's secret girlfriend. Sierra liked it. She said it added to her mystique. Sometimes Lily wondered if instead of the Laws of Cheese they should have drafted Rules about the Limits of Using Someone Else to Further Your Own Ends, but it stood to figure that if you *knew* you were being used and didn't do anything, then you were probably getting something out of it, too.

From inside the Rosko house, curtains rustled.

"Sierra's new," Lily answered. Which was the point. Lily was out now, and everything was different. With Sierra, she didn't have to check the rearview. "She said she'd milk this hero thing for all it's worth."

"There's a whole world between milking and accepting a bit of credit." Gran shook her head, and then pushed up her sleeves like what was to come would involve serious manual labor. "And this neighborhood's been good to me. This year—" Gran fussed briefly with the fall of her hair. "I'd have curled up kaput without neighbors to make sure I didn't. So here's me, basking in all this community . . ." The weird accent was back. Apparently, that was how Gran did dramatic. "While right next door someone's struggling and I never even noticed. I don't like the kind of person that makes me."

The door opened then, though Ms. Rosko kept the chain latched. She looked a good deal thinner through the chink.

Gran's greeting was bright. "Mona."

Ms. Rosko eyed them. She had long, curling lashes, blond to the point of near-invisibility. The waste of it was almost Columbine tragic. "Sadie."

"And Lily, my granddaughter."

The door closed and Lily heard Ms. Rosko fiddle with the chain. She opened it again. "Lily. Of course. You must be the one I've been meaning to thank." There was a soft, controlled quality to her voice.

"You don't have to thank me. Really."

"No. I do."

Gran stood beside her, so full of pride she looked inflated.

Lily shouldn't have come here. Not after blowing this woman's secret. She should have *told* Gran what it was like. How she kissed Lindsay Clements at the back-to-school cookout. How Lindsay's mouth soured. She went heavy on the lipstick, matte when she should have used gloss, and it made the expression infinitely blatant. The red curl of her mouth, seconds before so appealing, pursed around something delicious. Not the kiss but the fact of it. Lindsay was going to tell. Everyone. So Lily told first. And then she did Lindsay one better. She told the whole Internet. Once she was an Official Lesbian, her page views soared. Everyone at Day was reading *Lipstick*. So yeah, it worked out okay for Lily.

But for Ms. Rosko? Probably not so much.

"We brought you some dinners," Lily lifted the trays. "They're frozen." Usually she was better at talking. In Health and Human Relations, they'd had a week-long unit on self-esteem and why it was important. They'd had to write down twenty-five things they were good at. They'd had to read their lists in front of the class. Talk about a day to lie about cramps. Lily started making things up around number seven, but by the time she got to the twenties she remembered and wrote *I give good grownup*. Everyone laughed when she read that part, which was kind of the point, but the laughing didn't make it less true.

"You brought us some dinners," Ms. Rosko parroted, as though she were translating from a language she knew only slightly.

"Yeah. I mean, yes. We did."

"Chicken Tetrazzini, some stuffed shells, and a veggie lasagna." Gran pointed at each tray in turn. She sounded like a flight attendant, but at least the reggae leprechaun was in check. "I tried to pick things the little fellow would enjoy."

"Tyson. We call him Ty."

The papers hadn't said that. They were all about preserving *Der Führer*'s anonymity, which if you thought about it was completely naïvecakes. Take his grandmother's name, add half an hour with a search engine, and you could probably figure it out.

Ms. Rosko accepted the dinners. "Come on in. Ty'll want to thank you." She had shockingly nice cheekbones. She'd probably had a good chin too once upon a time, gone loose now with soft skin. The house smelled citrusy and was scary clean. Carpet strands stood orderly from recent vacuuming. Tasseled throw pillows punctuated the sofa at precise intervals and a blue vase erupted with tulips.

"I should have brought flowers," said Lily. "Or maybe a teddy bear for Ty." The nickname felt dishonest in her mouth.

"We were so glad to hear he was okay," said Gran. "The papers all said—"

If Gran were Sierra, Lily would jut a quick elbow into her ribs. Look at the woman's face. Ms. Rosko wasn't the least bit happy about the newspapers and the things that they said. Lily interrupted. "Look, I'm sorry if I got you in trouble."

"You saved my grandson."

"Even so. If it puts you out any."

Ms. Rosko laughed, a staccato, joyless caw. "Ty's in here. We were having breakfast."

They followed her down the hall. Lily wished she'd taken off her sandals. Every step crushed a new patch of immaculate carpet. "We should go," she said, her voice louder than she intended. Ms. Rosko and Gran both stopped. "I only wanted to say sorry. I really am. If it means you'll have to move and all."

Ms. Rosko let out another bitter bark. "I've only been trying for ten months. You think I keep my house like this in real life?" Sunlight from the windows beyond turned her shirt transparent. Soft flesh rolled over her slacks and Lily could see the shape of her bra, one of those horrible old-lady ones with freestanding cups.

"Realtor ready." Gran sighed. "I sure don't miss that."

Ms. Rosko gave her a look like it was *Gran's uber*bra showing. "I bet the last house you sold was on the market for all of a minute."

"A few days."

"Huh. A few days. How about that?" Ms. Rosko folded her arms across her chest.

"Different market." Gran shrugged apologetically. "Peak of the boom. That's when we *bought*."

Lily felt better knowing there was a logical reason for the Rosko crazy neatness. Lindsay Clements of the Regrettable Kiss kept freesia-scented hand sanitizer in her locker. Lesson learned. It was never good to tango with the innately tidy.

In the kitchen, Tyson sat at a table that had been polished to a warm gloss. Up close he had a cowlick, which made his overall look less *sieg heil*-able. He spooned Cheerios into his mouth with intense focus. His right arm was in a sling. He offered an unsmiling hello, then asked his grandmother for more cereal. He said please. Ms. Rosko poured. It wasn't Cheerios after all, but those generic Os that came in a ginormous plastic bag. Tyson said thank-you without being prompted. Ms. Rosko settled Gran's trays into her freezer, then ran a hand through her hair, which hung unabashedly gray past her shoulders. Gran's was bobbed and bottle brown. Lily wasn't sure which was sadder, growing old and giving up or going around thinking that you were fooling people.

"Ty, it was Lily who called the ambulance when you fell," Ms. Rosko said.

Once again, the kid knew that thanks were expected. He made eye contact and used her name. Giving good grownup would probably be high on his skills list when he got to Health and Human Relations.

"I'm glad you're okay," said Lily. She meant it, but she was also glad the kid was pale and proper and self-contained. She might like him otherwise, and she felt bad enough already. He chewed with milky little slurps. "Can I see your cast?" Kids liked that, right? Ty raised his sling without enthusiasm. Lily offered to sign it. He met her eyes again. He had his grandmother's invisi-lashes and a furrowed pair of blond invisi-brows. "Can you draw?" he asked.

"Not well."

"No thank you then."

"I could try."

"My mom can draw. She draws on her letters."

Gran and Ms. Rosko were having some kind of neighborly conversation of their own, but at the word *mom* Gran threw her a cautioning glance. Like Lily wouldn't know that asking the and-where-*is*-your-mother question was only one step down on the rude-ness scale from a truly thunderous bout of flatulence.

Ms. Rosko was saying something about keeping the hot tub empty for showings, which had probably saved Ty's life. She caught Lily listening. "Along with your quick thinking, of course."

Lily shook her head. "I'm sorry it's in the papers. And about the HOA and all of that. It's probably discrimination, them wanting you two to go. It might not even be legal. I had Civics last semester."

Ms. Rosko laughed again. A real laugh this time, from her gut.

Ty laughed too, not wanting to be left out.

Only Gran didn't. That stupid proud grin on her stupid proud face. It was embarrassing. When Lily was old she was going to go the Rosko route, fearless and gray.

"Truth is, I'm almost relieved," Mona Rosko said. "At least it's out there now."

"That makes sense. Secrets aren't any fun."

A pinched look. "You're how old again?"

"Fifteen. Sixteen this October."

"Fifteen. Huh. Well, enjoy it."

"I'm gay. I try to tell everyone right when I meet them. I don't want to sit around wondering how they'll act once they find out. So I guess I know a little bit about how it feels." Lily, don't *do* that, Mom always said. Wait till you get a read on folks. The world doesn't work like Forest Park Day School. You can't guess who might have a gun out in their truck. Poor Mom. But if it wasn't this, it'd be something else. At least now she wasn't up nights worried about Lily coming home pregnant.

"You're gay."

"Yup."

"We're very proud of Lily. She's very courageous." That was Gran. Pride in Lily seemed to be her go-to response to any given stimulus.

"You could say that," Ms. Rosko said. And people did say it. Like Lily had done it in hopes of receiving a high school medal for valor.

"We're very proud," Gran repeated.

"Well. What I do wonder is how she spotted him. I'm grateful, of course, but—"

"I was up on Gran's roof. Tanning."

Ms. Rosko made a face. Cue the melanoma's-no-joking-matter talk.

Instead: "Hmm. Unsupervised minor unattended on the roof. Maybe someone should sic a social worker on *you*."

"Gran didn't know, and I—"

"Joking, joking," said Ms. Rosko. The shape of her mouth said otherwise. "Besides, they only go after the guardians."

From his perch at the table, Ty perked up. He set down his spoon. "My mom is in the army."

"That's right, puffin." Ms. Rosko's posture softened briefly with her tone.

"Is she abroad?" Lily asked, afraid of saying the wrong -ibad or -istan. Her Civics teacher said it was embarrassing how few Americans knew any kind of world geography.

Ms. Rosko looked over at Ty. "Yes."

Gran said, "That's hard."

"Her name is Carrie," Ty said. "Carrie and she likes carrots." He laughed because, yeah, to a little kid that would be funny. He hopped down from his chair.

"Afghanistan?" Lily guessed. The capitol was Kabul. She'd only got a B+ on their world geography unit, but she was pretty sure she had that one right. Last year's senior class had held a pencil drive for girls' schools over there as their service project.

"Yeah," said Tyson. "I can show you on my map." He tore off down the hall.

"Don't bother, Tyson," Ms. Rosko called after him. "Our guests are on their way out."

Something had shifted. Lily felt socially short bus. "I hope she'll be all right. And I think it's cool she's in the army. Being a girl and all."

"Yes. Well. I can see how you'd be keen about the army."

"Mona . . ." Gran sounded a lot like Dad before he launched into one of his steely Lily-we-expect-more-of-our-daughter talks.

"That and marriage. All of those—backbones. The things that keep the rest of us standing tall." Ms. Rosko's smile was brief and achingly sweet. It dissolved with a derisive snort and what she was *actually* saying jostled into place.

The world doesn't operate like Forest Park Day.

Lily had a 3.87 grade-point average. She'd rocked her semester of debate. She should be able to rebut.

But it was Gran who spoke. "That's unfair. Lily did your family a tremendous service."

"Let me tell you about unfair. I grew up here. My granddad was one of the original ranch hands. My folks ran a Feed 'n Seed that folded once you people swarmed down here. Then the taxes alone—" Her words catapulted quickly one into the next. "My husband and I stretched to stay and without warning"—she clapped once, a gunshot of a sound—"he's gone and I'm on my own and underwater for a place that'll sell for three-fifths of what I put into it and that's if we're lucky." A breathy hiss. "And now you people want to kick me out and go about your happy little lives." She shrugged. Like nothing in the world could possibly matter.

Lily giggled, like she always did at the worst possible moment. When it came to fight or flight she was (c) none of the above, which would easily make the top five if Health and Human Relations asked for a corresponding list of flaws.

Ms. Rosko shot her a look that could invert nipples.

Gran's hand came to rest on her shoulder. "I think an apology is in order. It's hardly Lily's fault you overextended—"

Ms. Rosko turned her back on them. "You want to know where I was when Ty fell? The papers sure do." She picked up her grandson's bowl. She rinsed it out and chased a few errant Os down the drain. "Job interview. I covered the earth with resumes. Hundreds of them. Thirty years I ran medical records down at St. Joe's and I get the one little nibble."

"Nevertheless. That sort of talk isn't called for," Gran said. "We're glad your grandson's well. Goodbye."

"Have a lovely vacation, Lily." The word *vacation* sounded more bitter than anything Ms. Rosko had said before, which meant it probably wasn't just the lesbian thing. Lily knew what she looked like. She did the math: the cost of her shoes and her highlights alone.

"I'm sorry," she said.

"Lily," Gran said, "do not apologize to this woman."

Forest Park Day School had celebrated its centennial this year. They'd hung banners all over the place. One Hundred Years of Shaping Students. Sierra made the joke, oh so cynical, oh so Sierra, oh so sophisticated. One Hundred Years of Sheltering Students. Dusty sunlight spilled through the windows and across Mona Rosko's pristine floors. On the off-chance of prospective buyers, she'd have to wipe them once they left.

Gran let the front door slam behind them. "I had no idea she would be like that." She wiped her palms on her pants. "If ever a woman was weaned on a pickle."

Almost a year now since Lily first came out. Cocooned at school, people fell over themselves to accept her. She was overdue for small-mindedness. Everyone and their dogs called her courageous. If she rose above this, she actually would be. "It's okay," she said.

"It's light years from okay."

"Gran, it's fine."

"Look at me. You didn't deserve any of that."

"Okay." True, she hadn't. But it didn't follow that she deserved all the good things that had come her way either. Her earlobes itched, heavy with—real—gold hoops, and she felt fluttery-frantic to *do* something. Gran called her the Angel of the Commons and angels only ever held still and pretty on top of Christmas trees. Angels were terrible and forgiving. They wrestled, they fell, they rebelled and avenged. Angels were all about the verbs.

Hello, Chickie-dolls. Yes, I'm back. Yes, this is the authentic Lillian, *not some off-brand cotton-poly blend. Rumors of my demise/ new gig as columnist for* Teen Vogue/*forced enrollment in one of those de-gay-ifying camps are completely and utterly cuckoo for Cocoa Puffs. I'd set you all straight (yes, that's a pun. Yes, you can deal with it) but you seem to be having the time of your collective lives going feral in the comments. Besides, I've got something important to say, so put down your nail files and listen up, ladies and Midwestern perverts pretending to be ladies.*

We're attractive, not dumb. We all know there are things that matter more than looks (and no, I haven't turned into any of your mothers. Believe me, I've checked my mirror).

This is one of those things.

LIKELIER THAN BARCELONA

BEN LIKED THE SIMPLE SAMENESS of his Commons mornings. A walk with Sadie, tinkering with his espresso machine, then hunkering down at his computer to do the crossword. Every day, he and his daughter-in-law did the same one online. She'd yet to beat his time but said it didn't matter. She liked the way it got her mind warmed up.

Today though, Anjali might actually win; it was damned near impossible to concentrate. A news van had parked across the way. Ben watched a reporter, pretty from a distance, ring his neighbor's bell. A cameraman hovered close, encumbered with technology. Marvin and Ed, Ben's golf buddies, were parked in his drive and playing looky-loo, never mind their tee time in twenty minutes.

It was the Rosko thing. Of course it had gone big. Ben had guessed it would three lines into the *Crier*'s first report. Not a sure thing like another pretty housewife evaporating on the eve of a national holiday, but the odds were up there. Young kid, local grandmother getting royally screwed over, and a smug patina of judgment. There you had it. Headline stew.

Ben finished his coffee and crunched a last bite of toast. He watched Sadie and her granddaughter saunter down the street, armed with tennis rackets. The girl swung hers in a wide, lazy arc, courting the cameras. Someone had taught her a proper grip, but she'd need more than that to land on TV, and oh boy did he know. Years ago, a summer storm had felled a century-old fir on his street in Portland, taking out a hefty percent of the city's power grid. A news van came for footage and Ben had run into the rain with a picture of Tara. He'd asked the reporter, please, if you could broadcast this for even a second. If you could run our home phone beneath. No dice. The reporter had worn a yellow slicker, Ben remembered, a childish thing that looked like it ought to be paired with bumblebee galoshes. The one across the way was in yellow, too, a bright blouse beneath a somber, nipped-in jacket. No one real ever wore that shade. They must teach you in journalism school that it makes you stand out. The reporter rang again. Her companion did something with his camera. Ben smiled. Evidently, Mona Rosko wasn't answering the bell.

And good on Mona for that. Making *them* work for it for once. He didn't know the lady well, but this morning he sure as hell liked her. There was a gritty brand of dignity to tending to your own troubles. Lord knew that employing professionals (the name of their private detective came to mind here, followed closely by the name of their marriage counselor) got you nowhere.

A moment or two passed. The reporter cottoned on to the fact that Mona wasn't answering. She had the cameraman set up on the Rosko lawn, which probably was in direct violation of a strident clause or two of the HOA. Marvin and Ed loped over to brownnose. The reporter was gracious with her handshakes. Ben wondered how long it would take for her to do her thing and get gone.

Then the quick glint of light on glass. Mona Rosko, opening her door. She had a large hammer slung over one shoulder and a sign of some sort rucked up under the opposite arm. Long pants and what looked like a denim work shirt, the last thing you'd want in this heat. She moved with a startling, cool fluidity. An Arizona lifer, so who knew. Maybe heat actually worked the way idiots said heartache did: Live with it long enough and whole days can pass without it registering. Mona stood a moment beside her door, gathering herself and their attention. She stepped out to the center of her lawn.

Her stance had him very aware that she was holding a hammer. Her stance had him wondering what it was for. She hefted it higher. The camera, he thought. A rush of child-like glee. One hit and it's a splintered assemblage of wire and casing. But no. Mona busied herself with the sign. A simple, red For Sale sign, the kind you saw in neighborhoods where such *departures from our shared Southwestern aesthetic* weren't prohibited by the Flamingo Police. Mona swung hard. There was thunder in her shoulders. Ben thought, for the first time in ages, of those yellowing pinups he'd found taped to the underside of his father's workbench. Tame things, even back in the day, big-busted dames with toolboxes and lug wrenches, Rosie the Riveters with legs. Those girls were pretty where Mona wasn't, tarted up where she wasn't, but as far as specimens went, his neighbor was the more impressive, beautiful in her hardworking context instead of simpering along beside it. She checked the sign over to make sure it was even, stood a grim moment with her hands at her hips, pivoted abruptly, and went back into her house.

She never spoke a word.

Everyone on Mona's lawn began scurrying at once, as if they'd been wound with a key. Marvin and Ed gestured furiously in his direction, and Ben let himself out into the street.

"Ben! Over here!" Ed Runch waved as though hailing a Manhattan cab. You can take the man out of the city and so on. Ed told the reporter, "Here's the guy you'll want to see."

The reporter had blunt blonde hair and several inches on most of the surrounding men. She walked his way. The cameraman followed as if tethered. Marvin and Ed, too. A bunch of damn ducklings. Ben forced his face into a cracked plate of a smile. Don't blame the press, Veronica always said. If it weren't Tara, would *you* be interested?

And that was Veronica, resolute and practical, except when she wasn't. Between Olympics, she had a friend over at Nike, someone she knew from the Women in Business Council, collect tapes of figure skating that didn't air on U.S. television. Whole weekends passed freeze-frame by freeze-frame, Ronnie scanning the faces in the crowd. When she was small, Tara had loved the sport. His wife wore contacts for the workweek and glasses on the weekends. The screen reflected in her lenses, and he wondered if she actually believed they had a chance of spying her, easy as that, cheering from a stadium in Barcelona.

"Did you *see* that?" Ed asked. "How's that for drumming up interest? This guy caught it all." He jerked a thumb toward the cameraman, then ran a hand through his hair. He still had plenty. "House'll sell now. Like they say. Silence. It's golden." He said it like a slogan. Ed used to be in advertising.

"This is Emmy," said Marvin, his voice cutting high across Ed's. "You know, like the award? Feel like helping her get one?"

"Emily Rourke." The woman extended her hand. The coloring was off—too fair—but she had the same careful, Gallic prettiness as Veronica and that caught him right in the throat.

"I know Mona a little, if that's what you're asking."

"Would you be willing to talk with me a bit?" Emily Rourke made it sound like she was asking for just that, a chat. No clip-on microphone, no signed releases. None of whatever else media attention entailed. She leaned in, smiling, and he—because you never get over being a sucker, never get over that hindbrain—was glad he was taller than both Marvin and Ed.

"Be sure to film in black and white," said Marvin. "Get a load of those pants."

Ben looked down. Your standard-issue garish golf pants, a Christmas gift from Veronica. Every year post-divorce, she sent him a new pair. Because she made a joke of the holiday, Ben did too. He sent umbrellas, knowing damn well that in Portland only out-of-towners used them.

Ed chuckled. "We told you he was a funny guy. Hey, Ben, tell us again what brought you to The Commons."

Emily Rourke beamed, an on-purpose expression that worked on him despite the fact that he *knew* it was working on him. "The pants are fine," she said. "I think that's the plaid they use for my stepdaughter's school uniform."

"I'm not sure I'd be much use to you. Mona's my neighbor, that's all."

"We'll just talk. Casual as can be, okay?"

Casual as a person could be with a microphone threaded up his back. Ed and Marvin stood off to the side. Ben couldn't think of a thing to say. Look at me and not the camera, Emily instructed. That should've been easy—decades of Ronnie bristling when he looked at pretty women and here was license to do exactly that—but it wasn't. He saw the camera. He saw the guys. The things his ex would say about the whole scenario. Benji, you do know you're only going along with this because those two goons wish they could, don't you? Christ. You'd think with the divorce finalized he could get her voice out of his head. The interview started with him stating and spelling his name.

"Tell me a little about your life here at The Commons."

Golf and tennis sounded so frivolous in list form. He must have said *um* twenty times in the space of two sentences. "I used to be a veterinarian," he added, because he needed gravity from somewhere, "up in Portland. I did a lot of pro bono work with service animals."

"And what brings you to The Commons?"

If Marvin and Ed hadn't been right there, beyond the camera he wasn't supposed to be looking at, it never would have slipped out. That stupid joke they liked so much. "Well, I'm newly divorced. And without my ex, I need the HOA to tell me what to do."

Emily Rourke would never get far without work on her poker face, but he wasn't her father and he wasn't going to lecture. She recovered well, which was something. "Have you found the Homeowners' Association intrusive?"

"That was a joke. Not even a very good one. I hope you won't use it."

"You're doing fine. Can you talk a bit about the HOA? All those rules . . ."

"Everyone jokes about it."

"Why?"

"Like you said. All those rules. It's funny."

"Funny how?"

"Because it comes down to have a little taste, don't be stupid, and don't be rude."

"Do you think that applies to the Rosko situation?"

"Look, I said I don't know Mona all that well."

"You're doing great," Emily repeated. The more she said it, the more he knew he wasn't.

"I'm sorry. I know this isn't going well."

"How has Mona Rosko been as a neighbor?" The cameraman stepped back. He at least knew a dud when he saw one.

"Quiet. Nice enough, I suppose. People are always having barbecues and things like that, but she doesn't show up all that much." He sounded like every neighbor, ever, describing every serial killer, ever, on the news. At least he knew better than to express that particular thought. "That makes sense now, knowing about her grandson. It's a pretty big secret to keep."

"And how do you feel about that?"

"Bad luck all around. For the kid that he doesn't have anyone else, at least if what you lot are saying is true. For Mona, too, stuck until her place sells. I don't know what they're going to do."

"What about personally? How do you feel about this? As a neighbor or as a—do you have grandchildren?"

"No." A sore twang beneath his breastbone: the truer answer was none that he knew of. "No," he said again, because you didn't admit that you had no earthly idea to a stranger. You didn't cop to the daydream: Tara and some kindly boy in a shelter—not something crueler, and not something she did to survive—the shock of it waking them to responsibility, to her parents at the ready to help them along.

"Okay then," said Emily. "Thank you for your time."

"Wait," Ben said. Mona Rosko had them all fawning to help her, a full cast of marionettes. And then not a peep. There was pride, he got that, had plenty of it, had allowed it to make a mess of him time and again. There was pride, and then there was the sweat and dirt of the world they actually lived in. Time was, he and Veronica would have liquidated their portfolios if it could have bought this kind of attention. And Mona flounced off. "Wait, please." Tara was gone, probably forever. Rand said so. Veronica, drunk, once even said the words aloud. But if she was out there, she might be near a TV. Tara might see him. It wasn't likely, but it was likelier than Barcelona. "I have something to say." Ben shut his eyes and thought of a newsreel bomb falling in black and white. The bigger the blast the wider its radius.

The cameraman stepped closer.

Emily Rourke nodded for him to continue. His mind went kaleidoscopic with everything he should have said in his life but hadn't.

Marvin and Ed paid no attention at all.

Ben wasn't nervous. A debate scholarship had helped put him through college and his ex said he was the only man alive who actually thought in bullet points. He took a breath and looked straight at the camera.

"That Mona Rosko is a vinegary old cunt."

THE OPPOSITE
OF SHALLOW

IT WAS WAY TOO EARLY for SAT words, so when Gran said, "I believe you have a swain," the best Lily could manage was a slurred *huh?* and a series of thick blinks.

"That young man." Gran indicated the window. "I doubt he's here for me." Her weird accent was back and she brought a hand theatrically to her heart. "Clearly smitten. He must've spotted you from afar." If Mom ever spied a lingerer she'd be dialing nine-one-one and saying stalker. Dad, too. The parentals had some highly detailed theories about what happened to little girls who played on the Internet.

Lily said, "If he's here for me and he's a he, he's out of luck."

"Poor fellow." Gran tapped the window. Sure enough, the guy stood smack in the middle of the street like an out-of-uniform traffic cop. And not just any guy. Rocky. Rocky Ludlow. Sierra's Rocky. Holy Little Black Dress.

"I know him," Lily said, running scenarios, all of which hovered around the Gouda level of extreme cheese. A pregnancy test, positive, Sierra's. They were en route to elope and wanted her as witness. A pregnancy test, positive, not Sierra's. He needed her to intercede before Sierra castrated him with a melon spoon.

"Oh?"

"From school. I'm going to see what's going on."

"Let him down easy." Gran winked. If plotted on a graph, her swoony silliness would peak each morning before her walk with the per-vet. They'd watched him on the news last night. Some brief per-vet platitude about being sorry for Mona Rosko. Then the lady herself, large and stern. She hadn't been ugly though; her stillness transformed her. Her silence, too. The way she'd crossed the lawn. She'd worn beat-up sneakers, but she moved like a bride. The hammer split the air and Lily felt all flutter and gauze in the face of the woman's *I am*. Gran didn't get it. She wondered why they'd only used a few seconds of Ben. There needed to be a verb. Crushversate: to obsessively bring up one's crush in conversation.

Of course Gran thought Rocky had come a'courtin'. Her whole mind was wired that way. *Let him down easy.* Har-dee-har. "Things aren't always about that," Lily said. Her parents' friends always teased her about dating, like talking romance was the accepted shorthand for acknowledging she wasn't a kid anymore without having to actually engage. In the street, Rocky bounced foot to foot. Trust the Rockster to get himself the thousand miles to Arizona and then forget her grandmother's address.

"Things aren't always about what?" Gran asked.

"Love." Lily made a sour-milk face and wondered if Grandpa would have started crushing so soon if Gran had died first.

"I know. But wouldn't it be better if they were?"

Lily was spectacularly unqualified to say. Her one kiss had been a disaster. She went out into the morning bright. Rocky's head whipped around. His features resolved: almost Rocky, but not quite. The mouth was broader, and arranged into an expression of completely un-Rockified pensiveness. He waved, which if Lily were ever crowned Queen of the Universe, was a gesture she'd ban about twelve seconds into her reign. There was always that moment of social panic: how to be one-hundred-percent sure you're the intended recipient. She didn't wave back. For all she knew, the guy had a dandruff problem and was raising his hand to scratch. Rocky II came sprinting over. "Hey, check it out. That's my paper!"

"No way. It's my gran's." Aside from his mouth, the resemblance to Rocky I was terrifying: the hair, the chin, the slightly crooked nose. The absent-from-kindergarten-the-day-they-taught-sharing impulse to waltz on up and say *mine*.

Rocky II laughed. It made his Adam's apple prominent. "Yeah, sorry. I meant that's the paper I work for. Nicky Tullbeck," He extended his hand like a mayoral candidate.

"My grandmother said you were lurking."

"I'm *reporting*," Nicky said. He wiped his hand on his pants when it was clear Lily was not about to shake.

"This just in: local granddaughter gets the paper."

"Your grandparents live here?"

"My gran."

"Little Red Riding Hood." Rocky did that same smug thing with his chin when he thought he'd said something smart. If she had her phone she'd take a picture for Sierra, who would promptly drop dead at the blissful prospect of two of them. Nicky attempted a flirtatious grin. "To grandmother's house you go? Like in the story."

"I'm not stupid," she said. "I just didn't think it was funny."

"Fine. Sorry. You been visiting long?"

"I'm not visiting. I'm living here in secret."

She hadn't had a sense of how lousy his posture was until he straightened. "For real? Like that kid?" His phone came out, with a doofy stylus for notes.

"Yeah. Just like him. And we aren't the only ones. Bin Laden's hiding at *his* gran's house, too. You're not really a reporter, are you?"

He colored. His eyelashes were long like both Roskos' but bold and feathery and dark. Further evidence of an unjust universe: no mascara in the world could get her that look. "I'm an intern," he admitted. "I start at Rice this fall."

"That's nice, I guess." A curtain rustled in the Rosko house. Little Ty, playing secret agent. Mona Rosko, wishing that strapping fellow would kiss the dyke and cure her already.

"It's a good school. I'm looking forward to it." His blush receded and his grin returned. Like Rocky, he had an underbite. Ten bucks said that on the way from his eardrums to his brain her *that's nice* turned into a breathless, mushy, Sierra-to-Rocky-style *omigosh-you're-smart*. A breeze rattled the chimes on a neighbor's porch and a quick, deep *damn!* carried from the golf course. "I'm doing a follow-up on that kid who's been hiding out." Nicky made Tyson sound like a cops-and-robbers bandit. "This is his street."

"I know that. I told you I wasn't stupid."

"Have you met them?"

She shrugged.

"You have. Do you think you could throw me a quote?"

"Isn't the *Crier* sending someone real?"

Nicky examined his hands, front and back. "I'm pretty sure I *am* real."

That was kind of funny, actually.

But Lily knew the formulae.

Laugh and it's encouragement.

Say I'm not interested and hear back *bitch*.

And half the time he'll take the God's honest I'll-never-be-interested-no-offense-it's-a-question-of-chromosomes truth as a challenge.

The other half he'll ask to watch.

"My gran's waiting. I've got to go."

"C'mon." He took a quick step toward her. "Look. I was on the paper all through high school. I made editor my junior year. I got into Rice early decision." He rolled his eyes. "And I'm spending my summer doing jack-all for an editor I caught using the wrong *there* twice."

"Our school paper did that once in a headline." She hadn't actually noticed, but her English teacher had gone on about it. "The guy's a sleepwalker. He's got no idea I'm out here. But I figure, if I write up something good I might get to do something this summer besides watch my ex-girlfriend play FarmVille. Help a guy out? I'm dying."

The way he threw up his hands reminded her of Gran.

"That doesn't sound so bad," Lily said. "Mucking around online all day." She was pitiful. Her hand made the shape it would take to hold her iPhone.

"I'm dying," he said again.

The emphasis on the first syllable reminded her of Sierra.

If she let her eyes blur, he didn't look like Rocky at all.

Lily knew what people thought of her. Even before Miss Titty Tattlecakes' sob story. She'd overheard her parents. Dad to Mom: Who knows, maybe someday she'll do a post on how not to be shallow. Mom to Dad: That's mean. She's so confident now. It's helped her come into her own. Lily to parentals, if only she were *actually* confident: It's the opposite of shallow. Shallow would be hoarding her know-how. *Lipstick* helped girls across the country, girls across the Atlantic even. It wasn't an exaggeration to call it an essential service. Knowing you look good frees your mind for so many other things.

Like doing actual freaking good.

"Ty's a sweetie," she said. Sweetie would get better play than one-of-those-creepy-kids-who-seem-forty. "Epic sweetie pie."

"You mean the kid?"

"Yeah. Tyson Rosko." The papers didn't even have his name. No wonder Nicky was paying attention. "He's the most fantastic kid. I've got a Facebook group for him going." Despite the call from her parents, who were *thrilled* about it in a yes-I-know-it's-important-to-you-but-we-said-no-Internet-Lily-we've-had-it-up-to-here kind of way.

Nicky's stylus scribbled briefly. "And the grandma? It'd be great to get intel on her."

Boom. The word *intel* made her loathe him again. The kind of word Rocky would pick up from one of those video games where he pretended to be a soldier. And then there was Mona Rosko: her bare, clean house, her quiet boy, her daughter who actually served. Her hair, a coiling curtain of gray. The golden wasted length of her eyelashes. The fluid arc of a hammer brought unerringly down. "She's strong," Lily said. "Like you wouldn't believe."

Nicky scrawled. She could read his notes upside down with no trouble. No caps for Rosko.

"She's doing her best, you know? Her daughter's stationed in Afghanistan. Someone's got to look after the kid."

Afghanistan, Nicky wrote. That, he capitalized. She wasn't saying this right.

"She's strong," she tried again, and then, "real." Lily mimed Ms. Rosko with the hammer. Nicky looked at her like she was having a fit. "You don't get it. If you'd seen her on Channel Twelve, you'd get it."

Nicky smirked. Rocky II: the return. "I don't think you were watching the same Channel Twelve as the rest of the world." He fiddled with his phone. It was embarrassing how much she missed the solid, connected palm-feel of her own. Nicky tilted the screen toward her, shading it with his hand. "Footage from yesterday. Leaked, I guess. Obviously they couldn't air it."

The reporter from last night, hair bobbed at chin level to make her eyes pop. And beside her, the putty-colored face of Per-Vet Thales. "Wait," he said, "I have something to say." He shut his eyes, then bugged them out. Beside him, the reporter gave a brief, conversational nod. The per-vet inhaled. "That Mona Rosko is a vinegary old cunt."

A quick pan back to the reporter. You could pinpoint the moment she processed the word. "Sir—"

"And you're a cunt, too. I apologize for saying it, Miss, but it's true. And you—" he pointed a tuberous finger at the camera— "you're a cunt for listening." He brought a hand to his mouth for an improvised megaphone. "All you neighbors! All of you are cunts for even caring about this." His voice pitched high and mincing. "But we have *rules*." Something in his throat shifted. His voice was baritone now, but still whiney. "But he's a little boy and we have to be *nice* to him." His face contorted; his eyebrows wriggled like a pair of tortured caterpillars. A fly zoomed into the frame. It came to rest on his cheek and he swatted it away, his hands huge and pawlike. The fly made its erratic way toward the camera and then back onto his face. He didn't notice, even when it crawled over the bridge of his nose. "We know the little boy's safe, and he's a cunt, too. We all are, because nobody cares about the real problem, about children who—" His throat worked horribly, like he was struggling for air. His skin had gone from putty to meat. The fly turned small circles on his left cheek. "Tenaya Alder, sixteen. Last seen wearing cutoffs and a green T-shirt. Mimi Asencios, sixteen. Last seen wearing her Pizza Hut uniform." The fly edged toward the corner of his mouth. Benjamin Thales had gone completely robotic, his voice glazed and metallic. "Christy Aves, sixteen. Last seen wearing khakis and a red parka. Lisa Balish, almost sixteen. Last seen wearing her boyfriend's letter jacket. Meghan Bagnall—" His face was still, except for the small, essential movement the mouth needed to name its names. Beside him, the reporter drew a quick finger across her neck. The mic feed dropped away. Ben didn't notice. His fish lips kept doing their thing. He stopped, realized the mic was out, and leaned in toward the reporter, who had one clipped to the V of her collar. The camera caught him in profile, the fly silhouetted on his forehead. The microphone caught something about "denim skirt" and "Darcy Bremmen" and "high-top sneakers." Every time the reporter stepped away, the man followed, head bowed as if to peck at something in her cleavage. "—and a green pullover. Theresa

Cavanough. I don't remember what she was last seen wearing. That makes me a cunt, too." And just like that he stopped. Face slack and mottled. As if disoriented by the sudden quiet, the fly drifted from the per-vet's face and settled on the reporter's exposed collarbone. Then Ben's voice returned, courteous and lilting, tender as a lullaby. "I'm awfully sorry, Miss. There's a fly on your shoulder." He gestured to his own with a flat, open palm, as if to cradle something wounded.

Nicky snickered. "I'm awfully sorry, Miss. There's a fly on your shoulder." He was a lousy mimic. *Gran's* accents were better. When his hand came to his shoulder, he looked more like he was trying to cup a large and badly placed boob. When she didn't laugh, he said it again, "I'm awfully sorry, Miss. There's a fly on your shoulder." This time, he reached toward her.

"Don't touch me."

"Sorry. It's funny though. The fly's what *makes* it. The guy doesn't even notice, and then he's all, I'm sorry, Miss."

The Laws of Cheese dictated she ought to say something arch here. Get a load of those golf pants, or I guess we know who's hiding the bodies. A quick, dull ache bloomed at the base of her tongue. Her grandmother *liked* Ben Thales. She'd invited him into her home, baked her specialty biscuits, put out the plates with blue flowers on the rim. "I've got to go."

"Wait. Check this out. My buddy Kai did a remix."

"Sorry. Bye."

"What? Are you pissed about the *C* word?"

"I'm not pissed about the *C* word."

Nicky followed her up the drive, pocketing the phone. The roof of her mouth itched. Gran was inside, waiting for her daily walk. Gran, whose husband had known the secret to the world's best scrambled eggs. Who had collected maps with that husband of everywhere they'd traveled, the roads they'd used traced carefully in yellow highlighter. Grandpa had whistled old show tunes when he shaved and had a callus from a lifetime of holding his pen the wrong way. Grandpa had insisted Lily sell her Girl Scout Cookies in person instead of circulating a signup sheet at the office because even though the world didn't operate face-to-face anymore, it ought to. He and Gran had met at a skating party when they were both twelve. Thick flakes had clung to dark hair and now he was buried in a state that hadn't seen snow this millennium.

Oh, Gran.

She was coming out of a time capsule from before she was hormonal. She had no way of knowing that ped-obsessed jerkoraptors like Benjamin Thales even existed.

"You *are* pissed." Nicky tapped his temple. "I'm kind of psychic." He smiled. The insouciant look of someone who thought her shoulder was his to touch by right.

"Me, too." She tapped her own temple. "I can tell you'd kill for a byline."

He nodded.

"Well, listen. I was the one who saw the kid get hurt. I've been in the Rosko house. I'm actually kind of their official spokesperson." The lie felt good. The way his eyes widened. His hand went quick to his phone like a gunslinger. "And I'm leaving now." She barely stopped a bright *ta-ta.*

JUST A LOCAL GIRL

THE THEME FROM *INDIANA JONES* meant that Stephen was calling. Last Thanksgiving, Ben'd had Anjali set up the ringtone. "Why Indy?" she'd asked, inputting an unintelligible set of commands. "His favorite's *The Godfather*, yeah?" She'd hummed a few bars. Badly. Anjali was slight and vivid and omnicompetent, which made her musical hopelessness endearing.

He'd smiled. "The tune gets stuck in my head like nothing else. *Dah-dah-DAH-dah, dah-dah-dah.* Now when he calls, it'll stay with me all day."

"You dear sweet man," Anjali had said, and thereafter the tune was full of her as well.

Ben picked up halfway through. "Stephen!"

"So, Dad. I hear you made the news down there."

"For a second or so. On Saturday." He'd watched at twelve, at five, and again at ten. He'd seen his father, nine years buried last October, before he'd seen himself. Ben hadn't realized. He'd lost weight. His hands were all puff and knobs. The skin of his face was half a pulse behind his actual expression. And the waste of it. The utter waste. The things he'd said to that poor young woman. The only thing that had come of it was Sadie's granddaughter asking, ostentatiously, where on earth he'd gotten those fabulous pants. He was a fool. Yes, a withered old fool. Even if they'd had the stones to air it, his daughter would not have known him.

His son said, "I'm proud of you, Dad. All calm and succinct and dignified."

Stephen sounded like Veronica at her most ticked off. Ben's house, all custom-outfitted twenty-one-hundred square feet of it, contracted claustrophobic.

"Stephen, I—how did you even know?" His son'd had a college-vintage girlfriend from these parts, a volleyball-playing squeak toy of a girl. Zoey something. "Did Zoey tell you?"

"Zoey, Dad?"

"The volleyball girl. Does Anjali know you're still in touch?" Anjali hardly seemed the jealous type, but you know women. Ben had been with two girls before Veronica, Paula Derry his first year at Bucknell and Deborah Shale back home. It was a small campus. They ran into Paula a few times each term. Veronica was always airy and much too sweet, like the cotton candy their kids would beg for at festivals in the years to come. They graduated. They married and moved West. They visited his boyhood home very seldom. Whenever they did though, Veronica insisted on flapjacks at the Sweet Mountain Grill, where Deborah waited tables. Deb looked just as she had in high school, and then she looked like she was trying very hard to look just as she had in high school. Veronica tipped outrageously, upwards of thirty percent, and though Ben had never felt particularly well versed in the slights and symbols that made up the language of women, he knew it wasn't well meant. He never said anything though. He reckoned Deb could use the cash.

"I haven't heard from Zoey in years," Stephen said. "It's called the Internet, Dad. You're all over everywhere. Hugh and Enrique posted it and neither of them even knew it was you."

Ben failed to place the names Hugh and Enrique. His son lived a whole world apart. "It was just a local girl," Ben said. "That reporter. She's on all the time down here. School bee stuff. Dog shows. So-and-so entered the state fair."

"And you won the blue ribbon. C'mon. You know there's no such thing as local anymore."

"I guess not." A side effect of television: since the interview aired Ben couldn't speak without hearing his own voice. Good grief, the threadlike timbre. The leaden way he ended words. Try hard enough to beat out an accent and you wound up with a new one. "Don't hang up yet, Stephen."

"Hang up?"

"Please." Ben was missing something here. He'd only been televised long enough to say *bad luck all around*. No possible offense in that. "You're upset and—"

"I don't hang up on people. Christ, Dad. People don't do that."

"You're angry."

"I'm not. But, Dad—Tenaya Alder? Mimi Asencios?"

"What? That part didn't air." Though he did owe the reporter an apology. Flowers too, probably.

"The *Internet*. You know what? Maybe I *am* mad."

"I never meant—" Gall in the back of his throat and all along his molars. The rest of it must have gotten out somehow. Out and into the everywhere. "You know I'd never—"

"Christy Aves?"

"Stephen."

"What about Tara?"

Ben's throat constricted.

"What about Tara?" Stephen's question was quieter this time. It was telling, if you thought about it. His son had always had an easy time with women. He'd reddened, but not declined, when Ben asked if they ought to buy him a box of condoms before his first term at USC. Before Anjali, he'd had two definitive types: brittle, pallid Tara clones and the plumped-up, over-processed chicken-cutlet girls who were their explicit opposites.

"Tara," said Ben, massaging his throat. "I thought she—it's stupid."

"This whole thing is pretty stupid."

"I thought she might see it somehow."

"Yeah. I figured." It bothered him, in a way he was too keyed up to fully articulate, that Stephen guessed. It was a loss of sorts. There had been a wholesome kind of benevolence in being mysterious to his children.

Ben said, "If she was out there, I wanted her to *know*. It's not right how the whole world let her disappear."

"Dad."

"Because it's not. And this thing . . . the boy is fine, but the reporters keep on—"

"Dad. You should have said, come home."

He and Veronica worried about how uncomplicated Stephen was after Tara, how absolutely forthright. They tongued at that worry like a canker sore. But that was just Stephen. Their boy. "You're right," Ben said. Come home. The breath-catching simplicity of it. The only real thing he had ever wanted to say.

"Well. Long shot anyhow, right?" Stephen made a noise like he was swallowing a sigh. Ben heard murmuring in the background. Anjali? He thought of her eating breakfast at the IKEA table he'd help the kids assemble, lipstick blotting the rim of her juice glass. Veronica used to do that. He'd once been wild enough about her to raise those smudges to his lips.

"Is that Anjali I hear?"

"I'm calling from work."

Of course he was. Monday in Boston. Once, he'd known where his kids were every minute.

"She's worried about you though," Stephen said. "Anjali."

"Tara used to do that."

"Do what?"

"Use an intermediary. *Anjali's* worried. Instead of saying it herself. *Stephen* wants Frosted Flakes. *Mom* wants you to push me higher." Maybe they should've packed her off to a shrink. It sure as hell didn't augur well that she was five years old and couldn't even speak to them directly.

A hiss of breath from his son. "Okay. Yeah. I'm worried, too."

"You don't have to be."

"You didn't seem like yourself, Dad. You're not—you're okay, right?"

"Never better. Hand on my heart."

"Because Anjali has a cousin at Hopkins. He could find someone to take a look—"

"It's nothing to do with—the old noggin's fine. Your dad's a little foolish, that's all."

"You meant well."

"You can't see it, but I'm shrugging."

"Dad."

"And I'm sorry. If I embarrassed you."

"I'm not embarrassed. Really. In a few days someone will train their puppy to moonwalk and no one will remember you."

"Good. I'm glad."

"But, Dad? I'm trying to be Switzerland with you and Mom—"

"I know that. I appreciate it. Your mother and I both do."

"You know she's going to worry."

"I was thinking get really pissed."

"That too. But mostly—Dad, you really, really didn't seem—"

"I'm fine. Scout's honor."

"Dad."

"Stephen. I really am. I wish—"

"Yeah?"

"I don't know. That someone hurries up and trains their puppy."

They said goodbye and Ben—because of course Stephen was right—checked his voicemail. Nothing from Ronnie. Time was, he'd have relished the fight he knew was coming. There was never any guessing what might trigger Tara. But Veronica, Veronica was easy. Milk left out to sour. Talking while she parallel parked. Frivolous workday interruptions. They somehow kept things pleasant while their son was in high school, but hardly a minute longer. Ben began to pick at her on purpose. It was air at high altitude, sharp and pure and intoxicating, to fight with Veronica. That sweet, sure feeling, knowing—because he never had with their daughter—exactly what he'd *done* to unleash all that rage. By the time he confessed in couples' counseling, all that was just background din.

Veronica hadn't e-mailed either, though Anjali had. She had a trial coming up but even so had done the crossword. *7:34. A new personal best! How about that, Dad? Saw you made the news. Stephen sent it to me. Are you okay? Forgive my overstepping, but you know I'm a worrier and I want to make sure. Trial hell continues here but both of us should have some downtime at the end of next month. Want to visit? I could probably score some Pops tickets . . .*

Ben hit reply. He highlighted the word *Dad.* Hit control B. The word stood darker and more solid than any other.

Dad.

He'd had one of those *dreams* last night. Underwater this time, Anjali's hands on his body, slowed by the water and made slicker by it, too. They bucked and arched; their limbs entangled like seaweed.

His first thought on waking was *you dirty old coot.*

Only you had to hope that the subconscious was more gracious than that, that it crafted dreams as explicit missives: Here, right here, is the line you may not cross. You may never know what cost you Tara, and maybe you should count your blessings. You've had decades to get used to the question, and at this point your thick-hick psyche would buckle with the weight of knowing. So instead, know this: There's only one thing that would cost you your son, one, and that thing is an impossibility.

You have a nose-hair trimmer in your medicine cabinet, for God's sake.

Ben had stretched out in bed, happy and well rested. He'd had an erection and he'd taken his time attending to it. Approaching seventy now. Modern medicine was all very well but who knew how many more spontaneous ones he could count on. Only now, with the word *Dad* bold on the screen in front of him, was he troubled about Anjali. She hadn't been *her*-her in the dream, at least not entirely; he had the wispy sense that in sleepers' logic she had also been Sadie Birnam. Still, he ought to do some token thing to shake the sense he was turning into an overripe letch. Ben pulled up the crossword site and dawdled, taking on the twenty-plus letter clues first, watching the clock so that Anjali beat his time by over four minutes.

THE PRINCIPLES
OF REAL ESTATE

THE SHOWER DRAIN WAS THICK with Alison's hair and the soap in the soap dish was worn to a filmy sliver. Seth dialed up the hot water. Ali could go ahead and clear out the gunk. She could replace the soap, too. The extra bars were stashed in the cupboard under the sink, along with a Costco pack of Q-tips and Ali's half-empty box of Kotex. Along with the grief books, because Ali had a theory. If the books were displayed, then people would ask, and they'd come all this way to be Seth and Alison again, not that poor couple nobody knew how to talk to. Which, fine, made sense. But she hadn't so much as asked first. Seth grabbed a washcloth and his wife's shampoo. Like Ali would say, soap was soap and count yourself lucky: One hundred and fifty years ago, Adah Chalk rendered hers from tallow and ash. The stuff in the bottle smelled faintly of green tea. He rinsed and toweled off. Steam had fogged over the mirror.

Alison was waiting outside. Running shorts and a sports bra edged with sweat, blotches all over like Rorschach tests.

"Sorry," he said, "I didn't hear you get back."

"No worries."

Not too long ago, she'd have joined him in the shower. Residual fog met the salt on her skin.

Not too long ago, he'd have pulled her to him.

Her doctor had given them the all-clear six weeks after. She went along with it and made noises, but Seth could tell. She only touched him to wordlessly reposition his hands. She writhed, but only so he'd be done, already.

Add her morning pill to all that.

Better to take care of himself.

"You don't have to wait for me," she said. "I'll catch the next bus in."

Their first time together in the dorm room he'd kept tidy for a hopeful month and a half, she'd said, *Pay attention: This is what I like. Fingers like so. Remember my neck. My breasts will never be as fun as the skin beneath.* And now she stood there. Just stood.

"Clear your hair out of the drain, could you?" Seth had a hidden book of his own, a first year month-by-month, squirreled away in his office. It said new mothers should expect significant hair loss. It said Timothy would now be pulling himself up to standing.

Alison shrugged. "Yuck. Sorry about that."

She should've yanked Seth's hair out by the fistful. She should've wept.

Either or both. She should've known about the shedding. She should have explained. He wasn't asking for much. He no longer hoped she'd speak the name they chose instead of early favorite Ethan, instead of Joseph her father or Raymond his, instead of Charles for Dickens or for Darwin, depending on their mood. He kissed her goodbye without zeal and rode the bus alone for the first time since their move. Her shampoo made a cloud around him. The secretary the *Crier* shared with Marketing looked at him funny, and he wondered if she could smell it, too. Hoagland Lobel was waiting in his office.

Seth's boss wore cowboy boots and a silver bolo. "Howdy," he said. Seth had run a biographical feature on the man. Worcester born and raised, UMass undergrad, Chicago business: roughly as authentic a cowboy as George W. Bush.

"Good morning."

"Lost your intern, I see. Young Nick not showing up?"

"Off on assignment," Seth lied. He had no idea where Nicky Tullbeck was. He was surprised the big boss knew the kid's name.

Lobel adjusted the angle of the framed wedding photo on Seth's desk. "You been following all this, Seth? About Mona Rosko and the little one?"

"Yes, of course. It's a real shame."

"That's tofu talk."

"Tofu?"

"Doesn't taste like anything on its lonesome but takes on the flavor of the rest of the conversation."

"I wouldn't have guessed you liked tofu." Seth tried to approximate Ali's easy back-and-forth with Lobel. Given the state of the job market and the length of their resumes, Seth suspected that easy back-and-forth was what had landed them here in the first place.

"My doctor's idea." Lobel raised a hand briefly to his heart like a child about to say the pledge. "Now tell me what you really think."

"Like I said, it's a shame." Shame on Mona Rosko. The old bat. She'd been entrusted with a *child*. The whole of Seth clenched at the thought. He managed to control his voice. "It's a lousy situation all around. Of course, our aim here is to stay objective."

Hoagland Lobel hitched a thumb through each belt loop and rocked back on his heels. No Wild West buckle. The man knew his limits. "A damn shame. Mona was one of our Phase One buyers. Arizona lifer. You'd think she'd care a bit more about community."

"Taking off my editor's hat, I'd say her priorities seem a bit out of whack." The child had a concussion. A bruise rippling over his brain.

Lobel nodded. He leaned on Seth's desk and drummed his fingers. Seth should've gotten there first, sat, staked his territory. The way Ali said it worked with the Homestead Act. Garner Chalk at the dusty Claims Office, a blistering lifetime of ranch work before him, marking an *X* for the name he couldn't write, two slashes that spelled out *I am here and, therefore, this is mine.* Seth dodged Lobel to reach the chair. It was the wrong move. The other man towered now. Lobel said, "Thing is, it's bad buzz. The whole world knowing Mona's place won't sell. And it's a nice model. One of the original Rancheros."

Seth nodded.

"And that stunt she pulled on the news. Did you see Channel Twelve? I sent Groundskeeping right over to axe that sign. You can't leave a thing like that to mess with the neighbors' heads."

Seth nodded, though he'd been avoiding the local news. He wouldn't be able to get through the Rosko coverage without throwing something. No one saw the story that mattered. Even without the concussion, that poor child, boxed away for months. How pale he must be, how thin. Not that he said a word to Alison. Seth had only managed a B in Psych 101, but even he could recognize projecting. Their still, sweet boy. The nurses cleaned him and wrapped him in a blanket. Bless them for their kindness and bless that blanket, the blanket that meant Seth could see him bit by bit. His veins the boldest part of him, green beneath thin skin. The rest an assemblage of curls: his hair and lashes, the arch of his foot, the curve of his fingers, that failed twist of cord. He kissed Timothy goodbye but couldn't bring himself to look at his boy all at once. It shifted, always, which was worse. His cowardice or how cold his son would've seemed unblanketed.

Lobel crossed to the window and looked out at the grounds. His back was to Seth. "I want it put out there that there was a mistake in our central listing database. A typo by a data entry temp. Realtors could find Mona's place if they dug, but something stopped her property from popping to the forefront."

"Something?"

"A technical thing. A computer thing. I'm not entirely sure I understand it myself. Near as I can follow, folks couldn't see Mona's place was up for sale so folks didn't know they could buy it. It'll move now. The Ranchero's got a prime layout."

"I'll get a quote from IT."

Lobel shook his head. "Sure. If you like, but I don't think most of the *Crier*'s readers can make heads or tails of that kind of thing. Besides, you wouldn't exactly say that's the heart of the issue." Lobel shut the office door. In the second before it closed, Seth saw that Nicky had arrived. The kid settled down at his desk. Of course. That was why whenever Ali stopped by, the pair wound up chatting. Nicky's desk was by the entryway and it was as simple as that. The principles of real estate: location, location, location.

"You're telling me it was just a glitch."

"I'm saying I want you to put it out there."

Two weeks into each school year, Seth's students could recite his lecture on fact checking verbatim. He'd flunked a girl once for falsifying quotes; he'd stood firm with a student whom Shipley pressed to reveal sources. Lobel made a satisfied sound. Seth choked down an *unsatisfied* sound of his own. "You might be better served with a press release from your office."

"Nah," Lobel clapped Seth's shoulder. "Let's keep it in the family. They're all reading you anyhow. As far as I can tell, that's how the jackals got the story in the first place."

"Am I supposed to feel bad about that?" A child's *life* was at stake. For all anyone knew that Rosko woman was senile.

"Not at all, son." Lobel had to be gracious, considering that he was asking what he was asking. "You do your job."

"Of course I will," said Seth.

Lobel beamed as if he'd heard a promise. Seth walked him out. Nicky tried for his attention. "I'll have your editor back in two shakes," Lobel said, and something ugly bloomed in Seth's gut hearing the title. They waited for the elevator. No one ever took the stairs in The Commons. Lobel asked, "You kids settling in all right?"

"We're renting a place about ten miles south."

"Rockpoint Townhomes?"

"Parklands." Seth fumbled a little for the development's name, though he passed it twice a day, spelled out at its entrance in an ornate font. So many places here were like that. Grandly labeled and fenced in, as if the gate itself made what lay beyond worthy of taxonomy and display.

Lobel nodded. "Nice area. My pool guy put theirs in, too. Though between you and me, it's a buyer's market. You and Alison should look into something permanent. Especially if you want children."

Seth could rip out that tongue like a fat, wet root.

"No rush, though. You kids enjoy each other a while first. You'll miss it after, being just the two of you." The elevator door opened and Seth wanted it to swallow his boss. Hoagland Lobel stepped on. He held a hand out to stop the sliding doors. "I see Alison now and again. Thought she couldn't top that old Hollywood stuff she dug up, but this Adah Chalk—I've half a mind to rename Centerville Commons Adahstown, seeing as it's her hundred fiftieth birthday next month. That'll distract from all this fuss. A little rebranding goes a long way."

Adah Chalk came West as a mail-order bride.

Adah Chalk saved the herd from a flash flood.

Adah Chalk ran the telegraph office, cured rattler bites with a secret poultice, taught English to migrants, drove the first automobile for a hundred miles, corresponded with Susan B. Anthony, won blue ribbons with her slices of lemon pie. Dear God, was he ever sick of Adah Constance Ragsdale Chalk.

The elevator door strained against Lobel's hand. "Adahstown. Or maybe Adahstowne with an *E*. One or the other. No tofu, now. Which do you think is best?" Lobel was all unweighted affability. Evidently, it had not occurred to him that Seth might have a conscience.

"I'd say check with Ali," Seth said. "She'll know what's in keeping with the period."

"Will do, partner, and thanks for the talk."

Partner. The doors closed.

C U NEXT TUESDAY

Secanthelpit: mother teresa!

LilyBee: So very not in the mood.

Secanthelpit: nah, i kid. it's genius. like those pageant chickies. philanthropy stops the h8ters dead. This tyson thing's a gift from the cybergods. mater and paterfamilias will HAVE to let you back. lipsticklil 4eva!

LilyBee: If you're going to use words like *paterfamilias* and *philanthropy* I suspect you can also use caps like a big girl.

Secanthelpit: i wonder tho if comparing him 2 anne frank was a little much.

LilyBee: Anne Frank! Anne Frank!!

Secanthelpit: Sorry, Your Capslockness. Truly and sincerely.

LilyBee: Shut up. It takes maybe one second more to get things right. It leaves an impression. Think about it like a signature perfume.

Secanthelpit: think about it like ur parents only LET u have lipstick because u scammed them in2 thinking it would make u grammar girl.

Yes. Because Sierra cared so very much about *Lipstick*. You'd think her best friend would have dedicated five minutes to posting a general notice. No, Lily hasn't gone Amish; no, Lily hasn't gone to military school. She's been falsely accused and misses you all like moisturizer. She'll be back as soon as she can. In the meantime, remember: Even with the Most Delicate of Dusting Brushes, Thou Shalt Not Apply Multiple Tints above the Crease. But no. Sierra was busy. Apparently slurping on Rocky's fat stupid tongue took an inordinate amount of time.

Secanthelpit: Hello? Lily?

Secanthelpit: r u there?

Secanthelpit: Are you there, I mean. See? You win.

Secanthelpit: r u happy now? teehee.

LilyBee: I'm looking for something for my gran, okay?

The laptop weighed thirty pounds and was burning up her legs, which was biologically unjust. Guys didn't have to deal with that. Guys got a lucky protective mat of leg hair. She Googled *Benjamin Thales the commons Arizona news interview.* Pages loaded in slow mo and yielded only permutations of the whole Rosko story. That and a YouTube tour of The Commons where some fake cowboy they'd hired to play the CEO steered a golf cart around, heehawing his way through The Full Life Community You've Been Working Toward. Outside, Nicky Tullbeck was long gone. In the kitchen,

Gran waited for Ben, her sneakers laced and double knotted. Lily tried *creepy old man knows way too much about missing girls.*

No way was she going to search for *cunt* on her grandmother's computer. Even if she cleared the history, therein lay the road to traumatic pop-ups. She heard the sound of it though, in the clattering of her fingers across keys. Cunt, cunt, vinegary old cunt. C U next Tuesday was the closest she'd come to hearing anyone actually say it, and that was just Sierra on the subject of a girl who'd had the audacity to sit beside Rocky in study hall, sharing her flashcards of irregular German verbs.

Lily typed out *cunt* but didn't hit return.

Here was a violation of all the laws, of cheese, of logic, of basic linguistics. To refer to something so objectively excellent as if it was nothing.

Worse. As if it was vile.

Lily deleted the word with four stabbing keystrokes. She tried *crazy old man says c*nt on the news.* The asterisk looked wrong, like it was trying to turn the nastiness into *Twinkle Twinkle, Little Star.*

Secanthelpit: u find it?

LilyBee: Not yet.

Secanthelpit: what was it? knitting needles? granny panties? hemorrhoid cream?

LilyBee: That's my gran you're talking about.

Secanthelpit: some1s in a mood. need me 2 lend you a tampon?

Lily wondered if anyone had ever called Sierra a cunt. If anyone had called *her* one without her knowing it. Or those vanished girls Ben Thales had been rabid about. Lily's back ached. She'd read somewhere that a woman with presence never let her spine rest against the back of a chair. It had seemed like good advice to internalize, particularly since she was shorter than she'd liked. Still. It turned slouching into something only boys could get away with. Sad but true: hunching girls look like they're embarrassed to have breasts.

Boys.

She bet Nicky was off somewhere watching the Thales clip again. She bet he was smirking.

She bet Rocky would be watching it within the week. Ditto the smirk.

LilyBee: Sure, lend away. I promise to return it when I'm done.

Secanthelpit: eeeew. whats with u?

LilyBee: I'm busy. I told you.

Secanthelpit: fine. ta. meeting R in a sec

LilyBee: I see ROCKY gets caps.

Secanthelpit: always, lady, always.

LilyBee: Great. Have fun. Say hi for me. See you next Tuesday.

Secanthelpit: thought u weren't home till next month at least?

LilyBee: Sorry. That's what I meant.

Secanthelpit: counting down 2 it!!! c ya!!

LilyBee: I'm really sorry I wrote that.

LilyBee: Really, really.

LilyBee: Sierra?

LilyBee: I didn't mean it.

LilyBee: I'm worried about my gran.

Secanthelpit: Secanthelpit is offline and will not receive your message.

LilyBee: She's really into her neighbor.

Secanthelpit: Secanthelpit is offline and will not receive your message.

LilyBee: He's a dick.

It didn't have the same effect. *Dick cock balls.* The words were brassy and arrogant and only anatomically related to cunt.

LilyBee: He's a worm.

Secanthelpit: Secanthelpit is offline and will not receive your message.

LilyBee: A weak wan flaccid little worm.

"Well." Gran was in the doorway. "It looks like we've been stood up." She said it twelve times calmer than Sierra would've if Rocky (a) deigned to agree to a standing date and (b) broke it. She brushed her hands like a gymnast chalking up. She rocked up on tiptoe. Lily clamped the laptop shut. Mom and Dad would have a fit at that. House rules: all Internet business is to be conducted in communal areas. Gran shot her a look. Gran had probably heard the whole Safe Cyber Choices lecture in excruciating detail. Poor Gran. She must've made the parentals' shit list for letting Lily within fifty feet of a functioning computer. She hadn't said a word though. Every cell that comprised Lily hoped her grandmother had never been called cunt.

"Good," Lily said. "I'm glad."

"What?" Gran frowned.

"I said, good. I don't like him."

"Ben?"

"He's sketch city."

"I hope that's slang for generous neighbor."

A pause. A sigh. Gran sunk back on her heels and it was amazing the height that she lost.

"No. I didn't suppose it was. Lily, I'm—"

"He's always *around* and I saw a—"

"I'm sorry." Gran shook her head, all highlights and shine. Maybe Mona Rosko wasn't the brave one, letting her color leach away like autumn in reverse. Maybe Gran was, holding on to brightness while it lasted. "I've left you on your own too much. I should've—"

"That's not why I don't like him. He—"

"I thought you might want the space." Another sigh. "I know you're having a prickly time of it back home."

"I'm not. I'm fine."

"Your folks said a change of scene would be just the trick. Sunshine, sleeping in. A chance to take your mind off things. The last thing I wanted was to smother you, but if you prefer"—she spread her arms wide—"this old girl's ready to smother away."

"Gran. They didn't pack me off here like a delinquent." They'd sent her down for Gran's sake, so she wouldn't be alone as her first year without Grandpa passed. An open-ended ticket because it was anyone's guess how much she'd hurt, and how long.

"Nobody thinks that. Nobody."

"I'm not some kind of *project*." Lily was fine. Better than fine. She was SAT word *superlative*.

"Of course you aren't. You're a welcome guest. Always. Whatever the reasons."

"*You're* the reason." Only: Dad and Aunt Manda's plan came right on the heels of Headmistress Brecken's office. "*You're* the project."

Gran's expression was unreadable, or maybe Lily was lousy at reading them.

"I'm here because of you. They wanted me to check you're okay. And I'm going to tell them no, you aren't. I'm going to tell them you had a *boyfriend* over."

"Lily."

"I'm going to tell them about the walks and the barbecue. You cooked him Grandpa's favorite biscuits." Great. Another five seconds and she was going to cry. Four seconds. Three. "I hate him. He's always staring. He's got this creepy thing about girls. And he was *vile* to Ms. Rosko. He called her"—she wasn't going to say it in front of her grandmother—"the C word."

"I'm sure he'd never."

"He did. On television. A vinegary old—"

"Lily."

"I'm going to find it." She opened the computer. "It's online. You'll see. I'm not making it up. And he went off about all these missing girls. Gran. He's the emperor of sketch."

Gran shut the laptop, hard. She slid it across the table, yanked the plug out, and tucked it under her arm. "Enough. Ben Thales is a good neighbor. There must have been some misunderstanding."

"Yeah. Because so many things sound like—"

"Blunt." Gran's voice was light.

"I can't believe you're taking his side."

"Stunt."

"No, wait. I can. He's the *boyfriend*. He's got a *penis* and he calls you on the *telephone*."

"Grunt. Runt. Punt."

"He's *so* cute and he takes you places in his car."

"Brunt. Lily, I made the damn biscuits for you." She held the computer tight across her chest and drew a serrated breath. "Twice. I burned the first batch."

And here were the tears, only a bit behind schedule. "You didn't have to do that."

"It was my pleasure." Gran set down the laptop.

"I'm not making it up. I wouldn't be able to even think that up."

"With your grades? And I'm sure they teach fiction in that fancy school of yours."

"It isn't funny."

"Anything can be funny if you box it hard enough." Her dork-tastic grandmother assumed a Tae Bo stance. "Anything," she repeated, and she punched at the air.

"Grandpa."

"Dropped dead while I was in line for the ladies' room." She let out a mordant chuckle. "Not even a real washroom. A bank of Port-a-Potties."

"It's not funny."

"No, but I try." Gran's fists flailed. Jab-jab-uppercut. Lily recognized the combo from Sierra's stepmom's DVDs. She mirrored it. Gran repeated it, faster now. "That's my girl. Ben's a friend and—you know what the stupidest thing about this year was?" Her hands stilled.

Lily shook her head. She stood by one arm of the sofa, Gran at
the other, and she remembered the star and crescent bookends Gran
gave her when she was tiny and wanted to be an astronaut.
"People who said if you need anything, ask." Gran snorted.
"Like I'd done this before. My God. I could barely butter my own
toast and they wanted to know what I needed." If the moral of the
story was that she needed Ben, Lily was going to do the following
things in quick succession: hurl, pack her bags, and hitchhike to the
airport. "Ben never asked," Gran said. "Ben never gave me a look
like the one you just did if I found something to laugh about. He
was—a presence. He'd drop by."
    Great. So he was moving in on her from the start. "That only—"
    "Wait." Gran held up a shushing finger. "He's a friend. No, a
friend. And I won't have you up in arms over an unkind thing he
said to a woman who never even sent a card. No, wait." The finger
again. "I know that woman has burdens of her own, and I know that
child's turned your head. I don't understand it, but I know, and I'd
never stand in the way of your trying to do them a kindness."
    "But he—"
    "He has opinions that are damn close to my own after those
redneck things she said to my favorite granddaughter."
    "I'm your only granddaughter." The relief on Gran's face at that
weak old joke was ridiculous. Lily swallowed down her next barb
and the morning passed with an awkward string of moments nobody
commented on. Mona Rosko emerged for her paper and Gran turned
on the oldies station. The per-vet collected his mail. Lily didn't say
a word. The refrigerator schedule advertised a one o'clock beading
class and Gran suggested they grab a bite beforehand. Lily agreed,
even though her stomach felt gnawed away from within. Gran offered
to let Lily drive the cart and Lily pulled off giddy teen with panache.
Gran whipped out her camera for a picture. Lily giraffed her neck so
there'd be zero chance of double chin. She asked if the camera was a
real camera for the sake of having something to say.

"It's digital. I've been digital for years." Gran slid into the cart beside her. The seats were hard and plastic and much too hot. "I can program my own DVR, too. This is no ordinary grandma you're dealing with."

"I didn't mean—it looked like a real one. The shape of the lens and all."

Gran laughed, the same chesty huh-huh as Dad. "I like that you call the old ones real. Your kids sure won't."

"I'm not going to have kids."

"Oh, not for ages. And it'll be a different row to hoe for you. But there's always the sperm bank." To deserve all this, Lily must have been Stalin in a previous life. Everyone else made it to adulthood without once hearing their grandmothers say the word *sperm*. Gran winked and handed over her key ring. Junk outnumbered the keys: a plastic-encased school picture each of Lily and her cousins, a breast cancer awareness ribbon, and frequent shopper barcodes for half a dozen stores. Lily put the cart in reverse and focused on her guts' hard, bright, budding feeling. Pearl-like, it grew, layer by layer of bitter nacre. One layer for Rocky. One for Ben. One each for self-absorbed besties and anonymous complaints and parents with ulterior motives. One for the C word. Another for a batch of burned biscuits.

PEOPLE WITH NOTIONS

THE PHONE AGAIN. NATURALLY, VERONICA. It was the landline, after all, and only she and robocalls used it. Ronnie, pissed off, and on schedule. Someone had sent her the link. "Hello?" Might as well get this over with.

A silence.

"Veronica?" Ben kept his voice pleasant. When Ronnie was in a state, you didn't offer extra ammo.

He heard her breath.

And then the blare of a dial tone. Typical Veronica. In the thin, fraught months before their marriage ended, she'd imbued the silent treatment with so much elegance he'd almost had to admire it. He dialed her number, a subtle bud of defensiveness starting. Voice-mail. His breath caught, reflexive, at her recorded voice. And then the pang. No fool like an old one. Corbin instead of Thales got him every time. His hand was still on the phone—an ancient thing from their old den, none of the screens and bells and whistles you got these days—when it jangled back to life.

"Hello?"

Another protracted silence. The ungenteel clearing of a throat. She had a finicky way of rubbing her neck when she did that, as if such sounds were beneath her.

"Nice, Ronnie. Real nice. Grow up."

"This isn't Ronnie." A man's voice, bland and flatly Midwestern.

"Okay?" Ben asked, trying to place the voice.

"I don't know who you think you are."

"This is Ben Thales." A wrong number, maybe. Hadn't had one of those in an age.

A heated noise on the other end, edging toward a growl. And then his own recorded snarl. *Vinegary old cunt,* it looped, *vinegary old cunt.* Ben hung up. There was no sense reasoning with people. He'd watched the clip and it was no worse than he'd expected. The cursing, the fly, the way he'd built to a royal lather. You could see how people might take offense. You could get the impulse to look up his number. But the planning involved in that little trick. Recording his voice, cueing it, playing it. Even with the tech they had these days, someone had gone to a fair bit of trouble. It made Ben more jittery than he'd care to admit. People could be unspeakably nasty.

His limbs felt too long for the muscles that tensed along them, and he wished he'd ponied up for some damn curtains. He went to the computer and watched the clip again. So he'd sworn. So a fly had landed on him. So what? Ben rubbed his cheek. People were laughing in the comments. People were phoning his home. A fine world. A fine response to the sight of a man turning himself inside out. He watched again. He looked slack. He looked sick.

No wonder the kids were worried.

The phone again. A woman this time. She identified herself, which you had to respect. "Lois Kibben. You don't know me, and after how you've represented our community, I don't care to know you."

"Lois. Ms. Kibben. Lady." His hands had begun to shake. Only a little, but still. If Veronica were here, she'd sure as hell have spotted it. "You're the one who called me."

"People have standards and if you can't—"

"You called me." He felt his pulse, a hot, defensive tattoo. He hung up, then clenched and unclenched his fists, getting his fool fingers back under control. His body was a fight-or-flighty old bastard with no sense of proportion. It was only the phone. Toward the end of things, he and Ronnie had seen a counselor. A two-seventy-five-an-hour dud, but you didn't walk away without trying. Dr. Flynn would've had Ben break out some *toolkit* to manage this, forgetting that the human heart was nothing but a muscle, that it could go ahead and muscle through. All right then. Ben unplugged the phone. He wound the cord with exaggerated care. He'd like to see them pester him *now*. He unplugged the bedroom phone for good measure. His heartbeat was perfectly normal.

He let himself out onto the back patio. There had been good reason to buy here. A yen to start over. The whole, clean feeling of a safe and self-contained world. The built-in sociability, and the 2007-vintage confidence of an eventual tidy profit. But sometimes Ben thought what had tipped the balance was the clear, pure scent of grass. He inhaled, and the foul thing in his gut resettled. You didn't get wild or weedy notes here to muck up the smell. You got one thing only, and that could be very soothing. Out by the water hazard, a pair of golfers teed up. The ball made its neat, predictable arc. Ben's sister liked to tease that any game you had to buy more than a ball for was a game for people with notions. Maybe she was right, and maybe he'd become one. Well, he'd earned it. He'd worked hard for his place here. The Commons. He thought of the prissy way the Kibben woman had said *community* on the phone. How they'd had him list his home number for the directory. The second golfer swung, the ball skewing right. The callers were neighbors. Every last one, he'd bet.

The grass scent, at least, remained uncomplicated. He breathed, his body overstretched and spongy. That heart of his started hammering again. He went into the house and then the garage. He started up the cart but didn't floor it. His foot wanted to, but he'd show some restraint for once. Invent an errand so none of this would feel like flight. He puttered along. Immaculate grass. Sculpted rises and shallow dips. A whoop carried across the green, an unadulterated peal of joy. Ben felt a sullen barb of envy and allowed himself to pick up speed. Another cart approached and from its passenger seat, Sadie Birnam called his name. The granddaughter was at the wheel. She didn't have the best handle on the thing. When she braked, both women rattled forward. The carts drew up face-to-face. Ben eased to a gentle stop.

"Sadie! Where're you off to?"

"Jewelry making. There's a class at the Hacienda."

"I can't wait," said the granddaughter, only she said it *cunt*.

He pretended not to notice. Sadie smoothed her hair, which wasn't mussed in the first place. Lily looked at him as if he were something smeared on the sole of her best shoe. "I can't believe all the amazing things there are to do here," she said. Again, the inflected, not quite *can't*.

"It's a pretty special place," he offered.

"And I can't believe Gran's letting me drive." That *can't* again. Wasn't she a clever one.

Ben Thales was a decent man. He should be feeling the bright kindle of shame; this girl had clearly seen him, heard him, and there was a time when he'd have wanted to deck anyone who used that kind of language in front of *his* daughter. Instead, he bristled at the finicky pitch of Lily's voice. There was a fulsome sense of sheen about her, as if she'd come out of shrink wrap. "Drive safe," he said, and he indicated his chest. "No seatbelts."

The girl gave an elaborate shrug. "I can't imagine Gran would let me do anything dangerous." Except for the unsubtle *can't*, her tone was very prim.

Ben was approaching his eighth decade. It still surprised him, sometimes, how thoroughly what he felt and what he ought to feel diverged. History like his, you'd think he'd clench up in the face of an adolescent snit. Instead he felt a fluid, internal lightening and something like tenderness toward the girl. Let her have her moods and brackish places. She wasn't his daughter or any of his concern. The crank calls weren't either. A bunch of dithering busybodies with nothing better to do. Ben beamed at Lily. He offered a courtly little bow.

Lily scowled. Her hair made a dark halo, hateful and kinetic. The cart jerked forward.

Sadie's voice rose in reprimand and then the world went slow, peach lit and syrupy, as if ladled into a jam jar. Ben's eyes met Lily's, which were an extraordinary blue. They widened, white and shocked and unveined.

Impact.

The jammy world unstuck. And then the women were beside him, terrible and tall. Sadie knelt to touch his shoulder, which meant he'd wound up supine and on the ground. He gave a lung-stuck wheeze and struggled against the light of fantastic pain. "You with us?" Sadie asked. He nodded. Something leaden thrummed where his skull met his spine. Sadie's eyes were the same bold blue as her granddaughter's. Ben shut his own and the blue stayed, Bunsen burning, as an afterimage. Tara's eyes had been brown, straight-up brown, no romanticized flecks of green or gold. Still, they let her get away with claiming hazel. Veronica had said it was important for girls to feel in control of their looks. Christ on a bike. No wonder their family went wrong. Some things simply *were*. It was a waste of your finite life to pretend.

A FAMILY MATTER

SETH WAS IN HIS OFFICE, daydreaming. A letter of resignation, terse and dignified and cutting. A lesson for Lobel: saying something didn't make it so. He shook his head, as if words were marbles rolling around in there. Ali was good at this sort of thing, but he wasn't about to go running to her. Not after being an ass about the shower drain. He grabbed his *Roget's*. There had to be a way to say *personal and professional integrity* without sounding like an outrageous prig.

"Hey, Boss?" Nicky Tullbeck hovered, uneasy, in the doorway.

Nicky was a boy like any other boy, not big, exactly, but tall, hapless, and waiting for his body to catch up with his bones. The kid was okay. Still, every time he saw him, Seth felt pummeled. In Chettenford, he would have been kind. He'd found *something* likeable in each and every one of his students. He made himself gesture encouragingly. That grizzled fraud Lobel wasn't Nicky's fault, and the boy wasn't to blame for the thinning treads of Alison's running shoes. Seth's smile felt frayed, the curve of his lips thin and chapped. "Yeah?" he asked.

"I met a girl this morning."

"Okay. Congratulations?"

"Not met a girl like *met a* girl." Nicky waved a top-bound reporter's notebook and wrested a pen from its spiral. "She's the official spokesperson for the Roskos. Some kind of neighbor. Says she was the one who saved the kid and all."

"We're not going to be putting anything else about that family out there. It isn't news. It's a family matter." Seth liked the way that sounded. He'd use it with Lobel. Polite and resolute, but still *no*. He was an adult, after all. If you believed CNN, he and Ali had snagged the last two jobs in the Continental United States. Enough with the daydreams. It was time to act right. Be responsible. Play a few innings before calling the game.

Nicky said, "The *Daily Star* doesn't think it's a family matter. They had another article this morning and—"

"A family matter, Nicky." Seth would have liked the kid in Chettenford. He wouldn't have had to force it. Nicky had gumption. Nicky had stick-to-itiveness. Seth had a barely animated wife, a son who'd never drawn breath, employment at the whim of a venal cowpoke, and all the zing of canned peas. He tamped down a sigh.

"*USA Today* had it, too. As, like, their Arizona thing. You know how every day they do a few lines for every state?"

Seth didn't know offhand. The last time he'd seen a *USA Today* he and Ali had been in some nowhere of a motel on their drive out to The Commons, still working under the theory that because the move was new it was destined to be good. The sigh he'd been fighting escaped. "Okay. What've you got?"

"Two ideas, really. The main one is local response. You know, since we're all about what goes down here in The Commons." Nicky's voice slid deeper in an attempt at professionalism. Seth pretended this was office hours, that the town where he'd been teacher of the year wasn't two thousand miles away.

"Go on."

"Okay. So there was this man who freaked out about it online. One of the Rosko neighbors. It's pretty funny—there's this crazy fly—and it's getting a ton of hits. And Lily, that's the girl I mentioned, she has a Facebook group going in support of the family.

So I thought I could frame it as The-Commons-meets-cyberspace. Like, our little community is a part of the whole big world."

Back home, at least two students a semester had pitched some spin on the same idea. Once upon a time, Seth got a kick out of that. How happy they were, so sure they were thinking something new. He'd tell Ali about it tonight. She'd laugh the wry laugh she'd had back in Chettenford. She would soften then. She'd be on his side. And then he could tell her about Lobel. She would rail on his behalf. They'd either get out their suitcases or come up with a plan.

Nicky tore a page from his notebook. Two web addresses were spelled out neatly on it. The ripped page was the only one in the pretentious little book with any marks on it at all. That kid. Add a fedora and press pass and send him off to a Halloween party. Something viscous and nasty thickened in Seth's throat. He'd been a boy like that once. One in an ambitious blush of boys. Only, it wasn't right to say ambitious. It was more the lazy confidence that all would be well. Even into his thirties he'd assumed as much.

And then.

Nicky used vocab words, *source* and *lede* and *nut graf,* to explain that he'd also like to explore the military family angle. Seth told him to focus. One thing at a time. Seth indicated the piece of notepaper. He said he'd check it out. He did these things so that he wouldn't say something cruel.

"Seriously? You'll look into it?" The kid looked like he was about to break into song.

"I told you I would. Now quit hovering. I'll tell you if I think it's something."

"And I'll get to write it? If it is?" Nicky's frame filled the door.

"Maybe," Seth said and the boy retreated. He'd like a word with Nicky's journalism teacher. The Colliers had put that whole world behind them, but still, as a professional courtesy. Seth opened his browser and entered Nicky's first address. The page loaded. None of *Seth's* students would have come running to the editor for consent if they thought they were onto something. His kids would trust their damn instincts and dig. On screen, the clip began to play.

It had been evening when Ali was finally discharged from the hospital. She still looked pregnant, and she moved as if the sidewalk had been iced over. The world was dense with shadows. Three miles on surface roads and then eight on the freeway. On the radio, NPR appealed for money. Lights flared assertively from the opposite lane. Seth only got that they'd been flashing their brights when he pulled safe into the garage. He killed the engine and realized. He'd driven the whole way home without headlights.

And.

Ali's parents had come. Her mother said, tea, though he and Alison were both known to be java heads. Seth found a kettle. He filled it and placed it on the stove. He watched the flame and waited. Alison's father came into the kitchen to see what was keeping him. Evidently the kettle had been shrieking a solid minute or so.

And.

He had taken off his glasses. He'd set them on the nightstand. He brushed his teeth, then tried to pop out his contact lenses. His finger grazed his pupils. First the left, then the right, as the optometrist had instructed back in sixth grade. He tried each eye three times before it registered.

And.

And.

And.

And the man on the screen was as broken in his own right. Seth swiveled in his chair. There was no way in this world or the next that he'd let Nicky Tullbeck blunder this story. That husk of a man. Seth knew what grief looked like. There'd been times when a fly could have taken up residence in the well of his tongue without him feeling it. One fly, two flies. A whole business of flies. Seth put his head out the door. "Tullbeck! Got a name on the ranter?" Nicky beamed and checked his phone. Proof positive. The notebook was all for show. Nicky said the man was called Benjamin Thales. The directory listed a home number. Seth dialed. As the phone rang, he entered a few of the names Thales had mentioned—Tenaya Alder, Mimi Asencios—into a search engine, guessing at the spellings. Missing. And for more than a decade. He felt a pulse of vindication. Everyone and their busybody cousin told Seth and Alison to give themselves time. But look at Benjamin Thales. Ten years from whatever had happened and still a mess. Time was as true a balm as platitudes.

The phone was still ringing. It kept on and on. Benjamin Thales was the last man in America without voicemail.

And that was just as well. Seth would let Benjamin Thales be. He would rely upon the books beneath the bathroom sink. He'd work. With Lobel. Around Lobel. Simply work. The books all said there was consolation to be had in that. Seth glanced at the second address Nicky'd given him. From the looks of it, a Facebook page, someone tallying other someones in their casual support of the Roskos. Now that was the real story. The psychology of the absurd. The minimal effort it took to get that puffed-over sense of having done good. The phone was pressed close to his ear and still ringing. He returned the receiver to its cradle. Cradle. He tried hard not to dwell on the word.

NO PLACE IN PERFECTION

GRAN SENT HER TO FETCH Ben a glass of water, but the bitter slant of her mouth said she was sending her away, period. Lily walked from the hospital waiting room, carrying herself very erect. Swan neck, high sternum. The stance all the magazines promised would shave off ten pounds. She was going to be flawless from this moment forward: stay offline while she did her homework and abstain completely from swearing. Compost, floss, and use SAT words. She was going to be perfect for the rest of her life.

Perfect. And also, enrolled in some hippie mountain boarding school where the sole computer still took floppies and the uniforms were made of wool from sheep the students sheared themselves. With luck she'd have *Lipstick* back by 2060-never.

She passed one drinking fountain and then a second. No cups. Stay tuned for this week's episode of Bad Decision Theater: Lily brings her grandmother water in her own cupped bare hands. See the water run out the cracks. Watch the penitent mascara run down her cheeks. It's a nice image, ladies and gentlemen, supplicating on a quasi-biblical level.

Not that Lily would know. Her parents didn't really go in for all that church stuff.

They probably should have.

Maybe then they wouldn't have a freaknugget daughter who went around running men over.

Oh, and who stole.

She had Ben Thales' cell phone. She had honest-to-eye-shadow taken it to help the guy out. It was lying there beside the cart and he probably didn't want to lose it. Nobody saw. Ben had sat bow-shouldered on the grass, eyes tracking the busy back and forth of Gran's finger. He knew the day of the week and the name of the president. He took his own pulse and pronounced it fine. His pupils weren't dilated. He stood. He walked completely unaided. Lily should have returned the phone then, with apologies, as the man checked his limbs over, stretching and bending, swiveling his hips like an advertisement for extra-strength brain bleach. She'd been about to when he shot her a pinched, waspish look and asked if Gran might take him to the hospital.

Which meant that the two things Ben Thales and Miss Bra Strap Bigmouth-Blogkill back in St. Louis had in common were (a) skin so thin it hardly counted as epidermis and (b) an inexplicable urge to ruin Lily's life, and that consequently the hottest piece of tech Lily was going to be let near was whatever they used for telegraphs back in the day. Maybe this time Mom and Dad would respect her enough to *say* it was a punishment, not like this nice-little-visit-to-make-sure-Gran-was-holding-up.

Sure. And a fleet of Nigerian princes were dying to give her millions.

She couldn't *believe* she'd fallen for the parental line. Sign her up for a brain transplant already. A pair of women approached in blue scrubs, their flat shoes slapping efficiently on linoleum. They looked a little sick themselves, but everyone did under hospital lights.

Hospital. Fuck. Oh, fuckadee fuck fuck fuck.

She'd put a man in the hospital.

He was going to be all right. He had to be. You didn't have excess energy for slit-eyed glares of doom if you were dying or even hurt. He was simply spinning things to his best advantage, salivating at the prospect of returning her, vanquished, to sender. No one now between him and Gran.

Lily one hundred percent hadn't wanted to hurt him. They had to know that.

She wasn't some kind of sociopath.

She wasn't even going to spit in the water she brought him once she found a cup.

She found a vending room. It hummed with refrigerator sounds. Sad sandwiches and pudding cups rotated behind Plexiglas. She checked her pockets for cash, keeping the ill-gotten phone pocket for last. In it she found two crumpled dollars. It took three rounds of smoothing for the latte machine to accept the bills. Lily chose hazelnut at random—she didn't drink coffee, ever; who wants teeth like a high school civics teacher?—and a cup dropped into its slot. The machine made stuttering foamy noises. Lily sat. Drew her legs in. Chin on her knees. Everything was going to be fine. If the per-vet were really hurt, he'd have made stuttering foamy noises too instead of chatting with Gran the whole way over about some biography of FDR they were plowing through for book club. A loudspeaker sounded, paging a doctor whose name she didn't catch, and then it was Lily making the choked little keening sounds. She leaned back against the coffee machine, the latte steaming the air up above her. She dug a fist into her stomach and tried to control her breath. She'd only wanted to see him flinch. To know he'd bolted from a *girl*. Her foot had hovered above the accelerator. Her nails had glittered and she'd hesitated long enough to see that a green bead on her ivy-patterned espadrilles was coming loose. Then she'd met Ben's eyes and stepped down, hard.

The thing was, she was learning to drive her mother's '08 Odyssey. The golf cart was maybe one-sixteenth as heavy. And wow, was it ever responsive. Wow, was it ever fast. The whole thing was like one of those problem sets she'd always rocked. If cart *A* moves toward cart *B* at twenty miles per hour, what will happen on impact?

She bit down on a finger to stifle a giggle.

It couldn't have been twenty miles per hour. That was the speed limit for the whole Commons.

Ten at the most. Not that it mattered. Five, ten, fifteen, twenty, here she was, fetal by the light of a thousand Pepsi machines.

She shifted. The phone kept jabbing her. She got it out. A couple in robes and mortarboards grinned from the screen. The woman was seriously gorgeous, despite a goofball grin. The guy was a guy. Like Lily had any expertise rating them. One arm snaked proprietarily around the woman's waist. Probably Ben's son and thus genetically predisposed to pursue women who were out of his league.

Fantastic. He had a kid.

The man she'd *put in the hospital* had a kid.

She should drink the hazelnut stuff cooling up above her. She should clear out the hospital's stash of Ho Hos and M&M'S. Morph into a yellow-toothed chunkster, her face a moonscape of zits. It would be fairer that way to the rest of the world. Give people a heads-up they were dealing with someone seriously vile. The coffee tasted bitter and synthetic, and there was an inch of syrupy sludge at the bottom. It scorched her tongue, then her throat. Three hot gulps drained the Styrofoam cup. There were tears in her eyes. She wanted her mom. Of all the crybaby ridiculousness. Mom, who always smelled of sunscreen and Aveda and the cinnamon gum that made it easier for her to avoid sweets.

But—extrapolating from recent data—Mom would get her a therapist or an open-ended ticket to Grandma Gillis in Pennsylvania or find some other way to make her Someone Else's Problem. Option two then. Sierra, since the whole point of having a best friend was being able to call when it turns out you're a USDA prime asshole. Lily gave the phone a vigorous wipe down—it was the per-vet's phone, and the per-vet probably had ear hair—with her shirt. His password—*quelle surprise!*—was 12345.

"Sierra's phone!"

"It's me," Lily said.

"Lily?"

"Yeah. Me."

"See you next Tuesday? Real nice."

"I said I was sorry."

Sierra sounded a dismissive bleat.

"Something happened," Lily said.

"Too right something's happened. I only texted you nine-one-one an hour and a half ago."

"I don't have my phone. Remember?"

"Oops, sorry. How are you even calling?"

Lily drew a steadying breath. "I stole a phone from my grandmother's neighbor after I ran him over with a car."

"Right."

"Okay, with a golf cart. He was in one, too."

Again, the laugh.

"I'm serious. We're at the hospital."

"Only you. You need a twenty-four/seven camera crew."

Wouldn't *that* be a catastrophe. "It isn't funny. He might die." He probably wouldn't, but saying the words made it feel officially possible.

"No one died from a golf cart. It would be like dying of ennui. What's your grandma's address? I can send you some of Christa's Valium." Christa was Sierra's Spandex stepmom. "Mind you, I'll have to pinch a few for myself to cope with the fallout when she sees they're gone. She's such a pill counter. I think she likes to prove she knows numbers higher than her fingers go."

"That's mean."

"That's Christa."

"It doesn't help me any," Lily said, mind vibrant with the sharp clarity of crisis. A staggering percentage of their conversations went like this. Tamp somebody down to buoy yourself up, like the world played out on a seesaw. It didn't help any. It didn't change things. It was a ludicrous equation and it didn't come close to balancing.

Sierra said, "You clearly haven't tried her Valium."

"I need a plan here. I need a real idea." She wouldn't stand and she wouldn't pace because that was the cheeseball response. "What happens at Granny's stays at Granny's."

"Sierra. I'm in real trouble." Her friend had, to use the Honors English terminology, a distinct tendency toward hyperbole. Sierra's crises were invariably one-eighth as dire as reported. Maybe she thought Lily worked that way too and that, adjusting for social Münchausen's, she was only in the midst of a *fractional* breakdown. "Please," she said. "Help me think."

"Okay. Maybe play it like she's going senile? Then you'll get bonus points for being all concerned."

"She's my gran."

"Right. You like yours." Over Christmas break, Sierra couldn't take a bite of pie without her own grandmother lamenting that such a pretty girl was getting an early start on the freshman fifteen. "So get her on your side. Work the subconscious. Maybe try to smell like something she loves. Did your grandpa wear aftershave?"

"I already *do* smell like something she loves. You're insane."

"I'm trying to help. And I've been thinking about what you said. About a signature perfume?"

"Sorry?"

"On GChat. About capital letters?"

"Oh yeah." Forever ago. Before the cart, the crunch, the wan hospital light.

"You're onto something. Because everyone knows the sense of smell's the most powerful, right?"

"I guess." Lily began to breathe through her mouth, so she would smell nothing, so she would not remember this.

"So I was thinking about Rocky." As usual. Lily almost said it. Caffeine surged vile in her stomach. Sierra said, "I love him."

"I know." Lily had to be perfect. She'd promised. From now on. She had to be kind. She made agreeable noises.

Sierra said, "He loves me too, but he won't always."

Lily's cue to trot out the list: high school couples, real and invented, who'd made it. She'd done it a dozen times. But Lily was in a hospital in Arizona, chemical coffee a riot in her stomach, the man she felled somewhere in the maze of halls. "No," she agreed. "He won't."

"Good to know my best friend thinks I'm lovable."

"You said it first."

"You weren't supposed to agree with me."

"This whole conversation is stupid. If you're not going to help—" Me, Lily wanted to say. Me, me, me.

"I'm thinking of using baby lotion. As a moisturizer."

"What?" The epic randomness brought her short.

"As an investment for the future. Rocky loves me now, but he won't always love me. So ten years from now or something, when he has a baby with someone else, he'll smell the lotion and remember me but he won't know why. And he'll wonder where I am—"

"In a mental institution, that's where."

"He'll be the one that's crazy. Always daydreaming about me. He won't be able to stop himself. And I'll be young to him forever. Still hot when his wife chubs out."

By rights Lily should've smelled coffee and industrial bleach. Hospital air, made of too many peoples' breath. She smelled baby lotion, pink and powdery. And she knew: Every time she smelled it now, she'd remember Sierra's stupid plan. How when she was fifteen and careening from one disaster to the next, the best person in her life couldn't be bothered with the worst thing in it.

The phone in her hand did a buzzy chirp.

It occurred to Lily that she was the one who called Sierra most of the time.

And that in a sanity-based universe, ER trauma trumped boyfriend trauma. The phone chirped again. *Per-vet Thales* had someone who cared for him more than Sierra did her. Two people at a bare minimum, considering how solicitous Gran was.

"Lil-lee," Sierra singsonged, "It's your turn to say something. That's how conversations work."

"I don't think you actually know how conversations work. I'm in a hospital." Call waiting continued to announce itself.

"And I'm a hundred thousand miles away. Plus, it's going to take at least ten years for me to get my MD."

"That doesn't mean it's okay for you to—"

"Twelve years, actually. I'm going to travel after undergrad."

"Great bedside manner."

"What am I supposed to say? Give me a script. I'm good with scripts."

"You're supposed to *know* what to say. And Rocky's wife won't be fat. She'll be pregnant."

"Yeah, then. But as time passes . . ."

The phone beeped. The caller had left voicemail.

"I still say you're nuts," Lily said.

"Be nice." She could *hear* Sierra pout. "I'm having a hard time."

"*You're* having a hard time?"

"You know you're going to be fine. If you have to, play the I-saved-little-Tyler card."

"Tyson." Lily wondered if Sierra had flubbed it on purpose. Right up until the morning of her father's wedding, Sierra kept fauxcidentally calling Spandex Christa *Trista*.

"Tyson, sorry. I guess he's your new best friend."

"That's low. Come on. What's up?" And *boom!*, she was wheedling. They should admit her to the hospice ward for the terminally pitiful. A man who hadn't shaved in about a year entered the room, nodded at her, and began to feed quarters to the Pepsi machine.

Sierra said, "I saw Rocky with Jennifer Vogler."

"Rocky *works* with Jennifer Vogler." It said something lousy about the state of the world that Rocky could get a job and Mona Rosko couldn't. Ms. Rosko might not be nice but she was formidable. Rocky was neither. He carried on like a surfer a thousand miles from either coast. The bearded man disappeared with his purchase.

"I didn't see them at work. They were coming out of that coffee place on Frontenac."

"Jennifer Vogler has a stupid neck." Lily's words came automatically and they weren't even true. She couldn't think of anything overtly wrong with Jen, except that she'd destroyed the curve in Honors German. But *neck* was specific enough and random enough to talk Sierra down. Last month, with Alana Patricelli, it had been chin.

"You think?"

"Total duck neck." Duck neck wasn't even a real thing.

"For real?"

"Quack," Lily said. "Quack, quack, quack."

"Quack," said Sierra.

Lily quacked back. Maybe someone from the psych ward would wander in and take her away.

Sierra said, "It's the third time I've seen them."

That seesaw: even if each Vogler sighting counted as a discrete problem, how slight that was against the Roskos, and Gran, and the veterinarian she'd left in the waiting room. "Were they, say, behind a counter any of those times? Wearing back vests? Little bow ties?" Rocky and Jen worked concessions at Cineplex 8.

"Yeah." Sierra laughed. It sounded like her tongue was sputtering through a well of Elmer's Glue. "The bow ties are awful for her poor duck neck. Even worse than the boho beads."

"The what?"

Lily knew, though.

It was crazycakes that her body did nothing to mark that knowing. No arterial ice, no freakout clatter knees. Only the image: the fall of Sierra's hair against Lily's neck as her friend read over her shoulder. She'd giggled at the cropped photograph and helped with the wording: *I'm worried about your necklace. Points for taking on that whole charm and bauble boho thing, but between you and me and the Internet it looks a little bit Etsy.*

Headmistress Brecken had made her take the picture down. There, in her office, in front of witnesses, since Lily was officially a miscreant and Not to Be Trusted.

She didn't even remember what the necklace looked like.

Or really the offensive bra strap.

Or even the Boob Fairy's bountiful gifts.

Only Sierra's glue laugh. The fact that the Boob Fairy was a patented Sierra creation. That Sierra'd said no, Bra-strap Boober-kins was way funnier than the other Fixit candidates in Lily's inbox, including Girl Whose Pockets Did Unfortunate Things to Her Butt.

Lily asked again. "Sierra. What boho beads?"

Her best friend covered. "You know. That thing she always wears."

The main reason Lily hadn't gone all CSI: Forest Park Day to work out the source of the anonymous complaint was that *Sierra* had said the only way to ID her would be to get a good look at her chest and that the school's collected population would freak and cry harassment if Lily started a serious inspection of boobage.

Sierra, whose cartoon drawing of the Boob Fairy had the same kind of side-swept bangs Jen Vogler wore.

Who was more than capable of snapping a picture and submitting it to *Lipstick* via sock puppet.

"Sierra?"

"Yeah?"

"Did you send that Fixit?"

"Why would I send you a Fixit? If there were ever anything *wrong* with me, you'd say." She sounded helium happy. She sounded like Saturday morning cartoons.

"Yes, I would," said Lily.

"Hey! You make it sound like there's actually something."

The per-vet's phone chirped again. "There's a call on the other line," she said.

"So? It's not even your phone."

"No. I lost my phone when I posted that thing."

"That thing?" A guilty catch in Sierra's voice.

"Um. *Lipstick?*"

"You'll get it back. Your phone, too. I'll *help* you. Once you get home. Trust me. And you're probably not even going to need my help. You're *you.*"

The volunteering cemented it. The cheerleading. The fact that it was all about Lily for once. Lily was one hundred and twelve percent sure. Sierra was the backstabbing bimbrain behind the whole mess. "Hey, Sierra?" The idea came beautiful from nowhere.

"Yeah?"

"Don't do that baby lotion thing. That stuff has a really high concentration of ispep. You'll break out like crazy."

"Really? But it's gentle enough for babies."

"Their skin hasn't started producing oil yet. It's a chemical thing. I've got to go now." She hung up. Sierra wouldn't hear it now if her voice pitched high and tight. Lily examined the phone. Its screen indicated two missed calls from Veronica (mobile). She pitched it in the hopper of the soda machine. Low move, but someone would take it to the lost and found. And she *had* to toss it. It was a question of personal survival. Lily was quitting Sierra cold turkey; she'd last maybe a day phone-enabled. She headed back toward Gran, her mind electric with should've-saids. The woman who would years from now be Frau Rocky owed Lily big-time. There was no such thing as ispep. The word was *Pepsi* spelled backward.

SOME LIST OF STRANGERS

SETH FELT THE SLOW TENTACLES of a killer headache. He should never have told Nicky he'd follow up on those notes. He had to log into Facebook now. Look over some list of strangers who thought ticking a box would make any difference at all to the Roskos. He pulled up the site. His password was *dlaonuiiesla*, a scramble of his and Alison's middle names. He entered it, and with every keystroke he remembered. How he and Ali had dithered about Timothy's middle name. How they joked about setting up a bracket in the teachers' lounge. How one morning Ali said *Lawrence* and they couldn't believe it took them so long to think of it. How it hadn't wound up mattering. How there had been paperwork at the hospital—forms with meager spaces and nursery-pastel triplicates—and how none of those forms had a thing to do with naming. How that hadn't registered until he went to close out their Chettenford safe deposit box. How he'd felt in the bank that afternoon, seeing their passports, their unassuming sheaf of graduation gift bonds, and, paper-clipped together, their marriage and birth certificates. Seth Daniel Collier, Alison Louisa Mackey, the font elaborate and brutal: Certificate of Live Birth.

All that from a simple password, and then the Internet went and gave him this: Nina McCordle Henry at the top of his feed. *I'd sell*

my left arm for a full night's sleep. Only then I'd have only one hand to deal with two teething babies. Gah!! Twins!! :)
For fuck's sake. Nina was one-half of the couple they were closest to back in Chettenford. She was a civil engineer and not at all the kind of woman who used emoticons. Seth's stomach roiled. He remembered a potluck at the Henrys' last year. The curve below Alison's waist had just graduated from possibly beer to definitely baby. Nina wasn't drinking and everyone guessed what that meant. The women laughed, one to another. They say it makes you stupid for the first year and a half. Now Nina's profile picture showed a loaf-sized bundle in either arm.

You poor thing, he wrote. *Alison and I slept BEAUTIFULLY last night. Peace and quiet at any cost! Love to Ross.* Seth hesitated, but only for a moment. The Henry twins' birth announcement had arrived three weeks after they got to Arizona. A postcard, the newborn pair snuggled and hazy. Their hats looked like the hat that the nurses had placed on Timothy's head when they brought him over to Alison's bedside. It killed him, that hat. The pretending involved in dressing a dead child. He clicked post.

That damn postcard. It was cruel. A letter would have at least had an envelope. A letter they could have trashed unread. This, they'd had no choice but to see. Ondine Violet (five pounds, thirteen ounces) and Linus James (five pounds, eleven). In their toothpaste-toned Arizona kitchen, Alison's eyes had gone gemlike, hard and bright. In the softness of the surrounding skin he could see the faint scoring he would come to know as wrinkles soon enough. "I hate them," she'd said. She made her voice nasal. "We're Ross and Nina. Have you met our children? Ondine. Linus." She'd kicked at the kitchen island. The surrounding cabinetry rattled, cheaply hinged. "Christ! I hope they wind up every bit as pretentious as their names."

"They're good people," Seth had said. "They didn't think." But he hated the Henrys, too. And he'd hated Alison, at least for the moment. When it was her turn to fall apart, it had to be his to be rational. She slumped to the floor. She tented her legs.

"They should have thought," she said. "Fuck them. Fuck them and their healthy perfect beautiful babies."

Fuck them indeed.

Seth leaned forward and clicked through to Ross Henry's page. *My third shirt in four hours. Move over, Linda Blair. There are new babies in town . . .* In Ross' picture, a baby—the daughter? The son? It hurt to look, actually hurt, there, in the space Seth used to think belonged to his lungs—wore a Yankees shirt that was a size too big. Seth felt a momentary nudge from his old life. The itch to get a gibe in there. There were people who loved the Yankees, and then there were people who actually loved The Game. Instead, he wrote *Paternity leave sounds like hell. Ali and I had it SO much easier.*

Seth tallied. He had one hundred and fifty-seven friends. One hundred and fifty-seven oblivious grinners. He typed quickly. North Chettenford's most beloved biology teacher was enjoying his first frozen custard of the summer and wondered why it had taken him so long. Seth wrote *Yum! I wonder what flavor my son would have liked best!* A girl he'd dated for about half a minute was setting off on a three-day bike trip. *Have fun, Jen! I used to daydream about teaching Timothy to bike.* His freshman roommate had posted a blurry ultrasound. *It's official. A boy for Maura and me.* Seth wrote *Wow, I didn't even know the two of you got married. Your son looks like mine did before he died.* One of Alison's cousins liked *Your Family Were Once Immigrants, Dingoes Ate My Anchor Baby,* and *What the Hell Are They Thinking in Arizona?* Seth wrote, *I'll tell ya, Sean, this Arizonian's thinking about how the hell to make it through another day with all this crushing grief. Also, dead babies aren't funny.*

A ping and a pop-up. *You there?* A photo of Ross Henry's stupid Yankee baby. Seth ignored it and refreshed. His high school lab partner would be in L.A. for the weekend and wondered if anyone

wanted to meet up. *I would, but I'm still in mourning.* One of Ali's
bridesmaids wished her mother a happy birthday. *Awww, what a
good daughter. I used to think our Timothy would be like that.* A
former student declared the sweet potato hash at O'Rourke's to be
the ultimate hangover food. *Ali craved sweet potatoes with Timothy. Remember Alison? AP European History? She and I had a son.
He died.* Another ping. Ross again. *Seth, want to talk? It's been a
while.* The asshole was probably typing one-handed, his other arm
wrapped around the warm weight of a wriggling infant. Seth took a
deep breath. The asshole probably felt his child's chest expand and
crest against his. The asshole asked, *You doing okay?*

As if the answer could possibly be yes.

Seth ignored Ross, typing away. He felt jittery and too-vivid, as
if edging toward a fever.

A grad school classmate had booked her tickets to Belize. *I'd
love a vacation from my reality. Did you hear? Timothy's still dead.*
The son of his mother's best friend put up a picture of a gargan-
tuan, meaty sandwich. *Easier to swallow than the fact my son died.*
A woman he couldn't even place had taken a quiz that identified
her power color as dusty rose. Seth typed *Wow, I'm so glad that
you're alive to waste your time on things like that. My son isn't.*
One Chettenford colleague thanked another for jump-starting her
car and someone he had never heard of made an innuendo about it.
*Long time, no talk, guys. Come visit me and Ali (just us. Our baby's
still dead) in Arizona any time.* His uncle needed a backhoe for his
imaginary farm. *That's great, Uncle Stu. I need someone to give a
damn about Timothy.* The guy who'd done all the cartoons for his
college paper couldn't get "Ice Ice Baby" out of his head, how randomly 1990. *And I can't get the fact that we lost our boy out of mine.
When you figure out a solution, give me a call.* The first girl he ever
kissed grumbled about the stress of med school. *Don't bother with
it; doctors couldn't even save one tiny baby.*

Seth? It was Ross again. *You there?*

He felt the seed of a scream beneath his Adam's apple.

Timothy was dead.

Timothy was dead and things like frozen custard still had the audacity to exist.

Seth closed out Ross' window. He clicked to Alison's page. Three hours ago she'd become friends with somebody named Mathieu Donaldson. Yesterday she had posted a picture of a watch and the words *I covet*. The watch was a runners' watch, black and bulky and covered with more buttons than the average dashboard. The day before yesterday she'd lauded Roy Halladay's perfect game. The day before that she announced she was finally getting a handle on Adah Chalk's handwriting. The day before that she bragged about clocking her best mile yet. Earlier in the week she'd posted a picture of a sunset that he hadn't even noticed her taking. That same day she'd asked for movie recommendations. She linked a review of a local gallery they hadn't visited and a hole-in-the-wall taqueria he'd never heard of. She appeared to have an ongoing list of Arizona wildlife she'd spotted on her jogs. She said that the cacti here looked like souvenir-shop cacti and that the sun was turning her into a giant freckle. She had registered for The Commons' Memorial Day Half Marathon. She said she was looking forward to it.

Seth may have made a noise. A mewl of sorts. He was leaning very close to the screen.

Life goes on. People seemed to get a kick reminding him. And so Seth wrote on his wife's wall. *I love you.* He wrote, *I get your thing about Adah Chalk.* It was simple. There were no rearview mirrors on covered wagons. When people left, they left, faces to the setting sun. Letters might yet wing their way: tidings of farms that failed, parents who returned to earth, a niece or nephew baptized under such and such a name. But all that was words and paper. Kindling.

Seth closed out his browser. He crossed to Nicky's desk, wanting nothing more to do with any of this. He handed back the slip of paper the kid had given him. He said, "I'm going to let you field this one. All of it. Your source, your story. Go with your gut."

Light came to the boy's face, and Seth ached all over. In another life, he had labored in a classroom, mining for that light. He returned to his office. On road trips as a child he'd had an Etch A Sketch. Even more than filling it, he had loved the moment of shaking it clean. He hadn't thought of that in forever. He took a full, rich breath. There was a logical progression here: If they were done, well and truly done, with all that had come before, that made this their life now. The Commons, Arizona. They had to make something of it. Alison had gotten that intuitively. She had started already; he'd seen as much online. His wife was waiting. All he had to do was catch up. So, a to-do list. He'd work out a fix for the condo's sagging built-ins and buy some decent patio furniture. They would explore Sabino Canyon and drive out to those graceful old missions. They lived in Arizona, for chrissakes; they had to Craigslist their snow-shoes. Lobel could recommend a realtor, and they'd decide if they needed to factor in school districts.

And Seth would run Lobel's bullshit, why not? A sound investment. The boss would owe them. He sat. He pulled up a blank document. He thought of his wife in her office upstairs, working away. The elegant sweep of her spine. Elbows on the table. Hair in an improvised knot. Notes and photos fanned out like tarot cards. Her lower lip paler than her upper because she licked it when she read and no lipstick had a chance. Seth typed. *Slow Sale of Rosko House Due to Internal Error.* It read a bit clunky and he'd always felt vaguely amateurish writing out the headline first, but who was he kidding? This was hardly the stuff of Pulitzers.

A VIRTUOUS START

INTAKE HAD BEN SHOW PROOF of insurance and sign a dozen forms he didn't bother reading. Sadie claimed a pair of hard plastic waiting-room chairs. The granddaughter was off somewhere, taking with her the *I didn't mean to, I didn't mean to* that had sounded like a metronome in his ear the whole ride over. Sadie stood when he approached, removing the reading glasses he hadn't known she needed. She popped them into the front pocket of her blouse and the cloth between the buttons gapped ever so slightly. He settled beside her to wait. She smelled subtly of grapefruit. Veronica used to eat half of one for breakfast so that whatever the day threw at her thereafter, at least she had made a virtuous start. Goosebumps stippled Sadie's skin. She'd gotten him to the ER without grabbing so much as a sweater.

"Cold?" he asked.

She shook her head.

"Liar."

Sadie smiled, but her eyes weren't in it. Her cheeks weren't either. "I'm fine," she said, but she rubbed her arms. She caught him looking and stilled. She folded her hands neatly in her lap. He could tell her watch had cost a pretty penny. Graceful. Silver. He heard it tick.

"You don't see those much anymore."

"Sorry?"

"Watches. It's a beautiful piece."

She fidgeted with the clasp. Odds were, the watch had been a gift from Gary. Ben's own wife had never liked jewelry that called attention to her hands. Veronica's nails broke easily and her fingers were stubby. She called them her plebe paws. Sadie crossed her legs at the ankles, uncrossed them, inspected her trousers, and plucked at an imagined speck. Posters hung at intervals around the room, encouraging him to quit smoking, to cover his mouth when he coughed, and to get more fiber, more exercise, and—because Knowing Is Sexy!—regular testing for STDs.

Sadie's foot tapped a nervy, erratic beat. "I was a debutante," she said.

"What?" Ben palmed the base of his skull, which still throbbed dully. Maybe he'd hit it harder than he'd thought.

"I've got a portrait floating around somewhere. You'd laugh. Crinoline. White gloves up to here." She patted the full swell of her bicep.

"Huh. I don't think I'd have ever guessed." A half lie. There was something country clubby to her bearing, now that he thought about it, more offhand sportiness than innate athleticism.

"It was an age ago and it was silly even then. But—what I mean to say is, I'm really good at manners. And that matters. If you know what's *done*, then you do it and it leaves more room in your life for everything else."

Ben nodded, remembering the note that had arrived in the mail six days on the heels of Gary's funeral. In it, Sadie had thanked him for the soups he'd had sent from an online gourmet company, the same company that Veronica always used when someone passed. Sadie's stationery had been thick and edged with scallops. Her handwriting was pure Palmer Method.

She said, "I could arm wrestle Emily Post." She flexed. "I could flatten her. But this. I don't know the polite way to ask. My granddaughter. Are you going to be pressing charges?"

"She doesn't like me much." Ben didn't admit it was mutual. He thought of the snotty moue of the girl's lips. The drawn out-cadence that laid exclusive claim to her *Gra-an*. An uncomplicated dart of feeling. Ben loathed the girl. Absolutely despised her. And he was allowed to. She wasn't his daughter. He didn't owe her a lick of nuance. Three years post-divorce and he still had his lawyer on speed dial. Picture the shocked, sullen look on Lily's face when the police arrived.

"No," Sadie agreed. "She doesn't." Veronica would have obfus-cated. *Lily likes you plenty. She's shy. She's always been a bit unde-monstrative.* Tara's first go at rehab? Veronica told their friends she was off at a summer leadership academy. Sadie's foot stopped its tapping. Whatever broken face Lily made when the cops came, her grandmother would surely mirror.

Ben said, "Maybe I have that effect on people. On teenaged girls." He swallowed. He'd been shooting for funny, but of course, it wasn't.

"Don't be ridiculous. Lily's"—Sadie cast about for the right adjective. He was disappointed when she settled for—"a good kid."

"A good kid," he echoed. He'd heard that plenty about Tara. A good kid at heart. A good kid but. Actual good kids were prob-ably called something else. On the other side of the room, a woman clutched her stomach and swore. Ben's skull felt too heavy for his neck.

"She was in a mood," said Sadie. "I shouldn't have put her behind the wheel. She was all up in arms about some Internet—"

"Valedictorians."

"Benjamin? You okay?"

"What they call the real good kids." The waiting-room floor was scuffed all over, a worn, familiar beige. Every hospital in the West-ern Hemisphere got its tiles from the same supplier.

"Let me get a nurse." Sadie was on her feet.

"Sorry. Sit, please." He tapped the seat beside him. "I was woolgathering."

"Aah." She resettled. "Should've guessed. You get this look sometimes." She indicated his head. "There's a lot going on in there."

"Sometimes, maybe. Not right now."

A nurse in pink scrubs appeared and summoned a patient who was not Ben, a narrowly built fellow with no outward evidence of injury. The woman with the stomach pains moaned.

Sadie said, "I do believe Lily when she says it was an accident."

"Yeah?"

"Yes. She's got the family temper, but I'd swear it's all backtalk."

"Girls that age are terrifying." Tara used to make her face colorless when they fought, eyes stolid shutters against any attempt to reach her. She was six pounds, fourteen ounces when first settled into his arms. And just like that his heart weighed six pounds, fourteen ounces. His sternum could never protect it again.

"Terrifying," Sadie agreed. "And Lily doesn't have the easiest path ahead of her. I tell you she's a lesbian? Came out last year. None of us had the least idea. She just wanted us to know. It wasn't—I don't know—laying the groundwork to introduce some Jenny with a rainbow flag she wanted to take to prom. Lily's always been like that. She's . . ." This time, the adjective was more worth the wait. "Adamant. Absolutely herself. Fifteen." Sadie sniffed and smiled, like the number was inherently funny. "That age, the only coming-out on my radar involved a white dress." Something warm swept across her face. "I went up to Chicago three times for fittings. It was the most delicious moonlight-colored silk." An easy flick of her wrist, as if to smooth remembered cloth. "I'm not saying I was some holy innocent. But I was young. It was more along the lines of figuring out regular sex."

Ben feigned interest in the nearest poster, a cartoon syringe that had something to do with H1N1, so that Sadie wouldn't catch the flow of his thoughts. Which were, no surprise, a lot like water seeking the lowest point. Teenaged Sadie, figuring out sex. The archaic smoothness of long gloves. Pearl buttons on a white dress slipping one by one from their slits. A twist of something must have shown on his face; a twist of something easily misread.

Sadie was defensive. Her chin jutted out. "I don't mean regular sex like Lily's kind is somehow abnormal. But young seems like it was younger then."

"It's young enough now." Bearing down on him, Lily's hands had been at ten o'clock and two o'clock exactly, a position you never saw outside Drivers' Ed. "It's plenty young." The fledgling frailty of fifteen. He'd forgotten. Or, rather: he'd stopped himself remembering. The ways a body could break.

"Ben." Sadie produced a pack of tissues. "Here."

He was crying. It had been ages since he'd done that. "I'm sorry," he said.

She brushed away the apology. "Hospitals bring it out in people. And for all I know you're in a hell of a lot of pain." She pointed at the receptionist. "Bet I could sweet-talk her into finding someone who'd give you a pill."

He took a second tissue. "I have a daughter. Had. Have."

Silence. Everyone he offered this story to accepted it in silence.

"Everyone called her a good kid, too. Only, you know how they say *everything before the but is bullshit*? Tara was a good kid but. Good but high strung. Angry. In and out of trouble. In and out of rehab. She ran off at sixteen. The police didn't give a damn. They made a few calls but that was it. Veronica and I checked all the shelters. We handed out her picture everywhere. Hired a detective. This was in 1995. We never saw her again."

"Oh, Benjamin."

"About your Lily. I'm not going to press charges."

"There's nothing about that story that isn't terrible. I'm sorry. What's her name?"

"Tara." You could tell a lot about people from whether they asked *is* or *was*. Their base level of optimism, or what they wanted you to think that base level was. "She's been on my mind. More than usual, I mean. I think seeing your Lily around—" He indicated the sodden shreds of tissues in his hand. "It's not the hospital. I hate hospitals, but—it's not the hospital."

"Eh. Hospitals are okay. They're clean. They're organized. Everyone in them tries their best."

"Maybe." He'd had enough of hospitals for a dozen lifetimes. The cheap, waffle-weave blankets, the Tommyknocker clangs of the MRI. "My wife and I—I hate that everyone thinks we split because of Tara. We hung on for *years* with her gone."

Ben heard how that sounded. Hung on.

Sadie said, "It must have been—I don't like to think about how that must have been."

"Veronica traveled a lot for business. All over. Six, maybe seven trips a year." That sounded like the setup for something licentious. That or Cro-Magnon. Thog want meat, Thog want fire, Thog threatened by career of second-wave spouse, and so forth. He spoke quickly. "I went along whenever I could. We'd research beforehand. It got a lot easier with the Internet. Where the missions were. Food pantries. The shelters. It was sometimes a trick to find the women's ones. They don't always publish addresses. A lot of times when women run it's to hide out from a man. So evenings, Veronica would be off for cocktails and networking and I'd hit the streets, hoping. We never actually thought—we're not stupid people. But she was our little girl." All those times he'd dressed, midsized hotel rooms in midsized cities—Minneapolis, Baltimore, Detroit. The clothes that he and his wife had selected with the specificity of theatrical costume designers. You didn't want to look sleek and prosperous. You didn't want to look shriveled and desperate. He wore a knit cap over the haircut Veronica had him spend more on than he was strictly comfortable spending. Jeans, about to fray but not quite there. Army-surplus parka. Off-brand sneakers. A too-big, no-color button down. "Four years ago, in Chicago, I was robbed and beaten by two men. In Hyde Park. We were under this footbridge. They said at the mission the overflow sometimes bunked down there. It wasn't even the worst neighborhood I'd been to that trip. It's right by the university, you know? They have that house by Frank Lloyd Wright."

"I can't believe you're talking about architecture. *Benjamin*."

"A first-year law student found me the next morning. I don't remember any of this. He was out for a morning jog. I was unconscious for nearly a week. That's why I wanted to come here. You have to be careful, you know? Have them give me a solid looking-over."

"You were out cold." She sounded appalled. He didn't know if she was talking about Chicago four years ago or The Commons this afternoon. "Of course you need a doctor."

"Maybe. Anyhow. They think now I might be predisposed to"—he made a vague gesture in attempt to indicate *breakable*. "Veronica had a hard time. She's a—she solves problems. She tries to make things balance. The kid who found me? We paid for his books till he made JD."

"That's lovely. A lovely gesture."

"I'm not saying it wasn't. But it shows the kind of person she is. Always an eye out for that one thing that will make things right. And that's fine, except—it's hard as hell, excuse my French, when *you're* the thing that needs fixing. When I got out of the hospital, she'd get this *look* like she was waiting for some kind of PTSD crackup. I think she wanted it to happen so she could put me back together already. She'd get real quiet in bad neighborhoods. Flick on the power locks. Or we'd be driving along, talking or what have you, and then we'd pass under a bridge and she'd clam up. Not even a footbridge like the one where—a regular old bridge. Like you use to get to the other side of the river. You know how many bridges there are in Portland?"

"No." A sad, shaky smile. "And I can't believe we're back to architecture."

"She was on me all the time to see a shrink; she got Stephen on her side so I was getting it from all directions. I'd mispronounce a word or forget the name of a street and she'd call in the brain docs like I was one breath away from another coma. I wanted—you know that thing they say about sharks? How they have to keep moving or die? I needed to go on and on. If I stopped—" He shook his head. "People never used to dwell as much. Have you noticed that?"

"It was a huge thing that happened to you. To you both."

"I know. But to talk and talk. That would make it huger. Sorry. I know that's not a word."

A focused flush had come to Sadie's cheeks despite the waiting-room cold. "Maybe not. But it's a feeling."

"Veronica started having these business trips pop up at the last minute. There'd never be a chance for me to reshuffle my appointments or plane fare would be through the roof. But these were conferences, right? She used to have to register months in advance. So I'd call up her secretary and it'd turn out they'd been on the calendar forever."

"I can see why she—"

"I know. I can, too. And I'm sure I wasn't a peach to live with either. I'm not trying to make it sound like it was just the one thing. It never is. We'd been fighting for years but we were *happy* in between. After Chicago, the in between got shorter and shorter. Less happy too." Beside him, Sadie waited for him to say more, but that was that. Another nurse summoned the stomach woman. It was bound to be a good sign that they'd let him stew in his seat this long. Veronica wouldn't have stood for it though. She'd have whipped through her cell phone contacts, found someone who knew someone whose daughter-in-law was a hospital trustee. "Your granddaughter's been gone a while," he said so he'd be saying something.

"I sent her for water. She'll be back." Sadie paled at the appalling casualness of what she'd said.

"It's fine." He laid his hand briefly over hers. Over the hand on the armrest, not the one on her thigh. "Really. It is."

"I'm glad you told me."

"Me too." It was true. Usually when he told people he regretted it right after.

They sat a while.

"So," he said.

"So. You've got that look again. Daydreaming."

"Nah. I wonder. What would Emily Post want you to say next?"

Sadie snorted. The last sound you'd expect from a white-clad bloom of high society. "I think it's fair to say you and I are somewhere beyond Emily."

"We probably are. Still."

"I don't know. She'd probably have me steer us to a less personal subject."

He bowed slightly as if to say, after you.

"Okay then. Let's talk about your putting."

"There's nothing wrong with my putting."

"Maybe. If you're up against a baboon."

The nurse reappeared then, scrutinizing her clipboard. She butchered the pronunciation of his last name. Ben stood so fast it made him dizzy. He didn't want her crossing toward them and saying something to show she mistook Sadie for his wife. He said, "Here's hoping the doctor's a bit older than twelve."

Sadie stretched, then nestled back into the chair. "Oh, I *like* it when they're young. The young ones are going to fight harder. They still take the bad stuff personally."

Ben looked at Sadie, really looked.

This was the only ER for miles.

They must have brought Gary Birnam here, post-collapse.

Her husband must have come here to die.

He took her hand again and squeezed. He said, "I'm probably still a little in love with my wife."

By her face, Sadie didn't know what to make of that. He only had the guts to say what was next because of the easy exit, the nurse on standby to lead him away. "I'm still in love with Veronica, but I like you more."

AN EASIER PLACE
TO PRETEND

SETH CUT OUT EARLY AND went up to Alison's office. It was empty. A single orange, its PLU sticker peeling, sat on the corner of her desk. It was the only bright thing in the room. A half-dozen books occupied the shelves, their spines muted gray and green and brown. *Azucena's Table: Feeding the American Frontier. After the Golden Spike. Tribal Groups of the Four Corners Region. Arizona! A Pictorial History. Coyote, Fox, Hawk, and Bat: A Compendium of Apache Mythology.* Two Stegner titles. For reasons he couldn't begin to guess at, a Danish-English dictionary. While Seth waited, he alphabetized them. Ali's office windows were smaller than his but oriented better. The room was thick with dust-flecked light. Two news vans—up one from the other day—were parked in the circular drive below. When she got here, he'd tell Alison that he'd given Nicky Tullbeck the Rosko story. He'd frame it as the kid's big break. Alison would like that. She was fond of Nicky.

Seth sat at his wife's desk. Her chair groaned under his weight. He leaned back and the groan changed pitch. More of a squeak now. It must drive Alison up the wall. He knelt and jiggled the seat, trying to pinpoint the trouble. There. Yes. It would take all of five minutes to fix. Seth lay down to better reach the undercarriage. Loose bolts. It wasn't even a question of WD-40.

"Seth? What are you doing on the floor?" He hadn't heard Alison approach.

"Your chair squeaks." The funny knobs of her ankles stuck out. Also her ears. There was something strange about her neck. He realized: "You've cut off your hair."

"Yes."

"It's cute." He sat up. Stood. A blunt fringe cut across Alison's forehead. The rest cropped close to her scalp. It made her eyes enormous. There was something different about the color, too. More yellow maybe.

"Well." She tousled it. It was better after. Less pristine. "Now you can quit complaining about my hair in the drain."

"Alison." His wife was fitter than ever. His wife was blonder than ever. And Seth was apparently no true blue American male. Because what he felt was cheated. Alison's had always been an unexpected sort of prettiness; if she were less confident, she might even be taken for plain. Ali was all those industrious colors of a summer road trip. Hair warm and variegated like farmed grain, eyes the cool gray-blue of quarried shale. Even her freckled skin. Nothing one color or the other. Her attractiveness came from that tension, and from the vividness with which she held it all together.

"This morning, I shouldn't have said—"

"No. It was bothering you. Of course I want you to tell me when something is bothering you." Her voice was dangerously bright. It matched the unfamiliar scent that hung between them, all zest and false flowers. Chemical undertones. Eau de salon.

Seth sneezed.

"*Salud.*"

"Thanks." He looked around. Back home in Chettenford, Alison always kept a box of Kleenex on her desk. The school was constructed in 1923 and his wife was allergic to some lingering interior mold. And of course her desk saw its steady stream of weeping girls.

Ms. C, it seemed, was as essential post-breakup as a pint of Ben & Jerry's. "Kleenex?" he asked.

Alison shook her head.

He'd thought she might have some on hand, that maybe she cried in private now and then.

"I'd like my chair back," she said, tucking her bag under the desk. "I used my lunch hour at the salon. I've got to catch up." A false lightness buoyed her tone. Chances were he was in trouble. It was bound to be his mucking about with the chair. She'd see it as an attack on her unquestionable competence. That was Alison all over. Chivalry was wasted on her.

"I can wait around," he said

"I'll be a while. Hoagie sprung this thing on me—he's renaming the main town here for Adah Chalk. He wants to announce at the HOA meeting tomorrow, and then have a big to-do for Founder's Day." She sat, swiveled away from him, and got out her stack of Adah Chalk three-by-fives.

"Tomorrow? And here I thought you couldn't rush history."

"When you get a brainwave . . ." Her shrug was sharp without the softness of her unbound hair. Or perhaps all the running had sharpened the curve of her shoulder. *Brainwave* was a Lobel word; if Ali started saying *folks* he would know the pair had been spending entirely too much time together.

"It's a nice haircut," he said. "It suits you." It did. Seth was the one it didn't particularly suit. Ask him again when he was used to it. Alison brushed a hand across the back of her neck. Attention there drove her wild. He wondered if the skin would start to lose its sensitivity without her hair to shield it from everyday touch. He pressed his lips to the knob at the top of her spine.

She scooted away. Her chair squeaked. "I promised Hoagie I'd get him a draft presentation on Adah ASAP."

"*Hoagie.*"

"It's his name. He wants us to use it." Her tone edged toward curt. "I've got to get to work."

"Sure. Let me run out and get you a sandwich. Or maybe a wrap from that place by The Homeplate? And an iced tea, right? With lemon. Or do you think you'll need more serious caffeine?"

"Seth, I'm trying to be nice. But what I really want is for you not to be in my face right now."

"Huh?"

She turned the chair to face him. Sunlight coalesced around her. "You'll never guess what happened while I was under the dryer." She patted her newly sleek head. She beamed. She had on earrings. She usually didn't bother. They were silver things, shaped like graduation tassels. "My phone rang. Any idea who it was?"

She was using her teaching voice, which seldom boded well. And all at once he knew who'd called. Ross Henry, math teacher, Yankees fan, father of two. Aspiring do-gooder. Seth hoped the twins developed a lifelong affinity for the Sox. "Ross Henry," he said. He should've left when Ali told him to.

"Ross Henry, that's right. He seemed to be under the impression you were hurting—"

"Ali—"

"I mean more than usual. He was very kind. He made sure to say of course you were hurting. But maybe the tiniest something more was troubling you?" She held her thumb and index finger close together. That Ross. Sometimes it was worse when people said precisely the right thing. It meant that they weren't quite your friends anymore. It meant they'd memorized their lines in advance. "It was nice, actually," Ali continued. "Playing hooky in the middle of the day, all this gorgeous sunlight, stylist swooning because he's got someone in his chair whose next stop isn't a hip replacement. And it was nice catching up with Ross. Tons of gossip. Shipley's come up with some unenforceable student cell phone policy for next year. We took state in softball. Would've done baseball too, but Mark

Sarrachino blew his shoulder. The twins are thriving, but Ross knew enough not to go on about it."

It wasn't just the twins that got him. It was the casualness of that *we*. We meaning Vermont and the North Chettenford Minutemen, the weight of her life still two thousand miles away. And yet like an idiot he'd filed the story Lobel had asked for. It would run tomorrow above the fold, next to a sidebar detailing the many activities associated with Founder's Day. He swallowed. He attempted lightness. "Well. You always said Sarrachino was going to need reconstructive surgery before he hit twenty."

She shrugged. Again. He hated that gesture and he hated that she hadn't done anything with her office. There was nothing to look at here but Alison. Her profile reflected in the window. He had to squint in the invading light. She sighed. The sound was unexpectedly content. "It was a good morning. The stylist didn't even ask if we had kids." Another thing they hadn't accounted for in the move. How to field that standard getting-to-know-you question. "A good morning," she repeated. "So I thought I'd treat myself. Ice cream." Her tongue darted out and swept across her lips. The unthinking intimacy of it rocked him. "And as I'm paying, *bzzzt!*, a text. What do you know? It's Bronsted, remember? From across the hall junior year? He used to have the biggest crush on me." It said something about Alison that she'd choose this moment to remind him, and it said something about Seth that he'd have remembered anyhow. "Eric Bronsted. Never subtle." Alison shook her head, like she was actually fond of Eric Bronsted. "Can you guess what he wrote?"

"Probably nothing complimentary." Bronsted had never liked Seth, but Seth had been human about it. Gracious in victory and all of that.

"Ali. Hey. Think your man might be cracking up." She made her voice husky but didn't sound a thing like Bronsted.

"The guy never liked me."

"Are you, Seth? Cracking up?" There was a claylike cool now to Alison's voice, as if she were still working out how to shape it.

"No. I'm really not."

"See, I wondered. Because my phone's sure been busy." Ali rummaged in her purse. Her skirt hitched up. He knew better than to reach for her. She found her phone. "Kerstin Buell: Are you guys okay? Jessie Jarvis: What's up with Seth? Give us a call. Oh, and this one's new. Aaron Fisher: Everything all right? And not one, not two, but three voicemails I haven't had a moment to check."

Seth was glad she'd cut her hair. It was like someone else unloading on him.

"Neil's call actually rang through." Neil was her brother, who played shortstop for the AAA IronPigs. He should have been out on the diamond. He should have been in the weight room. He got to live outside, lungs full of clipped grass and worn leather. He had no business whatsoever checking Facebook midday.

"Okay then," Seth said. There was no point dissembling. Alison knew. She'd seen it. They had WiFi everywhere here. The brochures had gone on and on about it. Alison leaned forward and the chair squeaked its protest. She ran her palm along the edge of her desk. Her hand skirted the orange. He wanted to take it in his. That or pick up the fruit. Peel it. Loose the scent of something other than hair gel in the room. Alison pointed and flexed her sandaled foot. Her toenails were painted soft mauve. He'd lain in bed and watched her apply that paint last weekend. She'd done it at home in Vermont, too, but back then he was the only one who'd known. Shipley had rules about open-toed shoes.

"What's up with you, Seth?" This came out a tired whisper.

"I may have pissed off some people." She wasn't meant to be one of them. Alison. She was meant to be on his side.

"Try everyone. Try may have committed social suicide."

"*Virtual* social suicide."

Alison gave him a look.

"I honestly didn't think you'd care." She didn't care for much these days. This, he had the good sense not to say.

"You honestly didn't think. Period. These are our friends."

"They were so smug, Ali. So smug and so happy."

"Facebook's smug," she said. "That's the whole point."

"It should be us. Complaining about spitup."

Alison said nothing. She curled in on herself like a comma. The only thing stopping him from laying his hand on her shoulder was how it would feel if she shook it off.

"It should be us," he said again.

"It's not." Alison looked at her palms, like her life was actually spelled out there. "And I like Facebook. I like seeing that the people I love are okay."

"It's so showy, Alison. It's all polished and rah-rah and unreal."

"I like that, too. It's an easier place to pretend."

"It's not a place," he said.

"Well. Whatever. It's an easier context to fake in."

"What do you mean, to fake in?"

An unsteady laugh. Her smile was a studied thing, deliberately crafted.

"You didn't really sign up for that marathon, did you?" He hated that he'd fallen for it, bought into the happy illusion she'd crafted of zeros and ones. The patio pictures and intriguing local restaurants. The road race she was looking forward to in three months' time. He was her husband. He should be impossible to put one over on.

"Look at me," Ali said. He did. Maybe it was the shorn hair, or the relentlessly waning curves. The particular thinness of her wrists. She looked like a little boy. "Here I am." She stood. She pointed at breastbone. Her clavicles made ridges beneath tan skin. "Me. Alison. Your wife. A real, live human being. Can you try to remember that?"

"Where's this coming from? Of course I—"

"No, you don't. I don't know what you see when you look at me, but it's not a person. Because a person, an actual human, wouldn't have to hear from some idiot she knew back in college that her husband is out of his fucking mind."

"The hell, Alison?"

"All our friends. Every single one."

"We never even talk to them." It hurt, the furious concern she had for them. Them, not him. The ones who chugged blithely along.

"That's not the point and you know it."

"We came here to start again." He shook his head but it didn't clear. There was usually an underlying logic when they fought, a dance of sorts. But this. They were in real trouble. It was like trying to argue with a Magic 8 Ball.

"Start over, sure," said Ali. "But I never said we should salt the earth behind us."

She never said anything. He might as well live with an ornamental plant. Seth said, "At least I'm making an effort."

"*This* is making an effort?" She brought her hand down, hard, on the desk and he hoped she'd shatter one of the fine bones of her wrist.

"You have no idea the effort I make." He saw it, in sixteen-point font. *Slow Sale of Rosko House Due to Internal Error.* Those were some fundamental fucking principles he'd laid down, easy as he'd set a bag of groceries on the kitchen counter. All for Alison. All so she could come back to herself, here, in the deliberate, painless place he had found for her.

"Sure," she said. "It's so hard, finding new ways to make an ass of yourself." She smoothed her skirt. Heat had come to her cheeks.

"You're *embarrassed*," he said, like he couldn't quite believe it.

"You bet your sweet ass I am. The last one to hear that my husband is out of his gourd."

Good to know she could actually feel. Cold perfectionist bitch. He said, "Oh, go have a run."

Alison stood. A comma no more. An exclamation point. One of those upside-down ones, with her round, close-cropped head and lean, straight body. There had to be a word for those, and there had to be a word for this feeling. He wanted to shake her until her insides resonated with the shaking of his own.

Alison had graduated *magna cum laude.*

Alison had made teacher of the year her second year on the job.

Alison remembered names and birthdays. She kept in touch with former professors. She'd sweet-talked their old landlady into replacing the ancient orange carpet and negotiated an extra fifteen hundred off their Camry. She could change a flat tire and check her own oil. His wife. In certain lights, she literally made him short of breath.

A petty smallness within him triumphed. For once, he was better at something than Alison. He was better at mourning Timothy.

He almost said it, but there are things you can't take back.

Alison knew that, she had to. She was always so careful with her words. Still, she could be ruthless. Still, she forged ahead. "I'm supposed to be mothering a baby," she said, and her arms cradled air. "Not someone who acts like one." Seth left without a word. Halfway to the elevator he heard her chair squeak. It was all too stupid to even be a metaphor.

A SIMPLE, BASIC HUMAN RULE

IN THE DIVVYING OF THEIR possessions, Veronica had wound up with the Thales' aging Mr. Coffee. Ben, as if to insure against a solitary life of single cups, had acquired what his son and daughter-in-law called the Chrome Monstrosity: an Italian-made coffee and espresso machine with built-in tamper, grinder, and steamer. The Monstrosity could drip twelve cups of coffee at a go. It could spit out hot water for tea, could froth up proper lattes at the press of a button, and, for all he knew, had the power to retroactively regulate those bastards at Lehman. He topped off his mug and sponged the Monstrosity down; the auto-clean setting, alas, applied only to internal components. Across the way, Sadie Birnam came out of her house. Ben blew into his cup and sipped. Sadie had a neat, deliberate walk. She passed the foot of her drive, and Ben felt the shy, seeping spread of bashfulness. She usually just collected the paper, her scoop and pivot married in seamless motion. He wasn't, thank goodness, a blusher, but he felt a flutter of heat. He knew her morning postures. He'd been watching for weeks now without really thinking about it. She was in the middle of the street and coming closer. Chin up, eyes fixed as if to return the cumulative weight of his gazes.

His house felt like it was built entirely of windows.

Sadie reached his lawn and cut across mown grass. He opened the door. No sense pretending he didn't know she was coming. A quick breath, hers, and too-bright, high-pitched *hello,* his. Yesterday's declaration snaked bald between them. They said good morning. The greetings were just off of simultaneous.

"I made coffee." He raised the mug. On it, bold letters warned: Don't Mess with Veterinarians. They Know How to Neuter. It could've been worse. He had another that said Save a Horse, Mount a Vet. Both had been gifts from Stephen. "Can I interest you?" he asked, and the question hung there, more layered than he'd intended.

"Smells great, but no. I, ah—"

"Do you want to come in?"

"No, Ben. I, um—I guess I should check. Are you feeling all right?"

"Yeah. I'm fine." There was something at play here that he didn't quite get. Something too intentional in her bearing. He asked, "To what do I owe the pleasure?"

"Okay, well. The thing is. I saw your interview online."

He saw the granddaughter in her then, mercurial and sullen. "Ahh, yes. I guess you were bound to."

"It wasn't for kicks, Ben. I wouldn't have bothered, only—it did a number on Lily. She's under my roof. I had to see what upset her. And, well. I'll tell you. It was quite a—"

"Disaster." He was glad Sadie had not come in; he felt a fool to have even offered.

A patrician smile. "I was going to say performance. But yes. You have a mouth on you."

"Not generally."

"I was shocked, hearing you like that. It was shocking."

"I never talk that way. I don't think I'd said that word before in my life."

"I don't do offended, Ben, but that was ugly." Above them, the sky was the irresolute blue of early morning. Sadie's eyes were bluer by far. Ben felt a cottony pang for the boy he'd been, who'd have felt a drunken, romantic pulse at that, who hadn't seen enough of eyes and skies to know that sometimes that was just the way they looked. He said, "You don't have to tell me that."

"I do. If I—"

"No, you don't." The hazy boy he'd been would've simply apologized.

"It'd be *there* otherwise," Sadie said. "Every time we talked. Ugly and there. I didn't want that."

"So, what now? You going to run me down with a golf cart?"

"That was ugly, too. You know that Lily never meant—"

"You know what? I *feel* ugly." He shifted a little to bar the threshold she'd made no motion toward crossing. His home. There was a sectional in the living room he'd bought because it looked like the one he'd bought with Veronica. The kitchen cabinets were crammed with dishes he and Ronnie had registered for way back when. Keep the lot of it, his ex had said, and Ben reckoned her post-paperwork restocking was propping up the economy's homegoods sector. "I feel *damn* ugly," he said. "You come to my house to tell me—"

"I told you, and now it's . . ." Sadie exhaled and spread her fingers wide, as if to pantomime dandelion spores on the wind.

"No, now it's *here*." He motioned at the space between them, where, for the moment, no tender thing unfurled. "And you know what else? Inviting yourself over to tell me off wasn't the prettiest maneuver on your part."

"Well, then. Sir. I humbly take my leave." Sadie gave a low, elaborate bow. Even Veronica seldom achieved that level of baroque bitchiness. So perhaps this was the alleged wisdom of age: You got a faster, firmer sense of how the people in your life would make you crazy. Sadie was blunt. She could pat her back and dress it up as virtue. Package and rebrand it as forthrightness. It didn't matter what she called it. He still felt bulldozed.

"I had my reasons, you know. For saying all that."

She pufferfished her cheeks and sighed. Ben braced. With Veronica, sighs were the stepping stones to screaming. "I know," Sadie said. "I figured. Your daughter."

He didn't want to admit she was right. He didn't like how obvious that made him.

Sadie asked, "Why didn't you mention *her*?"

"My son said the same thing." He should have led with Tara, no matter the girls he had memorized alphabetically. It was a simple, basic, human rule: family first.

"Stephen?"

"Yeah. Stephen. I don't have a secret third."

She gave him a wry look, freighted with all he'd withheld. She said, "He seems like a lovely young man."

"He is. His wife's lovely, too."

She nodded. They weren't fighting anymore, somehow. A release of tension from his limbs, followed by the quick flare of something like disappointment. Then exhaustion. If this—whatever *this* was—was ever going to happen, there was a whole language he had yet to learn. Sighs meant something else when Sadie sighed them.

He felt like sighing himself. "About Tara. I guess—we tried to be private about it. As a family. Old habits." It was out there, of course. They'd had to ask everyone they knew. Presumably the cops had too, and thereafter, Rand Danovic.

Sadie said, "I'd have told everyone. On the off-chance—sorry. I don't mean to second-guess you." She fiddled with a loose lock of her hair, rolling the ends between thumb and forefinger. How was that for a language lesson? This was Sadie ill at ease. She realized it and stopped. When you got to be their age, you knew your own tells. She looked at him, earnest as a proselytizer. "I'm sure—I *know*—you did everything you could think of." Chicago glinted between them. The sun on Lake Michigan the day he flew home, ribs still knitting back together, bruises still mottled, his slurry mind straining for the blacked-out days that would never be returned to him.

He said, "You can always do more."

"Ben." She sounded like Veronica, though Veronica would've said Benji. In the ICU and after, Ronnie had harped. Absurd. If there was any one thing that did them in. The borders of his bruises grew indistinct and vanished. His sutures dissolved, leaving behind the fine white vein of a scar. Months passed and then one day he found he could breathe without pain. And still Veronica wanted to talk about it, the way she never had with Tara. On and on. To everyone they knew. To the goddamn world and his dog.

"You can always do more," he repeated. "Always. We did what we could, but . . . Veronica thought—we thought—that the quieter we were about it, the easier it would be for Tara to slot back into place. You know, when she came back." They'd kept her room in stasis. Tara's closet brimmed with clothes so far out of date they'd be on trend again any day now.

"I guess I can see that." Sadie felt sorry for him. He could tell by the line of her jaw, soft, but strangely eager. Another reason he didn't talk much about Tara. Once you shared, people expected you to keep sharing. The same way he'd thought, gawking at girls way back when, that as soon as you got the first one to lie down with you, the rest of your life would be hot and cold running sex.

He swallowed a lukewarm mouthful of coffee. "After a while it was habit. Not talking about her. Habit. So don't tell me we did everything we could."

"I never meant to imply—"

"And then it was more than habit. You get so damn tired. It's lousy being that sad, crazy couple everyone avoids at parties."

"Of course you're sad."

"Yeah. But after a year or so, nobody wants to hear it."

"Oh, Ben. I can't imagine that's true."

A bitter flash at her prim piousness. "Sure," he said, "and folks are lining up these days to talk about Gary."

"Huh. You really go for the jugular. I wouldn't have guessed." Her face betrayed no emotion; it hadn't at Gary's funeral either. She simply touched her neck, right where the vein was.

He said, "You get mad. You can't help it. Seeing how the world trucks along. Hence my . . . disaster."

"Performance." She softened a little. "Those girls you mentioned. Mimi, Tenana—"

"Tenaya. Tenaya Alder. Mimi Asencios. Christy Aves. Lisa Balish. There are lists out there. Whole databases. Like I told that reporter. No one gives a damn. Meghan Bagnall. Renee Bench."

"You memorized them all?"

"No. You'd need to be a supercomputer. These are the ones who went missing right about when Tara did. All the girls her age. Noelle Cabley. Sarai Cabotaje. I'm never sure if I'm pronouncing that one right." He shut his eyes. "I used to run through the names before I fell asleep. All the way to Gabby Vullo."

"Like counting sheep." Once again, he'd missed the pivot point of their return to civil conversation.

"No," he said. "Like prayer. Like when you were a little kid and you felt—I don't know—comforted?—kneeling down before bed."

"Now I lay me down to sleep. I pray the Lord my soul to keep." Sadie's voice was singsong. There was motion in the Birnam house, Lily ricocheting through her morning. He hoped Sadie would notice, then skedaddle. He hoped Sadie wouldn't, and stay.

"Right. Like that. But real. Instead of what you did there, rattling off words. It felt like—I know it's silly but—if I was thinking of these kids, maybe someone out there was thinking about Tara. And that made her more real. It meant Ronnie and I weren't alone."

"Ronnie?"

"Veronica, sorry. She thought I was nuts."

"Do you still do it?"

"I don't. I haven't since—I can't recall. Maybe I should start again."

"It's been getting a lot of attention. Your"—Sadie didn't wink, but her eyebrow quirked—"performance."

"You're telling me. I had to disconnect the phone, and I'm afraid to even check my e-mail."

"Those other girls. Someone made a what's-it-called—a mash-up?—about them. Your voice and their pictures, how to get hold of their parents." The sun was up behind his house and its light fell across her face. She raised a hand to shield her eyes. An errant eyelash rested on her cheek. Tara used to wish on them. Ben brushed it away with his index finger. Sadie startled.

"Eyelash." There was no point in wishing. Stephen had seen it, Sadie had seen it, a whole host of crank callers had seen it. Inevitable that Veronica would. Pictures and parent info, Jesus Bartholomew Christ. Veronica would know the opportunity he'd squandered. Some measure of desperation must have shown on his face.

"Don't worry," Sadie said, misreading. "They bleeped out the— it was censored. So maybe it'll do some good. Maybe one of those girls will see it and come home."

Which would help not at all on the Veronica front, not when it could have been Tara. He was so tired, marrow-tired from yesterday's fall, and damned tired of caring what Veronica thought.

"Ben, you there? It's a good thing, Ben."

He was tired of talking, too. "I think your granddaughter's up." He indicated the house.

Sadie turned toward home. "Duty calls. Can I ask—?"

"I'm not going to do anything to Lily. I told you already." Sadie could put a bow on it and call it loyalty. That didn't change the way the girl led her around by the nose.

"I wanted to ask about Mona, actually. Is that really what you think of her?"

YOU COULD BE HOME BY NOW

The Rosko house was awake, too; a shadow skimmed the curtains. "I don't need a lecture," he said.

"No lectures." Her tone was so cheerful it back-bent around to brusque. Clear indicator that a lecture was, in fact, inevitable.

"I guess I should probably touch base with her. Send flowers." He thought of the soups he'd had sent to Sadie on the eve of Gary's funeral. Soothingspoons.com's comfort quartet: chicken noodle, minestrone, rustic potato, and something French and unpronounceable involving leeks. He'd never tasted a spoonful of their product. As far as he knew, Veronica hadn't either. Yet they sent them and sent them, every time somebody passed. "Flowers or something," he said.

"I think she'd prefer not to be disturbed." Sadie's tone was icy in a way he didn't really follow.

"Ahh, well. Maybe I'll catch her at the HOA thing today. She'll be there, yeah? I bet she'll want to speak her piece."

"She's certainly good at that." Sadie's sour mouth reminded him of Lily's.

"I don't really know her," he said. "I told the reporter that, too."

"Well, I've been getting to know her. What you said—she certainly deserves it."

"And here I thought you liked everyone."

"Not Mona. I don't mind about the boy, and I hope she can sell and move on fast, but—I think you were right on the mark about her. She was awful to Lily."

"That I'd have paid to see. Your girl can more than hold her own."

He was edging close to *too far* or had stepped beyond it. He didn't know Sadie as well as he might, but that much he could guess. You didn't mess with the granddaughter. But no. She grinned as if he'd meant to compliment. That bright Sadie optimism. She wielded it like a cudgel. Veronica was right. He should see a damn shrink. He should've been seeing one for years. Look at him. You were supposed to go after women like Sadie—generous women, warm, who went optimistically through their lives like kindergarten teachers. You were meant to be happy when things came easy. When you said your piece and forgave and were forgiven in turn. Veronica, or life, or his own fool nature had really done a number on him. All that Sadie sunniness and what hooked him, hard, was his neighbor's vitriol toward Mona, her unexpected snappishness, the intricate sweep of her sarcastic bow.

ANGELS AND ORIFICES

THE GODS OF EXCESS DRAMA evidently had it in for her. For lo, there was Nicky Tullbeck in all his stalktastic glory. He rang the bell; Gran jumped a little even though she was facing the window and had to have seen him approach. Multiple choice: Gran was (a) mentally casting Benjamin Thales as her very own wrinkled Romeo, (b) running through the list of third-tier relatives to pawn Lily off on, or (c) having a series of tragic but minor and wholly age-appropriate ministrokes. Gran opened the door. "Lily's unavailable right now," she said. "Lily is taking a bit of a break from amusements."

Translation: *grounded.* At least she'd spelled it out. The morning had been a case study in passive aggression. Lily had been the one to say good morning and she'd been the one to ask any and all questions. Gran's answers were pleasant, but not pleasant enough to balance out their terseness. And then there was the visual coding. Gran's laptop had—cue the spooky music—mysteriously vanished and the printed activity schedule had migrated from refrigerator to trash can, which only went to show that Gran was out of practice. Grounding was so much harsher if you saw the world buzz along without you.

Nicky Tullbeck apologized. "I hate to intrude on your family time, ma'am, but I'm here in an official capacity. I'm a reporter. From the *Crier*."

An intern. Lily let the fabrication slide, considering the self-puffery involved in elevating herself to official Rosko spokeswoman. Which, oh fuckadoodledoo, had to be why he'd come. Her guts felt jumbled and quick and sick. Gran smiled and let Nicky in. He was careful to wipe his shoes on the mat. Either they were new or he'd gone a little nuts with the polish.

"Lil-*lay*," he said, with the same smug inflection adolescent males the world over appeared to find so genius. It would serve Gran right if he actually was a stalker. He'd hack Lily to bits and scatter the various joints around The Commons' award-winning greens. The per-vet's property value would tank due to his proximity to the murder house and he'd reap exactly the sympathy he'd shown Mona Rosko. And Gran. She'd pickle inside, remembering how she'd flounced her way through the girl's final morning, conveying to the best of her ability that *Lily < Ben*. Mom's hair would go guilty white and refuse to hold dye. Dad would be hospitalized in short order with a roiling triple ulcer, but not before establishing a scholarship fund for Tyson Rosko in lieu of funeral flowers.

But Sierra. Sierra would speak at the all-school memorial. She'd wear blush half a shade lighter than her usual NARS New Order and mascara that was strategically not waterproof. When her eyes brimmed, even the stoners in the back row would see the streaking and think *that poor, brave, beautiful creature*. Teachers would cut her slack on assignments and she'd commandeer the *Lily Birnam 1995-2010* yearbook spread, selecting photos in which she looked better than the dead girl, or at least ones where the camera had caught her at a thinner angle.

Gran offered Nicky a cup of coffee, apologizing that it was only instant. Apparently there was a genetic predisposition toward that thing Dad did where you had no idea exactly how pissed he was until he squared his back to you and became pleasantness cubed to whomever else was in the room. Dad had learned from the best. Gran offered Nicky his choice of mug, spooned the powder in herself, stirred, and presented him with sugar in an actual sugar bowl. Nicky chose the Forest Park Day mug apparently at random, but who knew what might happen. Even now he was filing the school name away. He'd hitchhike to St. Louis, lurk by the entrance for the 3:15 bell, break out the chloroform, and bury Lily alive. Police would be stymied until Gran remembered how she'd let the slavering beast boy into her home. For the rest of Gran's life, even a whiff of coffee would set her retching.

Nicky sipped. He let out a commercial-worthy sigh. He took a chair at the kitchen table.

Lily resisted the pamby girl impulse to fold her arms across her chest. Talk about a cascade of causality. First you look weak, then you act weak, then you are weak. "What do you want?"

Gran shot her a look and mouthed *manners*. The intern was unperturbed. "This doesn't taste like instant. Thanks again. Lily's been such a valuable source. I wanted to firm up a few details." His voice was shiny as his shoes. Lily stood barefoot in her Cherry *Pi* pajamas. Critics, take note: If fashion were really nothing but fluff, that wouldn't matter. But it did. She wished she were confidently pencil-skirted. Nicky said he was looking for confirmation of the daughter's name. "You said Carrie Rosko, right? I'm guessing with a *C*?"

"They're going to *love* you at Rice next year." Brilliant maneuver, putting him on defense. Genius, really. No wonder Lily was universally beloved.

Nicky's mug steamed. Gran took a small sip from her own. "We don't actually know the Roskos that well," she said. Her face was open and apologetic.

Nicky shifted focus. "Still, you know her a little. What's she like?"

"Prickly," said Gran. She looked out at the cul-de-sac and the orderly green beyond. She faced the Thales house, not the Rosko, which was apt enough.

"How so?"

"She doesn't—" Gran paused. She picked up a spoon and clattered it around her coffee cup. Then she looked at Lily, proper eye contact and everything, for the first time since the accident. You could see her thinking, all those cogs and sprockets. No, I won't out my granddaughter to a reporter.

Lily's heart sprang seesaw. Pop quiz. Keeping it secret means (a) Gran loves you and has your back or (b) Gran's embarrassed. "Mona doesn't approve of me." Might as well spare Gran the trouble of saying it.

"You mean the job you're doing?"

Awareness sliced through Lily with the word. *Job.* Game over. Gran looked confused, and no wonder. She settled the spoon neatly onto her napkin. When she spoke, she looked at Lily, not the intern. "Mona's under tremendous pressure. Unimaginable. And pressure like that . . . some people turn into diamonds, but most of us turn into—let's be polite and say orifices." She laid her hands neatly parallel to the spoon. Gran, who couldn't say *gay* to a reporter but had no trouble with the Latinate plural of asshole.

Nicky's stylus was out and scrawling. Lily was pretty sure Gran had meant all that for her alone. "Don't quote my grandmother," she said, and her voice was hard and low. It had to be. It had to counterbalance the suntanned vulnerability of her legs, the boxers patterned with twinned cherries and 3.14159, the Greek letter–emblazoned circle-with-a-slice-out pie splayed over her breasts like a target.

"It's fine, Lily," Gran said, but it wasn't.

She wanted to die. Really, truly, and actually. There was a reason *mortal* and *mortified* had 44.444-forever-4 percent of their letters in common.

Nicky said, "I'm just here for the daughter's name. Maybe her rank and service branch if you've got them. You're sure she's Rosko, like the mom?"

Gran asked how on earth they'd know.

Nicky's attention shifted to Lily, joy of joys. Her bones rubberized, giving the flesh of her nothing to tense onto. "Yeah. Rosko. I guess."

"You guess?"

"I'm not really the official spokesperson." She pulled it off without the creep of blush. At least there was that.

"I figured as much." Nicky tapped his head and grinned. "Rice, remember? The Stanford of the South?" He made a face like he couldn't believe he'd said that. "I bet you never even met the Roskos."

"I did. I have." Lily sounded about five.

"So the deal with the mom—"

"Is something you'll have to ask our neighbor directly." Gran stood.

"She doesn't return calls." Nicky sounded about five, too.

A birdlike tilt of her head conveyed Gran's disinterest. Nicky tried Lily. "I can't get confirmation of a service record for Carrie Rosko. I've tried Caroline, Carolyn. So before I waste any more of my time on this, I'd like to know how much you were messing with me." He spoke like someone who watched a lot of cop dramas. Sierra would probably be weak with lust. "The only Carrie Rosko I can find is down in Florence," he said.

"So? We have bases in Italy." Lily was pretty sure, at least. And it sounded good.

"Florence, Arizona. As in, the women's penitentiary. Inmate number"—he checked his phone—"583446/RO."

"*R* and *O* aren't numbers."

"You know what? You're crazy. You're a crazy person."

Thank the Drama Gods for Gran, who indicated the door. She upped the wattage of her smile. "Off the record?"

Nicky hovered. "Yes."

"Completely?"

"Completely."

"My granddaughter's something of a drama bug. She's down here after being nearly expelled from her school for bullying. She got herself mixed up with the Roskos; yesterday, she practically put another neighbor in the hospital. She's just spinning you around." She touched his arm, conciliatory. "I'd head back to my desk if I were you."

He went. The screen door needed oiling.

Gran wheeled on Lily. "Official spokesperson?"

Lily made a squeak not unlike the door.

"Look at me."

Gran was fully dressed already: cream-colored trousers, silk blouse, low-slung necklace with a round fob. Subconscious stethoscope. She'd rather be across the street Florence Nightingaling. She steered Lily to the window. Lily could taste the warmth of her own mouth. Gran pointed. "That's the Romers' house. New car, right there in the drive. Convertible. Leather seats, like they always wanted. Why don't you go egg it?" Gran moved through the kitchen like a javelin, sharp, lean, designed for speed. She flung the refrigerator wide, popped open a Styrofoam clamshell and began grabbing eggs. "Here. Take them. Go." Lily's hands cupped by instinct. Gran said, "After, you can TP the Driskells'. Maybe play a round of ding-dong-ditch."

It was the combination of words that did it. First Sierra, then Gran. Lily was destined for a lifetime of getting ditched for some skeezy possessor of a ding-diddle-dong. Her nails clicked against an eggshell's white-blue curve. She wasn't going to cry two times in as many days. She said it simply. "I lied."

"Yes, Lily. I deduced that. Saint Louis University, remember?" Gran tapped her head in imitation of Nicky.

"I wanted him to feel bad." Right now, she wanted that for everybody. "He was being creepy."

"How?" Gran waited.

Lily talked with her hands more than she realized. She was completely inarticulate now that they were full of eggs. Mom would never ask how. Mom's general preoccupation with the many ways *Internet* and *pedophile* were predestined to intersect made *creepy* the ultimate get-out-of-jail-free card. "You really wouldn't get it." Gran liked Ben. Her sketch meter wasn't calibrated right.

"I probably wouldn't. I'm notoriously unsympathetic. Christ, Lily. I live here. I'll still be living here once you leave. What goes on in your head?"

That things were better yesterday. That an astounding number of things rhymed with *cunt*.

"And now we're going to have to deal with that woman again. Let her know you've loosed a reporter. It doesn't feel good to be blindsided. I'll tell you. It does not."

"He's only an intern." Lily wanted to crunch the egg in her hand. First the pop and then the splintering, then the bright ooze of yolk out her fingers. A measuring look from Gran said: I know your makeup entirely. Two-thirds water, one-third viscous fuckupitude.

Lily said, "I should apologize."

"To Benjamin, too."

A door-to-door campaign. Let the trumpets sound.

"Everyone will be at the HOA meeting. We can catch them there. Them and anyone else you manage to piss off." An electronic beep punctuated the words. Gran had left the refrigerator door ajar too long. She banged it shut with a quick jut of her hip. A clock once hung on the wall of Gran's St. Louis kitchen, its face sunk into the round belly of a happy sculpted chef. She must have left it behind when she moved. The clocks here were digital and the silence between Lily and Gran was itchy for want of that old-fashioned *tock* and *tick*. Gran sighed. She fidgeted with the tuck of her blouse. "I said some terrible things," she said, and laughter escaped, brief and blunt as a bottle uncorking. "I can't believe I said those things to you." She shook her head. Her earrings jangled and there was laughter in that sound, too, silvery and gentle. "Your grandpa and I always fought fair. You say what's upset you. You say why. Then it's done." She made a fist and slapped it into her open palm. "Angels and orifices. Too many people don't know how to fight fair."

"I didn't hit him on purpose. Ben. Mr. Thales."

Gran nodded, the earring chime a cue that Lily could set down the eggs. She lined them end to end, careful, as if they were irreplaceable.

"Benjamin lost his daughter at your age. I just found out. He doesn't like to talk about it. She was troubled; then she up and left and he never saw her again." Another head shake, the earrings' melody out of place now. "I can't believe I said those things to you."

Brainflash: the per-vet had better reason than basement bodies for the encyclopedic mess he'd made of himself on TV. For his freakish take on twenty questions: do you ever hitchhike? Have you studied self-defense? Today's special chez Commons: a plate of pan-seared context. Benjamin Thales was sad.

Brainflash squared: Gran liked him *because* he was sad.

It was a thought too intimate to lend voice to. Instead: "Gran. I'm not going to run away because we're in a fight. I'm not that big an idiot." One egg nested in her grandmother's hand. Lily picked up another. She hoped so hard it felt like prayer: Let the eggs be the reason they didn't touch, not the ugly things that hung between them. Gran returned her egg to the carton. Lily handed her a second and then a third. She reached for a fourth. She cast her mind forward to the HOA meeting and then to the guest room down the hall and along the row of hanging blouses for the neckline best suited to penitence.

THE GOLDEN COUPLE

WHEN MIDNIGHT CAME, AND THEN one, and Ali still wasn't home, Seth pinched a dose of the Ambien she never used and went to bed angry. He wasn't supposed to do that; just ask half the people who'd offered that chestnut, unsolicited, at his wedding. Yet the world still spun on its axis. He woke hours later to a soft headache and blanched light. There was soap in the soap dish now. There was no hair in the drain. His skin looked mottled and the inside of his mouth felt foul and plush. He was glad he'd taken the Ambien. He could blame the back-bottle list of side effects that he hadn't bothered to read. He didn't have to be the kind of man who felt physically wrecked because he'd fought with his wife.

The shuttle took a circuitous route and he was late to work. Main Street was closed to all but foot traffic as workers set up for Founder's Day. Aside from a Post-it that said Nicky Tullbeck was out firming up sources, Seth's desk was empty. He had no pressing matters to attend to. He was not usually a breakfast person but felt inexplicably ravenous. He ate the salad he'd brought from home and someone's lemon yogurt from the staff fridge. He heated water for the Top Ramen he kept in his desk for emergencies. His tongue felt corroded from the salt, and he longed for the orange that had been on Alison's desk. He took an early lunch break and dawdled over his burger. Back at the office he won several games of FreeCell. Out his window, the festival stage went up. A parade of golf carts were turned away from Main Street and puttered off in search of parking. Carnival booths unfolded. Three o'clock and he was hungry again. Plenty of time to grab an iced coffee and apple hand pie before the HOA meeting. He walked to the café. He walked back to the Hacienda Central, brushing crumbs from his hands. He hated that building. He'd hated it a long while now. He hated its clock tower and its terra cotta roof, hated every turquoise and buff tile in its mosaic window borders and the way the foyer had the hushed, echoing quality of a capitol rotunda. He passed a couple reading the plaque Alison had put up, commemorating the 2008 restoration of the building's original Mission-style details. It was the size and shape of a small gravestone and implied rather than explicitly stated that the building had been around long enough warrant such attention. He wanted to remind the couple that Hoagland Lobel broke ground on the place in April 2005. That or tell them how much of their HOA dues were going toward Alison's eBay price war over the 1906 cornerstone from some failed Kansas savings and loan. Lobel's contractor claimed it would be a piece of piss to fit the block neatly into the overall façade, making it look as if the building had been around that long.

No wonder Alison had made their life look sunny-sweet online. It was bound to come easy to her. His wife, the professional liar. His innards puckered. The man at the plaque slung an affectionate arm around his companion and Seth wanted to tear it from its socket. He followed the couple into the meeting room. His guts resettled when the pair no longer touched.

The meeting room was crowded, row after row of folding chairs, a wheeled cart of sound equipment, and a speaker's podium that bore The Commons' logo. All the men had the same haircut and everyone held cardboard cups of coffee. A table along the back displayed a carafe each of decaf and regular and a picked-over catering tray, more doilies now than pastries. Residents chattered, one voice layering over another. If it weren't for the occasional word he caught—*polyps, grandbaby, par five*—it could have been the din of a North Chettenford assembly. All the gunk he'd stuffed his stomach with congealed. Up toward the front, that man, Something Stouser, who'd made all that fuss when the *Crier* misspelled his grandkid's name, waved him over. Seth made his face affable, stepped forward, and tried his damnedest to think of a pleasant thing to say that was unconnected to the baby.

Then the world went black. Cool hands covered his eyes. The word *hiya* crooned low and lulling in his ear. His wife's voice, only Alison was in a towering fury and had never said *hiya* before in her life. He shrugged off the hands and there she was, shorn and smiling sweetly.

Stouser shook some other spry fellow's hand and sat. He hadn't been waving at Seth at all.

Alison darted forward to peck Seth's cheek, which didn't make any sense.

Maybe it was the Ambien. People sleepwalked under its influence. They drove across whole towns and cleared out their refrigerators without knowing it. Maybe he'd gotten down on his knees last night for Alison. Maybe he'd quoted Neruda at length.

Ali took his hand and rolled lightly onto the balls of her feet. She wore the suit she'd interviewed in. A single, wheat-colored strand of long hair clung to her sleeve. It would be years before her hair grew to that length again. She swung his hand in hers back and forth. That chip of a diamond he'd saved for threw back the light. For the cost of that glint, they could've bought plane tickets anywhere. He said *hiya* back. It made about as much sense as anything. This was a lotto ticket of a moment, an unearned, colossal win. Because this wasn't how Ali did kiss and make up. Alison didn't do cutesy and she didn't do slippery nonapologies either. When she had something to say, Alison said it.

And how.

It's *so* hard, finding new ways to make an ass of yourself.

I'm supposed to be mothering a baby. Not someone who acts like one.

Seth wrested his hand away. Alison reclaimed it and her smile broadened, taut as a tightrope. There was something wrong with her eyes. They darted minnow-like to the door. And there stood Hoagland Lobel. "Hoagie loved my presentation," Alison said. "He gave me a lift home and back so that I could freshen up for it."

"Gotcha," Seth said, because he did. They were to pretend in front of the boss because God forbid Alison feel embarrassed. He kissed her forehead because he was in Lobel's line of sight. He kissed her forehead because as a general rule she didn't like that. It was patronizing, she said, and it made her feel short.

Lobel worked his way across the room. He knew everyone's name. He had a vigorous handshake, full pump, but took tiny, mincing steps. He reached the Colliers. "Seth!" It came out sounding more like a nickname than a proper one, something he'd call a favored nephew, like Bucko or Sport. "I liked your piece this morning. Figure it should just about clear this nonsense up." He said morning *marnin'*. He flashed a toothy beam.

"Thanks," Seth said. He looked at Alison, chic and compact. She still had no idea what he'd done. It had taken all of twenty minutes to bang out a thousand words on Lobel's glitch. He'd worked in a quote from the man himself, some fabricated puff about being sorry for Mona Rosko's inconvenience; Seth was in suck-up mode and had the sense Lobel got a kick out of seeing his name in print. Lobel clapped a hand on Seth's back and Seth tried not to visibly recoil. He squeezed Alison's hand, harder than he knew was comfortable. He kissed her forehead again.

"The golden couple," Lobel said. "Between the two of you, this mess will blow right over. The missus tell you why she's here?"

Ali hated that brand of reductive naming: the missus, the little lady, the ball-and-chain. She hated it, but no one would ever guess that from her face. Seth draped an arm around her shoulder. Her body radiated unexpected cool, though it was well over a hundred degrees outside.

The woman was immune to everything.

"Not a word. What's up, Ali cat?" They didn't really do pet names and Alison loathed that one in particular.

Lobel answered on her behalf. No way in hell would Ali-of-old have stood for that. "We're announcing the name change to Adahstown at the start of the meeting." That *we*. They sounded like a couple.

"Adahstown or Adahstowne-with-an-e?" Seth asked.

"Plain old Adahstown." Lobel said. "Last-minute decision."

Ali said, "We couldn't decide. Hoagie flipped a coin." Again with the Hoagie and the first person plural. See if he cared. She could pack her bags and Lobel's too and run off to Gibraltar.

Only Alison was crap at packing. He was always the one who organized their suitcases. Well, fine then. Let them get to Gibraltar and discover they had no clean socks.

His life would be simpler, anyhow. He slipped behind Alison and began to rub her shoulders. "You're tense," he said.

"Public speaking. You know me." He did. Her case of nerves was roughly as genuine as the Hacienda's Mission-style details. Lobel probably thought it was charming.

"Imagine them in their underwear," he said. She really did have a knot in her shoulders; that much at least was true. He worked it, hard and round as a coin beneath her skin. He pressed and she winced. Another response that was actually real.

"That hurts." She wriggled away. "Seth, enough."

"Sorry. Just trying to help."

Lobel sauntered to the front of the room; everyone stilled. "I know most of you folks are here to talk current events, but I got a big announcement first. Was saving it up for Founder's Day, but I never could keep a secret. Some of you may know Ali here, our town historian. Well, this special lady's come to talk about another special

lady. And you heard it here first. We're renaming our town for her."
He held a hand out for Seth's wife. Before she could step away from
him, Seth gave her shoulder another squeeze. Gentle this time, with
all the tenderness he could muster. She managed a smile that was
credibly sweet. He did his best to mirror it. Why not? It could turn
true if they kept pretending.

AN APPROPRIATE
PLACE

A BRIEF PIT STOP ON the Lily Birnam Tour de Mea Culpa: the ladies' room of the Hacienda Central. HOA meeting minus three minutes, and Nicky Fucking Tullbeck was waiting in the hall. Lily retreated into the washroom. Nicky Fucking *Tool*-beck. Gran stood at the mirror, fluffing her hair. "Nicky followed me," Lily said. It would sound less like tattling if he went by something grownup, like Nick. "He's right out there."

Gran checked her reflected teeth for lipstick. Given the day's trajectory, it was statistically probable she'd insist Lily apologize to the intern, too, but no: "Don't give him the time of day."

"He's not going to be asking the time of day. He's going to be asking—"

Gran held up a hand for silence. She poked her head into the hall. "Young man, this is not an appropriate place to loiter." Lily didn't catch le Tool-beck's reply. Gran turned back to her and winked. Lily would need to run a soup kitchen while maintaining a 4.0 to properly deserve her grandmother. Gran returned to the sinks. "Let's give it a moment," she said.

A *glug* and a flush and a stall door opened. Mona Rosko, which explained the incredible lurking Nicky. He must be setting up an ambush. Ms. Rosko gave her an assessing stare. "Hello," Lily said,

all Miss Friendly Teen USA, Who in No Way Sicced the Press on
Your Possibly Jailbird Daughter. "How are you this afternoon?"

Gran stepped between the two of them, even though she had
this master plan wherein Lily fessed up and apologized.

Ms. Rosko held her palms below the tap. The sensor wasn't
working right. She waved her hands beneath it like a deranged
mime.

"There was a reporter outside," Gran said, even though it was
Lily's screwup and Lily's apology and Nicky Tullbeck was only an
intern anyway. Lily would need a 4.0, a soup kitchen, and an Olym-
pic gold medal to properly deserve her grandmother.

"He's just an intern," she said, because it needed saying.

"I'm not surprised. There'll be opinions today." Ms. Rosko said
opinions in a way that made her own very low ones abundantly
clear. The water hissed on.

"I was talking to this one before. About your daughter." Lily's
voice was in full-on revolution. Everything came out as if punctuated with a question mark. "I was trying to help. I was trying to
get people on your side." Ms. Rosko pumped the soap dispenser.
Lily said, "I thought if everyone knew she's in Afghanistan—it's
the kind of thing that would get people rooting for you. I thought—"

"Don't help me." Ms. Rosko began to lather. It looked like spit.

"I only wanted to explain how—"

"We don't need help from you." She rinsed.

"The guy outside—he wants confirmation of your daughter's
name. Carrie, right? With the army?" There were simple explana-
tions at the ready. No, I said Karen, dear. I said the Marines.

The water shut off without warning. Ms. Rosko's hands were still
coated with foam. She waved at the tap. "Know what they charge
a month in HOA fees? And they can't even get a faucet working."

Lily stepped aside. "I didn't have any trouble with this one."

"You've never had any trouble."

"Where's Tyson?" Points to Gran for deflecting.

Mona Rosko jerked a soapy thumb toward the next stall. "He's five and a half. Old enough to pee solo. I haven't left him on his lonesome, if that's what you're implying." There was no actual sign of Tyson, but then there wouldn't be. He was a slight kid. His feet reached nowhere near the floor.

"Gran was only asking."

"And I was only telling."

With a simple pair of questions, Lily could wreck this woman. Are you sure it's a good idea to have him in the ladies' room? Won't it lead to (gasp) gender confusion? She wouldn't be *Die Schaden Fräulein*—coming soon to a theater near you!—in front of Gran though. She absolutely would not. "You should speak out at the meeting," she said instead. "I really think people will be pulling for you."

The water started up again. Ms. Rosko rinsed.

"I really do. There are thousands of people on Facebook who think you should be able to stay here. I started the group but it kind of took on a life of its own."

"You want to help me?" Ms. Rosko's mouth was a blunt and colorless line.

"Yes. I do. I told you." She wasn't sure, actually, not anymore, but she couldn't not say it.

"Good. Great. *B-U-R-N* down my house and sort out the insurance paperwork." Ms. Rosko helped herself to paper towels with a series of quick jerks. In theory, Lily could get away with a charitable touch of arson. Mom and Dad had given her two hundred dollars cash for emergencies and if she used it instead of cards, the purchase of camp stove propane couldn't be traced. She'd buy marshmallows and bug spray so no store clerk would be suspicious. She'd wear a ponytail in case of security cameras. No one would connect it to her. Everyone knew how she felt about ponies.

"*B* is for bear," came Ty's voice. "*U* is for unicorn, but only in books."

"That's right, Ty."

Gran peered into the hallway. "The young man's gone. Lily?"

Ms. Rosko said, "You had no right talking to him in the first place."

"I was only trying—never mind. You know what? He told me that your daughter's in—"

"My daughter is in the army."

"What's her rank?"

"Don't you dare." There was nothing soft about her whisper.

"You lied to me."

"Everybody lies. It's kinder that way."

"You made *me* into a liar."

"You're the one who took it upon yourself to speak to reporters. I'm just looking after my grandson."

"What, so you told him she's in the army instead of—"

"My mom's in the army." Ty came out of the stall, thrilled in the it's-a-small-world-after-all way people got when they found out you'd gone to camp with their third cousin.

"—told him she's in the army instead of—"

"Don't," said Mona. "Don't you dare."

"The meeting's started." That was Gran. "I think we all need to take a step back."

"—instead of—"

"Please. That's her son."

"—instead of *J-A-I-L*."

Mona looked at her like she'd said instead of spelled it. Wordlessly, she crumpled her paper towels into the trash. It was true then. Poor little Ty.

"Do you for real know thousands of people?" he asked. Lily's mind felt thick till she remembered: Facebook. The Thousand People Who Want Tyson to Stay. Ms. Rosko ducked back into the stall to flush for him. He began to diligently scrub his hands. The sink he chose gave no trouble at all.

"Yup," Lily said. "Thousands. Well, two thousand. Almost. One thousand eight hundred and seventy-six. Maybe more by now. I haven't checked today."

"Wow. You know lots of people."

"Online."

"They're like imaginary friends, Ty." Ms. Rosko handed him a paper towel. Gran opened the door onto an empty corridor. Lily followed her out. Gran was right. She owed Mona Rosko nothing. And the woman was fantastically vile. She'd flushed for her grandson and hadn't rewashed.

A REAL DYNAMO

ALISON HAD COME TO THE part where Adah Chalk was appalled at the state of frontier medicine. Seth leaned against the wall and watched Lobel inspect his manicured hand. When Ali took her place at the podium, that hand had brushed her back and Seth's chest felt banded in iron. The Ali he fell for would have removed it from her person, intimating that he'd lose it, and painfully, if he touched her again. Lobel caught Seth looking and winked.

Alison didn't even mind the man.

Alison called him Hoagie.

Seth's guts felt like a mess of hooked worms. He was married to this woman. From his spot along the wall, he could only catch her in profile. She held a stack of pink note cards. The Ali he'd married would've made fun of the one standing before him. She looked like an amateur politician. She came to the part where Adah Chalk introduced inoculations to the native tribes.

The door opened. Every head in the room swiveled toward Mona Rosko and the grandson. Of course Seth recognized them. How many children were there in The Commons? How many thin, broken arms? Nicky Tullbeck—where had *he* come from?—edged toward her as if magnetized. He beamed toothily and offered his arm. The room was a collection of grandparents and want-to-be grandparents, and Seth caught variations of the same coo. A softening at the youth of the one boy, pleasure at the raised-rightness of the other. Seth came up blank on the collective noun for grandparents. A satisfaction of grandparents would do nicely. A smug.

Alison came to the part where Adah Chalk chased a claim jumper off at gunpoint.

Another pair of latecomers, an older woman and a younger one, arrived. They stood along the back wall.

Alison came to the part where Adah Chalk set a ranch hand's broken leg.

Hoagland Lobel jammed his fists in his pants pockets. The material puckered. His hands were twitchy in there, exploratory. In Chettenford, Seth had called the cops on a man who'd lurked just that way on the edge of the girls' soccer field. He shuddered, aware of his body, naked beneath its clothes.

Lobel was watching Alison.

Every hair on Seth's body unfurled.

Alison and *Hoagie* were destined for an affair.

Alison came to the part where Adah Chalk was the honorary recipient of the county's first telephone call.

A thin whistle sounded. A McCain up-front adjusted his hearing aid. Someone nearby was chewing spearmint gum. Seth's mouth flooded. Ali and Lobel. Ali and Lobel. He wished they would. He wished it.

You could leave without compunction a wife who slept with your boss.

Alison came to the part where Adah Chalk organized a volunteer fire brigade.

The possibility of leaving forked through Seth's brain like lightning. He couldn't look at Alison. The meeting room walls were painted yellow, maybe half a shade lighter than their old Chettenford kitchen. She'd look so at home against that color. So *like* home. He hardly ever saw yellow in Arizona. Most decorators seemed contractually obligated to go through the sandier colors by the gallon.

Alison came to the part where Adah Chalk lamented the lack of a local school.

Seth looked at her. Serene as milk. Beneath her clothes she was slimmer and stronger than she'd been when they met. None of that softness at the hip she used to pinch at, frowning in the mirror. If he were single he'd never have the guts to go for her number.

Alison came to the part where Adah Chalk raised the money to bring a schoolteacher West by auctioning her prize steer.

No one would listen to any of this if Ali weren't a real dynamo. And she was. But fuck, did he miss the heft of her hips. At the festival tomorrow, Lobel would make Adahstown official. He'd suggest a drink to celebrate, Lobel, Seth, and Ali on barstools all tic-tac-toe. Ali's drink was a 7 and 7. When she ordered it on their first date, Seth had asked why not call it a fourteen. So stupid. There almost wasn't a second date because of that. Lobel wouldn't be so inane. He'd pay the tab, his credit card a color beyond platinum.

Alison was quoting, at length, from one of the Susan B. Anthony letters.

If a town wasn't enough to land her, Lobel would suggest an Adah Chalk museum. They'd have to consult, late nights.

All around him, residents squirmed in uncomfortable seats. Some whispered. The speech had gone on long enough. They'd come for gossip, not history. Seth bit down hard on the inside of his cheek. Quiet, he wanted to say, that's my wife. He wanted to say it because maybe it would be one of the last times he'd ever say it. He was going to walk in on them at the office. Lobel could afford a hotel room, hell, could afford a hotel, but on top of the mahogany desk added to the fun. The expression of her face on the brink would be the same one it always was for him. Later, in some dim bar some three states away, Seth would tell whoever would listen that *that* was what had killed him.

People would understand. Poor Seth, they'd say, patient Seth, you've been through so much.

I gave her everything, he'd say. I gave it my all.

And the guy. I covered his ass with the press.

He'd be balls deep in pity fucks. He'd go for girls with generous breasts, thighs that bulged at the top. Throaty laughs and the overall sense of peaches in heavy syrup. He shifted, aware of the movement of his blood. That supple, building fullness. The thought of freedom. Of Alison getting it good from his boss.

In the front row, a man whispered, "I thought I was done with history class once I was out of high school."

His buddy said, "No teacher back at PS Thirty-Eight looked like that." He wore a fraying Dodgers cap.

Seth pushed himself off the wall. "Take off your hat," he said. "That's my wife."

SOME MANNERLY
INSTINCT

IT WAS NOT AN UNREASONABLE request. When Ben was a boy, you removed your hat indoors, end of story. Beside him, the man in the Dodgers cap shrugged, surly. People got that way when called on their bad behavior; just look at him this morning with Sadie. By way of apology, Ben had come to the Hacienda early with a chivalrous eye toward saving a seat. He'd reserved one for the girl for good measure, but the Birnams were uncharacteristically late. He'd thought about calling Sadie for an ETA, but he'd gone and left his phone someplace and then Dodgers plunked down without asking, making the whole idea moot. The historian continued, intrepid. "With the second wave of the Spanish Influenza threatening her beloved school, Adah—"

"I said, take off your hat." The young man's voice was louder now, carrying. Most folks hadn't caught it the first time, but now they were starting to look.

"This hat?" Dodgers passed a hand across the battered brim.

"Gentlemen, please." That was Hoagland Lobel. Ben didn't like him—slick as Jell-O—but you had to admire the gravitas.

The room stilled. The historian began again. "Adah decided to quarantine—"

"Yeah. That hat." The young man rocked forward, knees bent for maximum spring. Ben had never thrown a punch, but he sure as hell knew the posture for it. Dodgers was on his feet, too. For Christ's sake. He should remove the hat, proffer an apology, and be the adult his mother raised him to be.

"Gentlemen," Lobel cautioned again.

"A misnomer." The historian gave a tart little nod and just like that, Ben liked her. Shades of Veronica, of Sadie in a funk.

The young man took a looming step closer. The historian's tenor changed. "Seth, please." Her voice was small without the microphone's help. Only the first few rows heard.

Dodgers did. "Seth," he crooned. Ben cringed, embarrassed for him. And then Seth rushed forward. A swift flare of envy. The man's youth, the tumult that propelled him, the fierce clarity of his gait. It didn't occur to Ben to think *fight*; that didn't happen in well-ordered conference rooms, with podiums and deli trays. And technically, Seth never laid a hand on the other man. He touched only the brim of the hat. An indolent wrist flick knocked it to the ground.

Some mannerly instinct prodded Ben to stoop and retrieve it; Sadie might be watching.

Dodgers made a low throat sound Ben recognized from Chicago.

Veronica's trauma pamphlets would have a list of things to do now: visualize water, take mindful breaths, count to ten in every language that you know. Instead Ben watched another neighbor, paunchy, called Dan, maybe, or Don, step between the men, hands out to keep them apart. An aftershock of that initial envy: not too long ago *he'd* have been handy in a crisis like this. Around the room, neighbors rose in a crescendo of babble. Lobel brushed the little historian aside and took up the mic. His amplified permutations of *enough* and *ladies and gents* and *your seats, please* ricocheted. The historian pulled her young man off by the elbow, hopping mad if you could credit her hyperbolic gestures. Paunchy Don wrangled Dodgers from the room and, Ben hoped for the young man's sake, out of the building. Ben still had the man's hat, and he pulsed with nonsensical pride. Nothing to do with having weathered the altercation, though Ronnie would never believe he'd held so steady. It was the hat. He'd nabbed the offending hat, and with it the vague, schoolboy thrill of having pulled one over on everyone.

ROBERT'S RULES
OF ORDER

LOBEL GOT THE ROOM BACK under control. Lobel summoned Alison from Seth's side. "Please, continue." When he called for her, Ali went, instantly cool. She couldn't even be bothered to finish their fight. Lobel hovered at the podium beside her, a bodyguard or a cartoon conscience. Ali reordered her note cards.

"In the aftermath of the epidemic, Adah Chalk—"

"Forget Adah Chalk." That was Mona Rosko. She stood, weathered and immovable. One of those spirits carved on the ancient prows of ships. "No one came here for a history lesson that's bound to be BS anyhow. Let's get on with it. I've got a child to care for. If this nonsense goes on much longer, I'll be late getting his dinner." She smiled, but there was no light to it. The grandson's suit was much too big.

Alison tried again. "With the new fashions and attitudes of the nineteen twenties, Adah—"

"You can't go putting out signs, Mona." A woman, thin, tanned, and brassily hennaed, stamped her foot for emphasis. "The code clearly states that any signs or window decals that can be seen from public spaces are expressly forbidden." The whole thing had to be rehearsed. No one could come up with this stuff on the fly.

"Hear, hear," said someone on the other side of the room.

"This place'll look like a junkyard."

"Relax. It was only the one."

"We should *all* put out signs. Show some support for Mona."

"Yes!" Seth recognized the speaker: the broken man. The fly man. The man who knew the names of lost girls. "Well, we do support her. You, Mona. We do support you." His face was flushed and shining, his voice a tick too rapid. He actually bowed at the Rosko woman. Seth knew making amends when he saw it. Seth had amends to make before him. Ali stood at the microphone, slight and silent, a child stumped at a spelling bee.

"Support? Really?" The henna woman again. "For the sign she shouldn't have, or the child she shouldn't have?"

"Real charitable, Jeanne," somebody said.

Jeanne gave another imperious stamp. "The Commons is not a charity; it's a community."

A smattering of applause followed, a chorus of boos, and too many voices at once. Almost everyone was standing now.

"It *isn't* a community." The general din died down for Mona; it wouldn't have for anyone else. "It just tries to look like one." Her grandson stared out the window. Seth wasn't quite a parent, but it was obvious even to him: The more a child pretends not to listen, the better attention he's paying.

"A community," Jeanne repeated, climbing up onto her folding chair. "Built on agreed-upon regulations that serve to—"

"Built on lies. Community?" Mona made a choked noise that might have been a nascent, bitter laugh. She shouldn't have brought the boy to the meeting. She should've guessed how ugly people would be. Seth tried to catch Alison's eye. She'd agree with him on that much. She'd agree with him and all would be well. Ali looked like she'd swallowed chlorine. Mona's voice was low and mordant. "We're trying to leave this place—sorry, this community—believe me. But until we do, my Ty's no skin off your teeth. It took an outsider to even notice him. That's hardly community." The speech wasn't doing her any favors, but holy hell did Seth understand. It was easier on the soul to rail than to beg.

"We all agreed to certain precepts—"

"We can adapt," the fly man—Ben, his name was—said. His flush was gone but the sweat clung. "We can be human about it."

Someone toward the back said, "He's right."

And someone else, "Mona's playing for the cameras, you know."

Lobel's amplified voice called for civility.

Someone suggested *Robert's Rules of Order*, which nobody seconded.

"It's not right," another someone said, "kicking out a child."

"She knew the regulations before she bought." It was that Jeanne. Up on her chair with her petulant foot. A plain old folding chair, rickety as could be. The woman had a hell of a sense of balance.

"Communities don't have regulations." Mona again. "They got folks. Four generations my family's been here. That's *real* history. Why don't I head on up to that podium and set the rest of you straight?"

At that his wife bolted. Ali all over. Her boy was ashes; her husband, brawling. And what stirred her was the hint that someone, somewhere, could be better at something than she. Seth followed, angry, instinctive, pressing through the crowd. It felt good to jut his elbows out, to gloss over the excuse mes, to burn through the adrenaline of his almost-fight.

He caught some mention of extenuating circumstances.

From her perch on the chair, Jeanne derisively echoed the phrase. Another stomp. *Toddlers* were better behaved. Timothy would have been. Ali was picking up speed. He felt pink and overheated and strained to untangle the conversations around him. A McCain had made a bullhorn of his hands, insisting that if they relaxed the rules for children they should ease up on the ones for dogs. Someone could've sworn Mona's grandkid was a girl. Someone said, "Mona's doing her best."

And Jeanne, "That doesn't mean anything."

Seth's brainstem clogged with the fact that Ali had made it to the door. It was just a door. She passed through it. There was no reason for that to feel as significant as it did.

Someone said, "Did you see Ben Thales the other day? Charlie sent a link."

Someone said something that made Jeanne stamp her foot again.

Someone said, "I think I heard the daughter's serving, and that's worth keeping in mind."

A girl straightened at that. She caught the eye. Young, which was part of it, and pretty, if a bit overdone. A dime a dozen back in the halls of North Chettenford, though that didn't stop Nicky Tullbeck— who had no reason to be here; he and Seth were due for a chat—from blatantly puppy dogging. The girl knew she'd drawn her fair share of attention; girls like that always did. She smiled and said, in that petulant way specific to girls just coming into their own power, "Yeah, she's serving. Time." And then, with the flip-flopping of adolescence, the woman was a child again, overstating and overdramatic, unsure of ever being clearly understood. As Seth reached the door, he heard her press on: "Serving time. Like, in jail."

UNFORGIVING
NOISES

Ms. Rosko laughed. A full-body, pudge-wobbling, teeth-bared laugh full of crazy. She scooped up the little boy, who barnacled on. His pale brows made him look perpetually worried so there was no way to tell if he'd understood. Nicky Tullbeck followed stalker-close. His Rocky-esque face married hunger and smirk.

Ms. Rosko started toward her. Tyson squirmed. "You're mashing my sling."

The Rosko laugh continued, unpunctuated, but she shifted her hold on Ty so maybe a smidge of sane remained. Gran wasn't anywhere. No, Gran was pushing her way to the per-vet, whose face was the color of uncooked shrimp. Cue the Very Disappointed in Yous, because if *he'd* heard her all the way across the room there was zero percent probability that Gran hadn't. Ms. Rosko bore down, laughing. Lily tasted envelope glue.

Nicky Tullbeck grinned. She wished him snaggletooth. She wished him dentures.

Tyson Rosko cocked a finger gun at her and Lily remembered being small enough for that to feel like a threat. It felt like a threat now, with the laugh, the grandmother, the room full of people and their unforgiving noises. "Gran!" she called, but Gran was off with the per-vet, who was cultivating a very soap-operatic, middle-distance glare. Like what she'd done was unforgivable. Like *he* was one to talk. All the piping up for Mona mid-meeting didn't cancel out a single cunt.

The laugh devolved into breaths, big ones, like a kid with a cake full of candles. The glaring per-vet was right, the hypocrite. What she'd done was unforgivable. She hadn't known how thoroughly her allegiance had shifted until she went and opened her mouth. Nicky Tullbeck had his stylus out. Fair enough. Lily was a see you next Tuesday and deserved to have this documented. The nutbar on the chair broke out a rape whistle. Tyson covered his ears. Ms. Rosko was much too close. "You." She pointed.

"It's not a lie."

"I told you. Everybody lies." There was a hushed, singing quality to her voice. Too small for her bulk, too far away for her closeness. "Everyone lies. Even in this *community*. Community. That's a good one. There used to be *folks* here. Not queers and golf shirts and Adahstown." A laugh. The ghost of the *uber*laugh in it. Ty recocked the finger gun. Mona Rosko pointed again. "Adahstown. The old ranch wife used to come by our Feed 'n' Seed. *Guadalupe* Chalk. That first wife didn't last two summers. Miss Historian's as full of it as you are. And so pretty. Go after her. You'd suit."

Lily was electric-alert and tense on a cellular level. The boy shut his eyes and yelled *bang!* A horrible moaning started and she brought a guilty hand to her throat as if to feel it thrum. Nothing. The noises were Ben noises. She saw him gray and teetering. She saw him fetal on the floor.

PRIMATES AFTER ALL

BEN WAS CRAVEN AND CURLED in on himself. An arm over his face for protection, another across his abdomen. He heard his own raw wordlessness, and over that, his heart. That line they fed you about panic being blind was a great gob of nothing; Ben saw a thousand shattered details. The scuffs on the linoleum. Sandaled feet, well corded with veins. And he saw other feet in overlay, the Chicago ones, their eager boots ready to grind away at the soft space below his ribs. The rope-veined feet belonged to Sadie Birnam. A blotch of scale below her ankle. Ben, she was saying, Ben, Ben. His innards had turned liquid; pulverized, as if they could leach out his pores. Sadie got him to his feet; somehow he still had feet of his own. She steered him by the shoulders. People stood aside as if for a pall-bearer. The granddaughter trailed behind. He was still all liquid when she poured him into her cart. Her voice seemed more cadence than comprehensible words. He registered *hospital* though and he shook his head.

"Benjamin. You were on the ground." The cart jittered along. In a kinder world, she would blame that for the uncontrollable movement of his hands. "You're scaring me. I don't know what to do here."

"I want to go home." He sounded like a child. His body began to re-congeal, bone and fiber, shame. This should not have happened to him. He absolutely should not have allowed it.

"You were screaming." Sadie sounded exhausted. "You were—" she broke off and twitched in imitation. It looked as bad as he'd imagined.

"Please." A return to civility meant a return to self. Sadie had to see. "I'm zonked. Please take me home."

"You sure?"

He nodded. She turned toward Daylily Crescent. Veronica would have been adamant about the hospital. She babied him after Chicago. She told everyone he had been beaten savagely. It was the modifier that made their acquaintanceship give him a wide berth. How clearly it evoked the desperate, deliberate thoroughness. The humiliation. The streetlights came on. Times like this, the things your mind came up with. He remembered that alphabetized list of Veronica's, counselors who specialized in post-traumatic adjustment. At her insistence, he made an appointment. The first entry: Abelard, Dr. Yvonne B. He'd sat in her waiting room and wondered how broken you had to be to pursue her kind of career. He left before his name was called. He lied to Veronica. Said he'd found another doc. The only psychological professional he actually saw was the marriage counselor Veronica insisted upon once the fact that their insurance was never billed for his biweekly sessions brought the whole mess down around his ears.

But the thing was, he was fine. No matter what his wife believed. He coped. He could drive under overpasses no problem. He didn't flinch when ragged men approached him for change. He could stare at a window display of boots, brutal and ready, and count the grommets till his heart rate slowed. It was *time* that healed, not incessant rehashing. He and Ronnie went their forty rounds on that and then he moved south.

He coped here, too.

Lily was speaking. "—wasn't my fault. I was all the way across the room." The hurt she'd done him felt long ago and laughable. Bumper cars.

"Lily, hush."

"She's okay."

Sadie shook her head. Her profile was unlovely and he was glad. Her neck was ever so slightly fleshy, her straight nose masculine at this angle, and there was an unappealing slant to her forehead. He couldn't have stood it if she'd looked delicate. She said, "I'm guessing it was all that shoving up front. The pair of them should be put in a zoo."

"It wasn't their fault." It should have been. If anything in that room were going to cross his wires. Instead, he admitted, "It was the gal on the chair." His eyes felt alive with salt and shame. To Sadie's credit, she didn't say, what, that dumpling of a woman?

"She belongs in a zoo, too. Zoos for everyone."

He tried to explain. "I can't have feet above me." He hadn't known it till now. It wasn't the kind of fact you picked up simply going about your business. Sadie accepted it as if he'd said something as common as I-don't-particularly-care-for-refried-beans. In the back of the cart Lily had gone very quiet. Ben fumbled for the right words. "They kicked me. Even after I was on the ground." Veronica was right. The beating had been savage. There was still a modicum of humanity to a punch; we're primates, after all. We work with our hands.

"Oh, Ben. I'm so sorry that happened to you."

"I'm sorry you saw me that way. Everyone, actually. But especially you."

"That's the last thing you should worry about." She squeezed his knee and he didn't flinch at the contact. He felt tentatively normal, heading home beside her. A kid in the backseat, that was normal, too. The clouds were doing something new. They hung striated and staticky, as if projected on the screen of a television in need of a sound whack.

Sadie pulled into his driveway.

A woman rose from the stoop.

The mind is a trickster.

The mind fills in the heart's blanks.

And it *was* a face he knew. A beloved face, bare in unfiltered light. For one wild moment that bastard hope flared and Ben thought it was his daughter and not his ex stepping forward to greet them.

A DISTANT CLOUD
OF DUST

IN THE HOSTILE QUIET OF her office, Alison said she was going for a run. There was a gym bag beneath her desk, a battered thing with her unmarried monogram. She opened it with an angry zip. "When I get back, I'm getting out the Yellow Pages. Whether I call for a divorce attorney or a psych referral very much depends on the next few things you say to me, so I'd recommend you grow up and *think* before you speak."

No one used the Yellow Pages any more. He didn't point this out. He wasn't going to say a thing. He didn't know what words would sway her decision and he didn't know in what direction he wanted her decision to sway.

Ali didn't speak either. She shrugged out of her jacket. She yanked down her skirt. Seth lunged to close her office door. The hem of her blouse just reached the top of her thighs. Anyone could be standing in the hallway. Anyone could see. Wordlessly, she peeled down her stockings.

Alison.

She had come to him once in silence, in his dorm room one winter afternoon. He'd been at his desk, formatting footnotes. Ali had held a finger to her lips. Mutely, she had shucked her jeans and raised her grubby sweatshirt over her head. She'd clapped a hand over his mouth and he'd bit her palm. They'd gone at it furiously. The dying light had lanced the air around them.

And now.

He counted her buttons as she undid them. The shirt pooled on the floor. Her bra joined it. The ugliness between them had him nearly immune to her nakedness. She put on running shorts, a sports bra, an ancient T-shirt with the name of their alma mater. Some letters had flaked away entirely. If he hadn't shared her history, he wouldn't have been able to read it. Ali put on socks, little booties with a lavender pompom. His grandmother had worn the same kind. Her feet were always cold in hospice. Alison laced her shoes and shot out the door. Her feet pounded down the hall. She was at the stairwell. Her pace picked up with his first footfalls in pursuit. They were on the second floor, and then the first, and then out in the corridor, where the sounds of the meeting they'd bailed on carried. Down the sprawling front steps, where an older woman and a young one steered a shaky-looking man toward the parking lot.

Alison was a block ahead on Main Street.

Two blocks.

Some kind of bird call split the air. Seth began to wheeze as if that had been his cue.

Alison was three blocks ahead of him now. Three and a half. Four.

He couldn't remember if shallow breaths or deep ones were the way to avoid a side stitch. Alison passed a series of flimsy carnival booths and then the bus stop. Seth's belt cut into his stomach. He fumbled with the buckle and cast it aside. He reached the bus stop; in the distance, Ali veered left, off toward the Sun Wren Pool and Spa. He had to sprint to simply keep her in his sights. His shirt was soaked from pits to ribs. He undid the buttons and let it hang. Air eddied over the slick on his skin. Alison passed the gym and loped out onto the golf course's open green. Seth panted, his breath outpacing his feet. Ali arced around the kidney-shaped water hazard, launched over the decorative wall, crossed a thin ribbon of tended grass, and tore off into the scrubland.

Seth's feet ached in shoes he was never meant to run in. His lungs were aging, desperate bellows. He slowed to a sad half trot and crossed into the thirsty wild, where even the shadows were barbed. Dust dulled his shoes. Perhaps the same particles that Ali'd churned up as she passed. He sat, hacking. There was a hole in his pants below the knee. His phone jangled. Lobel. Like an idiot, he remembered that he could've simply not answered the instant he picked up.

"You dying, Collier?"

"Nuh-uh." Seth struggled for an even breath. He rubbed his eyes. It made no sense the way that sweat burned them. Tears were just as salty, yet they came gliding on out without pain.

"Well then, what the hell excuse you got, son?"

Seth had sweat in his *ears*. He began to shiver, hard, his bones in contention with their joints. "That man was talking about Ali. Saying things."

"That *man* was Ray Preble and I don't care if he was talking about your sainted mother. That's no way to conduct yourself." Lobel said Ray Preble like it was a name Seth ought to know. Lobel said every name like that, which made him, in his way, the most democratic man Seth had ever met.

"I apologize," he said.

"Tofu. Save it for Preble. You track him down tomorrow, you hear? See if he'll shake your hand. That's what you do."

Seth said yes and stopped himself before *sir*. He tracked his wife, a distant cloud of dust.

"I'd say print a little something in the *Crier*, sincere like, but the less attention this all gets, the better. So not a peep. Christ almighty. I'm drinking downstream from the herd here."

"I'll talk to Ray Preble," said Seth. "I'll shake his hand."

"Make sure you do."

"I am sorry."

"Enough. I reckon we can still blow this Mona thing over without my breaking out the old checkbook. But, son, you shouldn't have done that to your wife. Her stage fright and all."

"She doesn't really get stage fright."

"Well, she sure as shooting won't get it tomorrow." Lobel had missed the possessiveness of Seth's assertion. "She can hop right up on stage knowing it can't go over any worse. So hey, you distracted her. Got to give you that much."

"I really am sorry."

"Tell it to the missus. The missus and Ray Preble. Now get yourself home. Grab a beer, get your beauty rest, do whatever it is you do to yourself. I'm going to want you out and about tomorrow, getting juicy quotes."

Tomorrow. Founder's Day. Lobel's Commons-wide celebration of himself. Seth felt too frayed to even be annoyed. "Sure. Yes. And Happy birthday."

"*Mañana*, Collier. Not till tomorrow."

"Happy birthday tomorrow, then."

"That'll do. And mind you sit tight for the wife's big Adah speech. I don't care if Ray Preble shows up in Miss Piggy panties. You sit tight. I like you. I like both of you kids and I hope you know I'm cutting you a country mile of slack."

"I do. And I thank you for that. I mean it."

"'Cause I hired you to write the news, not be it."

When Seth said yes this time, the *sir* slipped out. Lobel. This place. This job. Of all the things for him to get a second chance at.

"And listen," Lobel said. "Bit of advice?"

"Sure."

"Wife like Alison, you got to get used to remarks. My Josie was like that too, God bless. Back in the day."

Seth hobbled his painful way toward the bus stop. The belt he'd discarded coiled, snakelike, beside the bench. There were real rattlers out with Alison in the brush. Even now, one might be hissing out, a quick unspringing, a pinprick at her ankle. He looked out toward the horizon for the rise of dust to mark her fall. A daydream of fleet-footing it to her side. The Wild West heroics of drawing out the venom. The contact of his lips on her skin. The bus arrived. He limped on, rebuttoning his shirt against the air conditioning. He was still shivering when he got home. He took stiff-kneed steps up the drive. He made for the shower, then slumped on the cool bathroom tile. The grief books were still under the sink. Seth read their indexes, alphabetical, page by page. He fingered the sticker on one front cover: a New England barn, red, its roof a tented hardback, the words "The Book Croft" spelled out on its spine. Seth had loved The Book Croft. The august Chettenford bookstore occupied a hundred-year-old barn. A café had been done up in the hayloft, dappled with sun from an anachronistic skylight, and a pair of aging cats—Aslan and Tybalt—patrolled the stacks. The week before he and Ali lost Timothy, the owners had acquired a third, a tiny, mewling stray. There'd been a running contest to name it. Seth peeled off the sticker. He rolled it between thumb and forefinger until it lost its tack.

The only bookshops within thirty miles of The Commons were a pair of rival Barnes & Nobles.

He thought about ringing Ross Henry. They'd had a standing Wednesday chess date at the Croft. He didn't want to apologize or coo over the twins and he sure as hell didn't want to catch up. He simply wanted to know what name had been selected.

A PAIRED-UP BRIDE
AND GROOM

BEN STAGGERED FROM THE CART. Veronica took a few quick steps toward him and stopped. She pivoted back to the house, phone raised to her ear. "Steve-o, Duckling. *C'est moi.*" Their son had been a solemn, sturdy, almost professorial child. He'd grown into a solemn, sturdy, almost professorial man. The last guy you'd call either Steve-o or Duckling. Veronica said, "Your pops is fine. No, no, no. Don't trouble yourself. He's been out on the town. Tooting about with his new friends."

"Tooting about, Veronica? Why the hell are you here?"

She turned to him. She'd bought new eyeglasses. She wore the gray, belted, un-wrinkleable dress she always wore for air travel. The sweater that went with it lay pooled on his front steps. At first glance he had taken it for a shadow. "I'm at his house, Snickerdoodle. He looks a-okay, Scout's honor. No gaping head wounds. No convulsions. I didn't even have to follow the vultures to track him down."

"That Stephen? Let me talk to him."

Veronica held up a single finger, signaling him to wait. "I'm sure he never intended you to fret. There's so much to do around here. His own puny Eden."

"C'mon, Ronnie. The phone." Ben held out a hand.

"Oh, so we care about phones now? That's terrific!" She beamed and tossed hers. Ben lunged and missed. A laugh floated in from the periphery. A sibilant *hush* followed. Lily and Sadie and thank God for that. He and Veronica could usually tone it down when they had an audience. He fumbled with Ronnie's phone and clicked send. The number that filled the screen was his own.

"You weren't even talking to Stephen."

"And that, of course, is the salient point."

He'd told someone, once, that he liked the way Veronica's vocabulary seemed to improve with anger. Ben couldn't remember who. Maybe Veronica herself, back when his compliments were still accepted as interpersonal tender. Ben scrolled through her recent calls. His cell and his home dominated the log, punctuated with the appearance of Stephen's cell, six times, Anjali's, twice, and an unfamiliar number with an Arizona area code dialed earlier this morning five times in quick succession. Back in the golf cart, Sadie kept her hands placid on the wheel. Lily had the dull, lolling look that girls her age got sometimes, caught up with some televised stupidity. Sadie raised a hand in too-casual farewell and the cart sprang forward.

"Wait!" he called. Ever the coward. "I'd like you to meet Veronica."

Sadie had been a debutante and Lily had a grandmother to teach her by example how to behave. So the Birnams parked. They approached. Sadie extended a mannerly hand. "Sadie Birnam."

"Veronica Corbin." Ronnie's smile was lean and on the prowl.

Ben was not an unintelligent man. Four years of college, four years of vet school, the internship, the two book clubs, the daily crossword; his brain should be more than a mute machine, churning out comparisons. Yet: Veronica was taller. Sadie was slimmer. Veronica's lips were fuller. Sadie's white teeth more even. Beside her grandmother, Lily jittered up and down as if her joints had been surgically replaced with rubber balls. When Sadie introduced her, Lily offered her hand in a passable imitation of her grandmother. He said, "Sadie and I are headed to the Founder's Day Festival tomorrow. Lily, too." They hadn't actually discussed this and he didn't even like carnivals. But Veronica had to be made to understand. This was a full life she was invading.

His ex sniffed. "A festival. Well, imagine that."

Sadie looked adrift, but went along with it, graciousness personified. "You're welcome to join us, Veronica. The more the merrier." Lily gave a confused half-squint, but for once in her life didn't question or contradict.

"Fantastic!" Veronica sounded like a very bad actress attempting to sound very drunk.

He said, "I suspect Veronica will be much too busy for us. I suspect she's in town for a last-minute conference."

Everyone tensed at that. Even Lily, who had no context. All around them, the evening was a study in soft light and safe noises. Gnats sparked up from the grass and from the golf course you could catch the first steady ruckus of crickets.

Veronica said, "Actually, she's in town because her husband's too busy gallivanting to answer his phone."

"Gallivanting? Veronica, please."

"You're married?" That was Lily. She made married sound lethal.

"Lily. Please." Sadie's voice was cool and adamant.

"No," Ben said. "We're not married. Decidedly not."

Veronica said, "Look at your phone. Look at all those calls."

"We've gone weeks without talking before. Like I said, we aren't married."

"And thank heavens for that."

"Weeks, Veronica. Maybe even a month."

"Maybe. But you always call back. Always."

"This'll be good. I don't pick up the minute you want me to so you fly down like a lunatic—"

YOU COULD BE HOME BY NOW

"Always." She sounded like Veronica now and not some frenzied theatrical interpretation of herself. Because of this, he felt more invaded than he had before.

"Like a lunatic. So I missed a few calls. You could've tried the landline."

"Check."

"E-mailed."

"And check."

"You could've—"

Sadie broke in. "We really should be going, Ben."

Veronica gave a perky, finger-wriggling wave. "We'll see you at the carnival then. Ta!"

He said, "You know, you really can be a gold-plated—"

"All I wanted was to tell you how things went with Rand."

"Fine. And?"

Her shoulders gave a little. "Same as always."

"Thanks. Now I know. Can I call you a cab?"

Sadie pulled into her garage across the street. In the few seconds before the door rolled down, he saw her tuck Lily's arm into the crook of her own. The women marched into the house like a paired-up bride and groom. Ronnie whistled a few malevolent bars of the Beatles' "Sexy Sadie."

"Oh, shut up."

She gave another vicious whistle, this time approximating the lethal fall of a bomb. Veronica had gotten the frequent flier miles in their divorce settlement. He hoped this insane jaunt had burned through the lot of them. "Why did you come?" he asked.

"Look at the calls, Benji."

He scrolled through again. "Fodder for a restraining order."

"Can it, you." She rolled her eyes, but there was affection in the look. You'd have to know her well to spot it. "I was worried. You weren't answering your cell. Your landline rang and rang. I called Stephen to see if he'd heard from you and he was worried, too. He sent me this . . . link." Her face curdled. Ben remembered. That series of anonymous phone calls. The way he'd stormed about and unplugged the landline.

"About that interview. It was a—"

"You didn't look like you. You were—you know what? You were hysterical." She steepled her fingers. "You were paranoid. You weren't making any sense."

Naturally Veronica had collected pamphlets. Your Loved One in the Wake of Trauma. Families and PTSD. They were facile, busybody, trifold things. Veronica went over them with highlighters. Two colors of highlighters, if he recalled correctly. Her own special coded system. He hadn't read a single one, but you could bet at some point his ex had highlighted paranoia as a warning sign. That and whole paragraphs about angry outbursts. Fixation on past slights. A quick upstep to anger. Get out of your own head, squint a little, and you could see where she was coming from. He didn't have to be happy about it though. He said, "I'm fine. I was actually pissed off."

"Believe me, I noticed. But—"

"No. Actually pissed off. Actually, as in not diagnostically." A light came on in the Birnam kitchen. Another followed. Sadie's living room. His neighbor and her granddaughter, doing something small and contented to unwind. A movie and a massive bowl of microwave popcorn. An affectionate dispute over how vigorously to salt it.

"Benji. The whole interview sure as hell looked like you were—"

"But I wasn't. It wasn't some kind of—I was just mad." He was grateful that the Birnams had gone into the house. It would be so like Lily to broadcast his fall-apart scene at the meeting. She'd do it in half a heartbeat for the pleasure of seeing Veronica wring him out. It'd be like Sadie to spill, too, although she would have kinder motives.

Veronica rubbed her eyes, like their children had done when they were past due for a nap. The movement set her new glasses briefly off-kilter. "That's what Stephen said. You were just mad. And I thought, fine. Only—"

"Only what? We don't trust Stephen now? You're the one who needs your head examined."

"Anjali said you missed your crossword this morning."

"Huh?"

"That crossword you do every day. She said you skipped this morning."

"Well God forbid I take a break now and then. Maybe stay offline when the whole damn world is against me." The words sounded paranoid and he regretted them. But better that than to say he'd quarreled with Sadie this morning and had been distracted. Veronica knew. Fighting could be as intimate as hygiene.

"And Anjali said she won yesterday. By a wide margin."

"So? She had a lucky day."

"She'd never come close before. So you see why I might worry about your cognitive—"

"I let her win."

"Nonsense. You're the most competitive—"

He lied, mind wild with the watery ghost of that dream. "She's got that trial coming up. I figured she could use the ego boost."

"She was third in her class at BU. Jesus Christ. I hardly think she needs—"

"You know what I don't need? The lot of you spying on me. Talking about me—"

"Listen to yourself. You know what you sound like?"

"Well, it's true, isn't it? The crossword's your clever excuse to check up on me. Make sure the old noggin's—"

"It's a sweet thing the two of you share. If it happens to—"

"Be some kind of failsafe?"

"You make it sound like we're all plotting—"

"Enough. I'm grand." He couldn't remember who'd first found the crossword site, whether the daily challenge had been his idea or Anjali's. "You can tell my daughter-in-law to stop her snooping."

"She likes you. And she didn't want Stephen to worry. She knew you'd get—well, that you'd get like this if he started checking in all the time. Anjali wanted to help. Married people do that for each other, remember?"

"Don't start." It was early yet for the moon to rise, which was a shame. For no reason at all, it felt vital that he know its phase.

"You can see why we worried, that's all. Stephen kept calling. I kept calling. Anjali did, too."

"So the three of you wait. I'd have called back as soon as I—" He searched his pockets. He must have left his fool phone inside. "Look. I didn't have my cell on me. It happens. It's no reason to hop on a plane and—"

"Damn straight, you don't have your phone on you. Because I called and called and someone finally answered. A lovely sounding RN. Turns out your phone was lying about some hospital snack bar—"

"I have no idea what it was doing at the snack bar, but—"

"He was kind enough to give me the hospital's main number. I spent forever trying to get someone on the line who could tell me why on earth you'd been there."

"Ahh, yes. About that."

"No one would say a peep. Not one word."

"Patient confidentiality, Veronica. And it was nothing. I'm fine."

"Do you know what I was thinking? Do you know what Stephen was thinking?"

The rant, the crossword, the two days of unanswered calls. The unyielding silence of the hospital switchboard. You could see how it might add up. "You didn't have to come," he said. "You could've—"

"If I hadn't come, Stephen would've. And you know the firm would've loved that."

"I still say the three of you scare too easily."

"Maybe. Maybe not." She shrugged and spread her arms wide. The gesture looked out of place, like it ought to be capped with a gleeful spin. "Hey. You *are* all right, aren't you?"

"It's been a strange few days. Do you have a suitcase?"

"No. Just the blue carryall." She gestured to where it waited beside the steps. "A change of clothes, a toothbrush. I didn't know what I was packing for. I figured that's why they invented credit cards."

"Bring it on in. I guess you can bunk down in the guest room."

"Ahh, chivalry."

"Tone down the sarcasm and I'll throw in breakfast."

"And a festival. I was promised a festival."

"Don't push it. We'll see." They went on up the steps and he turned the key. Veronica whistled again—when had she picked up *that* habit?—and pronounced his new digs very swank. She ran a hand along the smooth planes of the Chrome Monstrosity. Ben had planned for this, or for something like it. Veronica here, her sweater on the back of his kitchen chair, her purse on his gleaming granite counter.

Of course, the way he'd planned it, he'd had a week's advance notice. He'd had the chance to run the vacuum before she arrived and time to pick up a loaf from that bakery down the road. Veronica would like their bread; the older she got the more stock she put in grains that were visible to the naked eye. His plan had involved tuning up his old Schwinn and finding a rental bike for his ex. It involved timing the invitation so that they could attend one of the twice-monthly lectures by professors imported from Arizona State. He'd intended to stock up on Veronica's preferred shampoo and on the carrot-based hand lotion she always used in the summer. He'd meant to spend an afternoon going through his box of framed family pictures that didn't look quite right on his shelves. He'd meant to pick a handful to display.

A CHEERFUL CREW
OF PAIR-BONDERS

FOUNDER'S DAY. ONE YEAR EXACTLY since Grandpa died. Clearly an occasion best commemorated by taking your miscreant granddaughter, post-freakout possiboyfriend, his ex-wife, and her probably real Kate Spade satchel to an arts and crafts fair. Gran was nuts. She insisted Lily borrow a pair of Velcro-strap sneakers. Practicality was in order, she said. They'd walk over. Parking had been difficult last year.

Lily wasn't perfect. Ask Benjamin Thales (whose shoes, joy of joys, also employed Velcro). Ask Nicky Tullbeck. Ask Tyson Rosko and his grandmother, four calling birds, three French hens, two turtledoves, and a partridge in a pear tree. She was basically a one-woman interpersonal wrecking ball.

Still.

Really, Gran?

Parking had been difficult?

She wasn't perfect but least she hadn't signed up for a complete emotional lobotomy.

They stopped at a display of hardwood puzzles. A great white with a belly full of surfboards. An ark with a cheerful crew of pair-bonders. Gran hummed the tune from the ballerina music box Lily had loved as a child. It was probably something famous in real life, reduced to wind-up plinking. She caught Lily's eye and the humming stopped. "We're going to have a great time." Her way-too-happy, deep-fried Rasta leprechaun accent was back. Lily nodded, then complimented the ex's bag to distract from whatever was going on with Gran's cognitive processes. The ex said she'd gotten a discount through Anjali's sister, who did something for the company's website. Lily acted like she knew who the hell Anjali was, because apparently they were all such friends, tra la.

Ben traced the edge of the Noah puzzle piece. "You left out Mrs. Noah," he told the artist, because marriage was the best possible thing to allude to in this particular social context.

Lily pointed to the next booth. "Let's try on hats," she said, before either woman could respond to the per-vet and turn the whole conversation insta-symbolic.

Gran brandished her—off-brand—handbag. "Onward!"

Lily winced. In the face of a rival, calculation was in order, not descent into full-on, French-fried freakdom. She'd learned that much from Sierra. That, and how to play scorekeeper. Her grandmother's whackadoo accent made it *Die Exfrau* one, Gran zip.

Die Exfrau tried on a green hat that looked like a satellite receiver.

Gran's beige, feathery confection turned her into Big Bird's anemic cousin.

The per-vet donned a pink, rectangular, felted thing. He winked. "Very Jackie O," said Gran.

He winked again in response.

Gran one, *Die Exfrau* one. Tie game.

Die Exfrau exchanged the satellite for undulating waves of stiffened tulle. She pursed her lips. "How about this for the Turners' next Derby party?"

Make that *Die Exfrau* two, Gran one, unless she also scored an invite to the Turners' soiree. They moved on, past oil-paint mesas and ceramic Kokopellis. Every third booth featured pastel coyotes profiled against the moon. *Die Exfrau* inspected a funny tiled pot for succulents. Ben clattered a display of inert wind chimes. Gran fingered the hem of a gauzy tunic. On the festival stage a band of mariachis in glittering shoulder pads began to set up. Their little group came to a balloon vendor. Visiting grandchildren and their keepers clustered. Lily checked that none of the kiddos was Tyson. A handmade poster labeled the street just beyond as the Kiddie Korral. It was mostly empty. A woman with a foam clown nose applied face paint to another grandkid who wasn't Tyson. Photocopied coloring sheets waited next to buckets of melting crayons.

Die Exfrau indicated the Korral. She asked if Lily wanted to get her face painted, because she was absolutely the kind of girl who wanted to go around with a cute little cupcake on her cheek. She managed a polite "No, thank you." Company manners. Like they always used to go on about for elementary school field trips: everything you do on this excursion reflects on Forest Park Day. Everything she did today would reflect on Gran.

And on Grandpa.

She'd wanted to wear black for him, but Gran nixed it. Don't be silly, Lily. It's a hundred degrees out. And it was hot, the day brazen blue and completely breathless. All up and down Main Street, banners advertising she-had-no-idea-what hung limp for want of wind.

Per-vet Thales said, "Forget face paint. Lily's got her eye out for bumper cars." He winked at her now. Maybe it was some kind of facial tic.

"Benjamin!" Gran play-punched him on the arm, and he rubbed his shoulder at the point of contact.

Die Exfrau looked pained. "Ben holds grudges," she said lightly to Lily, and then, to Ben, "You've always held grudges."

Point to Gran. *Die Exfrau* was way overselling her past with
the guy.

Ben raised his hands in mock surrender. Gran, whose job today,
for the record, should in no way involve playing post-marital ref-
eree, said there hadn't been bumper cars last year, like that was the
carnival's noteworthy flaw.

Lily wanted to stamp her Velcroed foot and scream. Instead,
she said she was hungry. She put on her best smile and somewhere
back in St. Louis her orthodontist lit with pride. They stood in line
for frybread. Lily tracked the approach of a green balloon, tethered
to the wrist of a pudgy little redhead. There was a blue one over by
the Hacienda steps and a pink one back by the Kiddie Korral. Her
conscience seemed to have developed a serious case of latex-based
OCD. She needed to relax, already. Little kids liked balloons. So
what? It didn't follow that any of those balloons were attached to
Tyson.

Die Exfrau informed them that she'd loved sarsaparilla as a
child and had always bought a bottle at the state fair.

Lily wasn't sure how, exactly, that was meant to advance the
conversation. The line moved slowly. Ben fanned his face and
complained about the heat; Gran asked if he was holding up okay.
The score was tied two-two now, with a point to Gran for looking out for the guy. Bonus points to *him* for that matter. Post a
twitchy meltdown like yesterday's, Lily doubted she'd have the
guts to go out in public. She was fully dreading her return to Forest Park Day, the inevitable—and owed—conversation with Jennifer Vogler, and whatever drama bombs Sierra was going to lob.
She could learn a lot from Per-vet Thales' spine. Something like
a small door opened in her mind at that, a door she hadn't known
was there. She still didn't like Ben, but she could put on her big-
girl pants and acknowledge the possibility that she might come
to if he stuck around enough. He gave a great, hacking, old man

cough and she looked away. Just because a door was open didn't mean she had to walk through it. *Die Exfrau* paid for everyone's snacks like she was trying to buy an extra point. At the picnic table, Ben picked the seat beside Gran, making the score three-two. *Die Exfrau* launched into SAT word-worthy sycophant mode, the logic evidently being if-Sadie-poaches-my-person-I'll-poach-hers. No one above sixty should be that interested in any blog, much less one about how to dress at sixteen. Every time Ben looked their way, Veronica made a colossal deal of asking Lily another question. They worked their way through their frybread, which was now the Official Snack of Awkward Conversation. People stared, and not subtly. She should hold up a scorecard. Gran bragged about Lily's rooftop heroism, and Lily wished she could trigger vomit through sheer force of will. *Die Exfrau* mentioned an internship in the new media Lily should apply for next summer. Benjamin Thales licked grease from his fingers. On stage, the mariachis began to play. There were nearly a dozen balloons in Lily's direct line of sight. She took an aggressive bite of her snack. It wasn't like those balloons were out to get her, cartoon-thought bubbles closing in. What was she, four?

She should just calm down. Focus on Grandpa: the baked Alaska he'd made for family birthdays, the concoction of which inexplicably required the use of a hammer, the knock-knock jokes he'd collected years after she'd outgrown them, the wall of travel books he'd organized spatially by latitude and longitude.

Ben and *Die Exfrau* started an argument over whether the mariachis' instrument was called a *vihuela* or a *vinculo*. Tucked away in the woman's $500-plus bag was a $200-plus phone that could resolve the issue in less than ten seconds. Reason *numero uno* that virtual trumped reality: online you argued about stuff you actually cared about instead of quibbling over something that either was or wasn't.

She said, "My grandfather brought me back a mariachi hat from Mexico. I was six."

"I'd have said eight," said Gran. "There was a piñata too."

Lily remembered the piñata, a tasseled sunburst in orange and green. She'd been too young to express the way it made her sad. Someone had made something beautiful with the express purpose of cracking it open. "Six," she said. "I'm pretty sure. We smashed it for my seventh birthday."

Die Exfrau asked where in Mexico they'd gone. Gran said Cozumel and the women launched into a compare and contrast of every vacation they'd ever taken. Ben stretched. Lily heard the crackle in his spine. It turned out the Thaleses and the Birnams had stayed in the same hotel in London, two years apart. Both women chuckled at the memory of the maitre d's impressive moustache. Ben Thales gathered the grease-spattered napkins and stood. She couldn't tell if he was taller than Grandpa had been or shorter. She'd been a child; of course, her grandpa loomed large and rumbly and comforting and bearlike. Ben crossed to a trash can and threw the crumpled wad of napkins. He missed. Gran laughed; Veronica called, "Air ball!"

Grandpa would have made it.

Or if he missed, he'd have shrugged and thrown it out instead of trying again and again like a doofus.

Ben made it on attempt number four. He bowed. Jerk à la mode. Clearing the table hadn't been the point. Getting their eyes back on him had been.

Die Exfrau complained she was thirsty, getting their eyes all back on *her*.

Gran said limeades were in order, that they'd been delicious last year. Ben's eyes lowered and looked away at the words *last year*, the words like magnets with reversed polarity. *Die Exfrau* chirped on and on about a new bar in Portland that did a fantastic cocktail with lime and muddled ginger. Either Ben hadn't told her that Grandpa died here last year or she was an utter oblivibitch. The limeades were cloying to the nth degree. They walked along sipping them,

Exfrau-Ben-Gran, with invisi-Lily as tagalong shadow. They turned from the midway onto a side street lined with more booths. And, wham, there was Mona Rosko, halfway down the block, holding fast to Tyson's hand. No balloon. Of course not. Everyone knew she had no cash for frivolities.

Everyone knew, thanks to Lily.

She slurped hard on her straw and hoped for brain freeze.

Gran frowned, and took a genteel sip from her own cup.

"Sorry," Lily said, because it was good to say it to someone.

Gran saw where she was looking.

"I'm really sorry," Lily said, before Gran took it upon herself to say something kind.

Ben and *Die Exfrau* drew up beside an array of jewelry. Ben said, "This is the gal who made that bracelet I got Anjali last year." The jewelry gal acknowledged this with a smile. Gran fingered a turquoise cuff. The Roskos were too far away for readable faces. Grandmother and grandson stopped to watch a caricature artist at work. The unstinting light cast them in silhouette. Lily saw sunspots when she turned away.

"You okay?" Gran asked her.

"I'm fine," said Ben, operating under the assumption that it was all about him. His eyes darted, uneasy, to *Die Exfrau*, then to Sadie, then to her. Textbook guilty look. *Someone* hadn't told his ex that he was moonlighting as Captain Public Freakout. He thumped his chest. His voice went genial-hopped-up-on-Pixy-Stix. "I'm fit as a fiddle."

As a *vihuela*, Lily almost said, as a *vinculo*. But if Mr. and erstwhile Mrs. Thales started in again, the Roskos were guaranteed to spot them.

Gran held up a necklace, a cameo dangling from an intricate chain. "She looks like you," she said, indicating the cut profile. She asked *Die Exfrau*, "Isn't this absolutely Lily?" Six booths away, then five, the balloon-less Roskos closed in.

Die Exfrau said that Lily should try the necklace on. Lily shook her head. Gran raised a mesh lariat with a cascade of cut black stones. "This would look good on Lily, too."

"Yes! With that neck!" *Die Exfrau* agreed, straining her own up like a crane.

"And those collarbones!" Gran actually applauded.

Ben bent low over a tray of rings, evidently content for the first time ever not to be the subject of their adoring focus. Thanks so much, Per-vet. Really. Couldn't he do her the small favor of twitching out again? Maybe she should scream fire. Fire or terrorist. Anything to stop the Roskos from coming upon her like this, a spoiled child among expensive baubles.

"I've got to go," she said, dodging the jewelry. "You know, to the ladies'." She crossed her legs at the ankles and she looked at Gran and then her innards crisscrossed.

Lily was worse than Sierra.

She was a bottom-feeding, silt-dwelling sel-fish. Talk about oblivibitch.

The limeades Gran drank last year. The long line for the Port-a-Johns. The reason she wasn't by her husband's side when he fell.

Gran gave a controlled little nod. She held a hand out for Lily's empty cup. She took it like it was porcelain. "See if the Hacienda's open." Translation: please not the portables.

Lily couldn't say oh-never-mind without making it an even bigger deal. Shame seared her face. "I'll come right back." She sprinted. She heard Mona Rosko call her name. She passed the line at the Port-a-John. She cut across the food court, around the stage, and beyond the Kiddie Korral. Her dry breath caught and instead of Gran or Grandpa or even the pair of mismatched Thaleses she thought, like a little trained puppy, of Sierra. If she'd figured out yet that Lily was mad. If she'd strike first or try for the kiss and make up. In friend-mode or foe, Sierra's initial approach would be Gran's landline. The blue tangled desk phone would ring and ring.

AS READABLE AS
DICK AND JANE

BEN FELT PROPERLY SOLID AGAIN now that the girl was gone. He probably owed Sadie for the fact that she hadn't run her mouth. Veronica would be flying home tomorrow. They might yet make it without having to discuss yesterday's unfortunate conniption. Though with Mona on her way over it'd be fair to say the chance of *that* was diminishing. If ever a woman owed him no quarter. She planted herself square in front of them. You got the sense with Mona that the long hair was what got the big compliments way back when. It would be hard to let a thing like that go. Beside him, the fine lines around Sadie's mouth looked like wires holding her smile in place. "Hello, Mona," she said. "Ty."

Mona made a low hum of acknowledgement. Tyson looked up briefly, then away. "Your girl can run," said Mona. "Speedy Gonzales."

Veronica winked at the boy. "*¡Ándale! ¡Ándale! ¡Arriba! ¡Arriba!*" Even before Tara gave her something to prove, Ronnie could be a right pain around young folks, gunning for *good with kids* like it was an essential line for her resume. The boy gave her a small, baffled smile.

Mona said, "Let's guess. Lily's avoiding us for some mysterious reason."

Sadie shrugged. "As far as I know, it was just a call of nature."

"Sure it was."

"I'm next in line." Veronica raised her cup. Ice rattled. The dance floor trill of distant mariachis elevated the sound to festive. "We've been drinking these lemonades." His ex gave an exaggerated lip smack. Veronica probably thought she was his life's great mystery but she was as readable as Dick and Jane. Given the chance, she would side with any given teenaged girl. Christ. When she got like this, he needed an insulin injection.

"Limeades," he said. "We've been drinking these *limeades*."

"Sorry. Limeades." Veronica shook her cup again.

Sadie's answering shake edged toward manic. "Cheers!"

The boy made monkey faces in the jeweler's mirror. Mona seemed oblivious to the fact he'd let go of her hand. She said, "I have something to say to your granddaughter. I can wait until she returns."

"I'm not sure you have anything to say to her, actually." Sadie had real steel in her. It was good to know. She and Veronica drew closer together, allied now, friends almost, imagine that. The movement was subtle. A shifting on the periphery. The way their shadows now touched.

Mona raised a pale brow and he remembered what the world had heard him call her. The apology she was owed corked in his throat. She looked the lot of them over like they were a display of overpriced fruit. "One of you tell her then. In case she wants to *help* me some more. Your girl's been a real . . ." She cast a quick look at Ty, who scratched absently beneath his sling. Stephen broke his arm one summer, and when they'd finally cut the plaster away, the grime line had been a thing to behold. Mona thought better of whatever word had coiled in wait. "Well, little pitchers. Let me be as clear as possible. I was letting off steam yesterday, but that was all. I do not now, nor will I ever, want her to set fire to my home."

Ben chuckled at her ludicrous formality. Veronica and Sadie had deeper wells of self-control. The flatness of Mona's mouth outright dared him to laugh again. "Sorry," he said. "I don't have any idea what you're talking about."

"She does." Mona pointed.

Sadie blanched not a bit at that finger.

When Mona spoke again, she spoke blandly, as if reading out the minutes of a meeting where nothing vital had been discussed. "She's already done enough damage. That girl of yours. C'mon, Ty." The crowd parted for them, but that didn't mean anything in particular. It was simply the nature of this place. Everyone had been around long enough to know how to behave.

Veronica asked what on earth *that* was about; Sadie sketched in the basic details. The woman who had been his wife, the woman who might be—*what?* They were simply women now, bandying a bit of gossip. They had nothing to do with him. The jeweler said that Tyson was a sweet boy. Sadie said, "He's struggling." People had said that about Tara, too. For their daughter, there had seemed to exist a finite list of adjectives. The women's voices all had similar cadences. The jeweler, too, a comment here and there as she tidied her display.

Ben wanted to be among men.

It seemed ages since he'd even talked to one. He looked around. He waved to Ed Runch and called his name. To someone who looked like Marvin Baum in the distance. He nodded in the direction of a fellow in a Panama hat who he was fairly confident went by Bing. The young man who'd started all the trouble yesterday headed toward The Homeplate and Ben saluted him as well. Everyone waved back. Everyone smiled. It was that kind of place. It was a fine day. A scorcher, yes, but brilliant.

You could see Ronnie tallying the greetings. "Mister Popular," she murmured.

He said, "They're good people."

"Maybe, but they've got questionable taste in friends."

"You're right. No one actually likes me. I paid them to be nice while you're here."

"You didn't even know I was coming."

Hard to say which was lovelier: these tart exchanges with Ronnie or the unvarnished back-and-forth he'd been building toward with Sadie. "True," he said. "But I keep them on retainer. Just in case."

"You don't have that kind of money. I know. Diesler is very good."

Diesler was May Diesler, Ronnie's attorney in the divorce. The air went electric. That she could be so arch about it. He said, "You're forgetting the account I've got in Sweden. I had Rand Danovic set it up." A dud of a comeback and he knew it. Still, the PI's name was bound to cut. And he'd gotten the tone right: airy and flirtatious. Trouble was, Sadie had heard him use it. She'd think of Ronnie any time he trotted it out with her. His neighbor stood a little aside, letting them bicker with a semblance of privacy. She tried on a necklace, tugging at the chain as if to lengthen it. The jeweler indicated she'd be happy to custom adjust.

Veronica said, "Switzerland, Benji. Switzerland's the one with the banks." If you didn't know her, you'd never guess he'd scored a hit.

"That's what May Diesler thinks, but Rand—"

"Yes. Let's really talk about Rand right now."

"Look." He picked up an ornate, disc-shaped pin, the closest thing at hand. "Aren't these beautiful?"

"You just literally tried to distract me with something shiny."

Sadie's lips quirked. She'd heard the whole thing but would pretend she hadn't. She would allow him to pretend as much, too.

"You know Anjali's Christmas bracelet?" he asked. "The green one?" Veronica wasn't looking at the baubles. Sadie wasn't either. Their eyes were on him and once again he felt displayed for sale. "It used to be antique bottles, I think. This gal recycles things."

"Repurposes," the jeweler said. "Please. Recycles sounds like I'm using pop cans."

Sadie raised the necklace and let it fall against her chest. "It really is lovely."

"Garnet. I popped the big stone there off this god-awful filigree brooch."

Veronica rubbed her own neck, conspicuously bare. "Garnets. Those are supposed to be bad luck, right? If they aren't your birthstone." Now that she was done with the wedding ring, Veronica wore no jewelry. She'd had quite the collection way back when. They had bought a minisafe and put a rider on their homeowners' insurance. There was the engagement ring that she was fonder of the punier the rest of their successes made it look. The graduation pearls from her parents and the black Tahitian pendant brought back from vacation. The glittering studs she'd inherited from her father's mother that, as a bride, she'd used as something borrowed. A handful of glinting brooches she treated herself to with each promotion. A small, square-cut emerald pin she'd been uncharacteristically unable to resist. A Cartier watch. Bracelets from their trip to Venice. A choker from a gallery in Santa Fe. The earrings passed down from some great-aunt or other that they were shocked to hear from the appraiser were real. The anniversary gifts: an upgraded diamond shaped like a pear, a necklace of semiprecious stones set in hammered gold, the intricate globule that you could either hang from a chain or pin on a lapel.

Veronica fingered a delicate strand of mixed beads.

The worst small dark truth of his life was that they didn't know, not to the hour or even the day, exactly when Tara had left. She came and went that whole last fractious year. The overnight at a friend's that ballooned into three, that vanished week she claimed passed hitching to and from a concert up in Seattle. He and Veronica set down rules, an explicit curfew. They hid car keys. They switched out their mattress for the pitted guest room futon and forwent pillows. The point was to sleep lightly, to wake at her footsteps on the stairs. Tara's absences lengthened. Their frequency increased. They guessed it was for keeps when Veronica went for her pearls and found an empty safe. The combination had been a mishmash of Tara's birth date and Stephen's. They never filed a claim with State Farm. There were things you couldn't bear to write down.

The jeweler said the birthstone superstition was actually about opals.

Veronica frowned. "I like a stone with some zing. Opals . . ."

"They never seem like they can quite make up their mind." Sadie finished the thought. The women smiled, briefly in accord.

"You'd like this." The jeweler indicated a ring. "You hardly ever get rose quartz quite this shade."

Ronnie fingered the ring.

Sadie encouraged her to try it on.

Veronica did. Right hand, not left, which looked strange. She held it showily aloft. She didn't make her usual crack about plebe paws, but she wouldn't in front of Sadie. "It's beautiful." She sounded young, but she wasn't. Well on her way to old-woman's hands, veins obvious as earthworms. Sadie's were, too; he checked in the spirit of fairness. Ronnie ran a thumbnail along the stone. "I'm not sure about these threads here. With the pink and all. You don't think it looks like a giant shrimp?"

Sadie said, "I like shrimp."

Veronica mimed popping the ring into her mouth and swallowing. Sadie laughed and Ben bristled. Petty but true: it offended his sense of, well, of *something* how quickly they had slid into getting along. His sense of how these things were supposed to unfold, maybe. His sense of self-importance.

Sadie unclasped the garnet and turned the necklace over in her hand, inspecting the craftsmanship. "I really do think this would suit my Lily."

Veronica murmured her agreement.

"I love that piece," the jeweler said. "It's based on Victorian mourning jewelry. You see the craziest old stuff. All these bands and chains woven out of hair."

Sadie set the necklace down. Her skin had gone mushroomy; the faint freckles he'd always liked could just as well be age spots. "I can't believe I tried to put that on Lily." She scanned the crowd, and Ben remembered: the same crowd last year, Gary in his final, unknowing hour, waving, hearty, from across the midway. Ben was a thoughtless bastard. He felt bleached and ironed. Sadie rubbed her arms as if chilled. "I can't believe I did that to her."

"No, no, no." The jeweler was all assurance. "It's not real hair. I use a kind of synthetic floss. The only thing actually period is the stone."

Sadie fingered the necklace. "Her grandfather died last year. To the day. We're trying for a pleasant outing and here I go, reminding her."

Ronnie was either being discreet or seriously contemplating something at the far end of the display. Sadie shook her head. She rubbed her eyes with the heel of her hand. She shouldn't have come here. She wouldn't have if he hadn't blathered on about it in front of Veronica.

"Lily's tough," he told her. This was Sadie. Just Sadie, here and now. None of that usual sense of another Sadie along for the ride, younger, adroit, green within this one like a wick.

"Oh, I know that." She let her hands drop. She smoothed her hair. He inspected a pair of earbobs, letting Sadie return to herself by increments. "But sometimes . . ." She ended the sentence there, punctuating with a shrug.

And then Veronica's hand dove, a raptor on the wing, toward a stamp-sized square of green. It was set in an oblong metallic squiggle. She picked it up. Crazed light refracted. "Everything's repurposed?" she asked. Ben couldn't work out how the item was meant to be worn. Add a top tassel and it would become a very expensive bookmark.

"Yeah. I've always been into—"

"Where do you get the things *to* repurpose?"

Veronica was being kind now, distracting the jeweler, giving Sadie a chance to resettle. Veronica did that sometimes. She didn't suffer fools, but if she'd decided you weren't one, well, she could be wily on your behalf. She could be ferocious. He'd thank her, later. He'd explain about Gary and his ex would give him the same grief she always gave when he let her walk into a room without knowing the full social context.

The jeweler said, "Oh, everywhere. Around. Estate sales, eBay. Sometimes pawn shops."

"Pawn shops?" The keening quality of his ex-wife's voice jolted through him. Her finger grazed that square green smear. He knew what she was thinking. Oh, Ronnie. He knew it with the operatic clarity of a high *C*.

"We should dance," he said, to distract from the hurt he knew was coming. A person's heart was a muscle, yeah, but that invisible thing that yearned, that was a sponge. Go upright about your business and it goes around with you, sopping up hope. Which was fine, as far as the day-to-day went. It kept things clean and you got by. But there was always a saturation point. A squeeze and then a wrung-out flood of feeling.

Veronica ignored him; the jeweler prattled on. "Pawn shops, sometimes, yeah. I don't like to—there's this sadness—but you get these really cool pieces."

"We should dance," he said again.

"Dance?" Sadie pronounced the word as though it were new to her. Her color was on its way back. From the stage, a song began as if he'd cued it. Sadie grinned at the timing, herself again. She had that unflappable kind of vigor that would be called dashing in a man.

"*Local* pawn shops?" Veronica asked.

"Yeah, mostly. Sometimes I'll look around when I travel."

"Veronica," he said. He'd never been one for the dance floor, but he bowed like he knew what he was doing. "Come on. Please." The green gem in her hand was easily twice as big as the one that had vanished with Tara. The emerald his wife had bought just because. They'd had a good year. Cost hadn't been a major issue. Still, when quoting the price she had managed the considerable feat of blanching and blushing at once. Portland wasn't a flashy town, so Veronica didn't wear it as often as she would've liked. He hoped—foolishly, fervently—that the stone had gone toward the security deposit on a small apartment, a place with natural light and good locks.

Veronica asked, "What's the story with this one?"

The jeweler thought a moment. "eBay. I got this insane lot of eighties costume jewelry." She touched the base of her throat. "The green came off a horrible Lady Di choker."

He watched Veronica's face absorb the information, and then he watched Veronica rebuild her face.

"It's not real," he said. It sounded like he meant the gem, but he meant the story she'd been building, the one they'd both dreamed in a thousand permutations. The one where the green was emerald, not glass. The one where it was Veronica's emerald. The one where the jeweler remembered the pawn shop she'd found it in and the owner was the furthest thing from seedy. The one where the owner remembered the girl with the emerald, talkative, lively, and unquestionably wholesome. The one where the emerald girl had left an address.

"I'm not an idiot," said Veronica, which meant she was pulverizing herself and thinking that, really, she was.

He laid a hand on her arm. He hadn't touched her since her arrival. "We should dance."

She nodded.

Sadie looked away. "Lady Di," she said. "I remember getting up early to watch the wedding. The whole thing was garish, but even so."

"Was she ever beautiful," the jeweler said. "I had the paper dolls."

"Gary teased me, about wanting to watch the whole thing. But it was such a good story when you didn't know what was coming. Everyone fell in love a little."

A new wan pool of sadness seeped through Ben. Once a dumb lug, always one. He should've cottoned on. Sadie had thought he'd been asking *her* to dance, back then. And he should've. She was down and in need of distraction. He and Veronica were beyond each other's helping anyhow. His ex-wife led him toward the floor and he allowed himself to be led. A brief crest of triumph swept him up. He was still young enough to make a mess of asking a woman to dance. Then, after the crest, the trough. All this time and you still haven't figured it out. He didn't look back at Sadie but the woman beside him did. Ronnie's hair brushed his cheek as she turned. Its texture was different somehow. Friable. The encroaching whiteness was at fault there, that or the chemicals she used to cover it.

EVERY LAST OUT

SETH MINCED DOWN MAIN STREET, feeling yesterday's run, sore and swollen in all the places that his body came together. And ravenous. He hadn't managed an actual dinner last night. Ditto breakfast today. Ditto lunch. And this festival was the last damn place he wanted to be. He was on thin ice with Lobel though, so when the man said *go*, Seth went. He had quotes to get. Proof of residents and their families having a grand old time. And it was too goddamn quiet back at the office. Just another Post-it from Nicky Tullbeck. *Be back later, boss. Out on something big.*

What Seth wanted was something small and normal. It was Wednesday. He and Ali always ate at The Homeplate on Wednesdays. Already the thought had a dull, nostalgic grub to it. Something he'd done with his wife, long ago, when they still sought each other out. He headed toward the café. Shin splints on top of it all. Their waitress, Cara, said she was glad he was here. He'd kick himself if he missed this, she said, indicating the screens where a game played live. She showed Seth to his usual table, where Alison sat, still and erect, as if this was the kind of thing she often did in the middle of the day. For all he knew, it was. "Hey," he said. He didn't look at her too closely. He was sick to death of looking at her closely. Analyzing. What her hair meant, her clothes. They used to talk. He never used to piece her together by clues. "Who's playing?" he asked.

"Tigers–Indians."

"It close?"

"Yeah, let's talk about baseball right now. You never came up last night."

"You sack out on the couch plenty."

"It didn't look slept on." It hadn't been, much. He'd tossed about. But Seth didn't say so. He thought of Ali, inspecting the creases of the afghan he'd returned to the back of the armchair, turning the pillows in search of the dent where he'd laid his head. It meant something, that she'd done some detective work. It was the kind of thing he might have done. Alison said, "You left without even saying good morning." No rancor at all. She just wanted the fact of it in the world.

"Well. It's a big day. Adahsville."

"Adahstown."

"Right. You got your speech coming up. I figured I'd let you sleep." He hadn't thought any such thing. He'd tried not to think of her at all. He'd known only that he wanted to be out of the house when she laced up for her morning run.

"Seth," said Alison.

She wouldn't get away with that. Saying his name like it solved things. Just because so much had come to her so easily. "We're in trouble," he said.

She looked some place beyond his shoulder. "Maybe we *should* stick to baseball."

He shook his head. No.

"You know, I'm at a point," said Alison, then stopped. "No, that's right. I'm at a point right now where the only thing I think I *can* talk to you about is baseball."

The books all said not to press.

The books said healing was a marathon and not a sprint.

The books said that when couples fought, couples lost.

"Fine," Seth said. "Baseball. I think the designated hitter's an abomination. I think the National League's got the right idea."

Alison slitted her eyes. One time in college he'd actually been moony enough to check a thesaurus for their color.

He said, "I think Rose was completely screwed over."

"You really don't want to start in with me."

"I think Bill Buckner's a hell of a guy and everyone makes mistakes."

"I'm not going to fight you now, Seth."

Now or never would be a facile thing to say. And she might choose never. She *would* choose never. She would speak the word and then what God had joined together would be pretty well torn asunder. Cara approached to take their order, took in their postures, and left. Seth said, "We can't just not talk." He said this without regard for the double negative. He said it as though he hadn't slept on the couch to avoid a confrontation.

The commercial ended; play resumed. A home game in Detroit. Bottom of the seventh. Alison said, "Look at Galarraga. The cameras don't leave him alone for a second."

Galarraga. Seth didn't recognize the name.

"The Tigers' pitcher," she said. She had always been able to read his face. She sounded like herself again, the vibrant Alison whom everybody adored. They were off the edge of the map and *this* was what she wanted to talk about. "Think." She darted forward and tapped his forehead. Her voice was syrupy and condescending. "Seventh inning. Why on earth would the camera be following the pitcher's every move?"

"If he's working a no hit—"

She clamped a hand over his mouth. "You're not supposed to *say* it."

Saying *no hitter* was bad luck. So that was something his wife still believed in.

"No errors or base runners, either," she said, and her hand pressed closer. Desire jolted through him, electric to the groin. His synapses were treasonous fuckers. Alison's fingers were very cool.

They began to warm against his lips. She said, "Those two words you're thinking? Don't you dare."

The two words being *perfect* and *game*. He nodded. Ali moved her hand away. Baseball was religion to her family. It wasn't to his, but he'd had a pretty typical boyhood. He knew how not to jinx things. The air itself felt drier without the cup of his wife's palm. He swallowed. "I know better than to say it."

"Saying you're not going to say it is practically saying it."

No wonder their marriage had gotten to this point. The verbal gymnastics she went through to avoid actually speaking. Seth said, "I don't even know who's playing."

"Tigers–Indians. I told you already. Cara saw me through the window and dragged me in. She knew I wouldn't want to miss this."

"Don't you have your big Adah thing?"

"Not for hours. Hoagie wants to run through it again, but I just texted I'll be late. He can wait a bit, considering he sprang the whole town thing on me at the last minute. C'mon. Let's live dangerously. And it won't be long. It's almost the top of the eighth."

She sounded happy. Actually happy. First time in ages and it had nothing to do with him. "Alison," he said, "You and me, we're in the bottom of the ninth."

She acknowledged this with a brief incline of her head. She'd done herself up for the big day. Earrings, smudgy eyes, a sweep of tint across her lips. "Baseball, Seth. Baseball's my speed. We'll talk later, but—Please, can we just watch the game?"

Good God, was he ever a sucker. But he couldn't help it. Something about the way his wife had said *please*, about the virtue of playing every last out. Cara came back for their order, availing herself of the momentary calm.

"Could be the third time this season," the waitress said. "The Phillies last week, Brandon back in May." Cara was breaking the rule, practically shouting *perfect game.* Yet somehow, Alison wasn't ripping *her* head off.

"Braden," Ali corrected. "For the As."

"Braden, yeah. That's the one. "

They ordered onion rings. A Coke each. The kind of things that teenagers ordered in movies set in malt shops. The last out of the seventh played. Commercial break. Cara returned with their sodas. The game resumed. Galarraga walked out to the mound. He walked like any other player, not strutting toward the record book, not bowed by expectations. Just another person pretending that what was happening wasn't. Cara hovered, ignoring her other tables. The Indians' batter approached. Travis Hafner. Alison would know his batting average, his walk-to-strikeout ratio, the path he'd taken coming up from the minors. He gave a trial swing, testing the weight of the bat. Another superstition. It was bound to be. The heft of the thing wasn't going to change from one moment to the next. And it didn't do Hafner any good. Groundout to short.

Cara whistled, a tone or so down from a teapot. "Never been a season like this."

"Nope," said Ali.

"Miss?" called a woman from the neighboring table. "Our check?" If they weren't watching the game, Seth wondered why they were even here. Aside from some serious onion rings and the salmon burger special they had offered a few weeks back, The Homeplate's food was nothing to write home about.

Jhonny Peralta was next at bat. Galarraga fanned him. None of the announcers hinted at the word *perfect* or the word *game*. None of the captions did either. No one in the restaurant spoke the words. Forget religion. A conspiracy like this was the best possible measure of human complexity. Russell Branyan was up and Galarraga forced a groundout to second. Commercial break. Alison said, "You know that no one's talking to him. Galarraga, in the dugout."

Maybe Seth had been quiet a while, but so what? "Alison. I'm not not-speaking to you." He heard how stupid that sounded and he didn't care. "I was watching the game. Just like you wanted. And you know what? It's just a game."

"Seth."

"Just a game. And *now* I'm not talking. I'm out of things to say." He could make it more than a game, of course. He could assign stakes. Say Galarraga pulled it out. Seth would change everything. Hightail it for good. Chances were, he'd stay—hardly anyone pitched a perfect game—but there was still the possibility. He drew his hands together, then realized it looked like he was getting ready to pray. He cracked his knuckles instead, the sound louder than he'd intended.

Ali said, "I'm only making conversation. I didn't mean—look, it's another superstition. You don't talk to the pitcher when he's working something like this." She sipped her Coke. "I wonder when they stopped talking. The fifth inning? The fourth?" She looked at Seth like he'd actually know. He shrugged, straining to remember the flurry of adjectives he'd tried for her eyes all those years ago. This was it; one perfect game and he'd head to the nearest U-Haul lot. They'd assign him a truck and he'd look at the mural on its side. Whatever state was depicted there would become his destination. He gritted his teeth, keeping himself quiet. He didn't want the rash bet he'd just made to tumble out.

Alison set her glass down. "Nine innings. Teammates clamming up one by one." On screen, whenever the ball wasn't in active play, the cameras searched out the Tigers' pitcher. The composure on the guy. Alison sighed. "Nine innings," she said again.

"It's the way of the game." Two outs now till the top of the ninth. Five outs total till he knew for sure.

"But think. Once your teammates go quiet, it means everything they've said to you up to that minute is code for I-don't-think-you-can."

"That's not what it means."

"On some level. And if he doesn't make it, just think how much he will have let them all down."

"Yeah, but no one ever makes it."

"Young. Joss. Robertson. Larsen. Bunning. Koufax. Hunter. Barker. Witt. Browning."

"Okay. Hardly anyone."

"Martinez. Rogers. Cone, I missed one, fuck, fuck, fuck, fuck." A tremor to her voice. A crack. This is what finally did it. This. Flatware rattled. She must have kicked at the table legs.

"So much for immortality," said Seth. He hoped Galarraga pitched like hell. From some cheapo apartment on down the road, he'd write the man. This is going to sound crazy, sir, but your curveball set me free.

"MartinezRogers*Wells*Cone." Alison took a long, slow breath. "Johnson. Buehrle. Braden. Halladay." The couple one table over was staring. His wife's voice pitched higher with every name. Galarraga would pull it out, or not. Seth took his wife's hand. This would be the last time he ever held it, or not. They sat quiet for the next two outs. The whole bar did. Top of the ninth. Commercial. Galarraga on the mound, warming up beneath their countless eyes. "Look at him," Alison said. "Carrying all that hope. That's got to be the loneliest feeling in the world."

Seth was an imbecile.

Seth was in the bush leagues, emotionally.

"You aren't talking about baseball anymore, are you?"

"Of course, I'm talking about baseball."

She wasn't. Look at her face. Nine innings. Nine months. Galarraga pitched. A crack of impact. The ball was aloft, then caught. Perfect still. Two outs left for the record books. Seth squeezed his wife's hand. Bile rose in his throat, and with it the fear that he'd somehow be held to the thoughtless gamble he hadn't had the guts to give voice to. "It's been a fuck of a week," he said.

She gave him a look that said, *now* you bring this up?

"Let's make a bet. Perfect game means total matrimonial amnesty. We back off. We let things calm down. We just keep going along."

From Alison's face you'd think he'd laid out the other terms, the ones that meant a U-Haul and the open road. "I asked you to do one thing. One. Dammit, Seth."

Nine innings. Nine months. The suffocating press of hope. He said, "I thought we were getting somewhere. I thought we were finally talking."

"You were talking. I was watching the game." She stood.

The remembered brush of her hand over his lips. The superstitious weight she accorded those two words. He said, "This is the dumbest fight I've ever heard of."

"It was a vicious, nasty thing to do. The one thing I asked."

"Ali, please, just stay."

"It's ruined. And I'm just going to get more and more pissed sitting here."

She left. He missed Galarraga's next out. He marked it only with the bar's collective breath. One out till perfect. Alison wouldn't ditch this for anything short of her whole self cracking clean in two. His mind was a tumult of his wife. The stakes he'd set clattered together. Galarraga wound up. Seth brought his fist to his mouth. He didn't really believe, but Ali did, and because she did, he spoke a cursed and deliberate *perfect game* in the moment the pitcher loosed the ball.

THE STANCE
RESERVED FOR GIRLS

GRAN STOOD ALONE AT THE edge of the space that had been cleared for dancing. She gave a cheerful wave at Lily's approach, but Lily caught her expression before she had a chance to gentle it: unsubtle hunger, fierce and so out of keeping with the mariachi soundtrack that Lily felt the start of an inappropriate giggle. One of the mariachis yipped as if bitten. Gran's mouth pulled into something that might someday grow into a smile. She gestured at the dance floor and then at herself. "Well. Aren't *I* a wallflower?"

"Our headmistress says that wallflowers make ivy," Lily said.

"That doesn't make any sense."

"Ivy as in league. She thinks I'm all about trying to be popular."

"She sounds like a ridiculous woman."

"Mom and Dad think it, too."

"Well. Then they're ridiculous also." Gran gave Lily an assessing glance. "You have your problems, and you've made yourself plenty of extra ones, but homecoming queen's not the brass ring you're after." The song onstage ended. The bandleader said something accented that was hard to follow.

Lily said, "We don't have homecoming at Day. No football team."

"You always do that."

"Do what?"

"Make these prickly little corrections when I'm trying to say something real. It's lousy manners. Now. Say you were gunning for—do you have prom?"

"Yeah."

"Prom queen, then. If you were gunning for prom queen, you wouldn't waste time with the Roskos. You wouldn't waste your summer down here with me."

"But I—"

"You wouldn't have made your very brave announcement last year. You wouldn't let people see the truth of you."

There were sour and cynical things she could say: I guess we're back to pretending I'm here by choice. Or: c'mon, I could make prom queen. What about the direct-to-video success of *Lesbian Prom Queens IV*? The thing she hated most about herself was that her brain went immediately there.

A new song started. It was like workout music, the way the same beat carried throughout. She and Gran watched the dancers, who, if the assemblage of pit stains was to be believed, were feeling quite the caloric burn. None of the women wore normal colors. Elder chic seemed to be either genteel pastels, fabric fading in advance of its wearer, or audacious neon, raging against that inevitable fade. She was glad that Gran wore khakis, unwilted by the heat, that her shirt was a simple, saturated blue. Gran linked her arm though Lily's like they were grade-school BFFs. Dancing couples arced and curved around one another with no discernible pattern and then, with a shift and a slide, Lily saw Ben Thales, holding his ex.

Poor Gran.

Die Exfrau's hands rested on Ben's shoulders. His were light at her waist. They turned and turned, out of harmony with the music, which seemed less a song than an excuse to simply touch. Once, Lily had come across Rocky and Sierra at the edge of the lacrosse field, their tongues in an amphibious battle for intermouth dominance. His hands were on an exploratory mission up her cami, hers had vanished into the waistband of his soccer uniform. Weird that now even more than then Lily felt she had intruded upon something she had no earthly right to see. The Thaleses stood apart, revolving. You could fit a person in the air carved out between them, a whole person, provided she was slim.

Gran ogled outright, a dieter's-eye view of a rotating pie case.

Someday, Lily would forgive Sierra for the severe case of Sierranoia that had lost her *Lipstick*. For the brain cells she'd exhausted saying Sierra, chill, you're cuter than/hotter than/better than the proverbial Her, and for the drama that was yet to come. Because all that investment had yielded this small return: Lily was prepped with the exact right thing to say. She indicated *Die Exfrau*. "Talk about a woman with a fatal case of duck neck."

It was clear from Gran's expression that *she* knew duck neck wasn't actually a thing. "She made tea."

Lily didn't follow.

"Last night. At Ben's. I saw through the window. Her first time visiting and she knew right where he kept the teabags. I miss that. Having someone in the world just *know*."

Lily shut her eyes. "Teabags. Upper cabinet, left of stove."

"You're a sweet girl. Upper cabinet on the right."

"I meant left as you're facing the table."

Gran snorted. "We should dance."

Lily had an official policy about dancing with girls and that official policy was a full-on, plus-size no. Somehow, it always devolved into a game of bumper-tits for the benefit of some boy watching from the dim. Now she had no idea what to do. But Gran had attended cotillions as a girl; she'd met Grandpa at twelve and they'd twirled in country club ballrooms. She positioned Lily's hands, ceding to her the stance reserved for girls. "Box step," Gran instructed. "Forward, together; side, together; back, together; side, together."

They moved slowly, the music an exuberant universe apart. Gran asked, "Back at the necklaces. Did you really have to pee?"

Perhaps Lily *wasn't* the most subtle girl on the planet. "No. I just didn't want to see Mona."

"Good. Front, together. Side, together."

"What?"

"Back, together. I thought it might have been the necklaces."

"Huh? They were pretty."

Gran nodded and the spoiled, fetid feeling Lily'd had at the jewelry booth returned. Gran would think she was hinting for one. There hadn't been any obvious price tags, which translated to *a lot*. "They were mourning pieces," said Gran. "Side, together. I thought maybe you'd figured that out. Back, together. It's the kind of thing you'd know."

Lily heard *morning* not *mourning*.

Gran shuddered. "Front, together. Side, together. They used to make them out of hair. You learn something every day. Back, together. Side, together. No, other side." Gran laughed. "It probably put a dent in the open casket business."

"Gran." There was a bank of Port-a-Potties across the floor. Gran had stood there last year, unknowing, while Grandpa crumpled and fell. And Lily. Even looking right at them, she'd heard *morning* and not *mourning*. Dancing gave her an excuse to look away, down at her feet and Gran's, twins in their Velcro shoes.

Gran said, "Widows used to wear black for a year. Why on earth would they need their husband's hair in—I don't know—a needle-point locket?"

Grandpa'd been balding Lily's whole life, but she'd seen the wedding pictures. Gran's girlish dress, puff sleeves and a sash, a bow tucked up under her breasts like a secret, Grandpa's hair thick enough to lend him extra height. Her feet navigated another box and Gran said, "It's appalling. Just imagine. Having to make a big *show* of it. Appalling, but goddammit. At least you'd know what you were supposed to do. Let's try it up to tempo now. Ready? Front, together; side, together." The lead mariachi yipped again; his backups clapped in unison. Lily managed not to step on Gran's feet. "Coming here today was ridiculous," Gran said. "I know that. This whole idea."

"It's okay."

"I wanted a nice, sweet, sane normal day. I thought it would honor all the nice, sweet, sane, normal days we had." Gran didn't sound nice or sweet or even very sane.

"I'm having fun," Lily said.

"You're full of it." Gran sounded amused, or mostly so. A layer of amused over the rest.

"Maybe a little."

Lily was starting to get the hang of this. Front, side, back, side; lather, rinse, repeat. Her grandmother's gait was even, her arms strong-set and supple. With a better partner, she'd be a very fine dancer. Gran said, "I think you're ready for some turns."

"No," Lily said, because they couldn't possibly: a rotation of one hundred eighty degrees and Gran would face the outhouses. Ninety one way would be the mourning pendants; ninety the other, the incredible spinning Thaleses.

"Have a little confidence."

What was she supposed to say? I am the only thing here that it is safe for you to look at. She shrugged. A surprisingly graceless gesture, given the formal position of her hands.

"Okay, then," Gran said. "It's walk, walk, side-close-side." She executed a fast series of steps that Lily would be able to master shortly after her reincarnation as Anna Freaking Pavlova. And they turned: the jeweler, the Thaleses, the people in line. Her grandmother's face betrayed no pain. She muttered something though.

"Huh?"

"Paper, cotton, leather, silk. The anniversary gifts. I used to know a rhyme to help me remember." They'd reverted to simply box stepping. Lily couldn't see the Thaleses anywhere, which meant they were behind her, directly in Gran's line of sight. "There should be some sort of list to mark this. A year now he's gone. There isn't even a word."

"Reverse-iversary?"

"You're funny."

"I'm not trying to be." She should be thinking only of Grandpa and Gran, but brassy old Sierra elbowed her way in. All their gods and goof-words, their codified Laws of Cheese. The point of an inside joke was to put the lesser rest of the universe outside it. Which was stupid. Your friends should make your world expansive, not exclusive. When she was small, Gran had pushed her on the swing and the whole of Lily felt open and endless as the sky.

"My funny girl." Gran let out a whoop. She spun Lily and landed her in a low dip.

Lily let out a surprised, strangled sound.

"Oh, relax. I'm not going to let you fall."

"People are looking." Not that she could actually see them upside down. Only, there were Ben and *Die Exfrau*, leaving the floor. They didn't touch, but every casual step narrowed the gap.

"Let 'em look," Gran said, but righted her. "It's my paper reverse-iversary. I'm going to do whatever the hell I want." She watched the departing couple. They both did. Anyone could see their paths were not parallel and must therefore intersect.

"Okay," Lily said. "Whatever you want."

"Good. Let's do something terrible." It wasn't the heat but the vim of all Gran's years that shimmered around her. She stepped back from Lily. "Something just—terrible." She nudged her with an affectionate elbow. "You're on a roll. You'll come up with something." She giggled like she was Lily's age, lips pressed against her knuckles. Time was a funny thing, or maybe only posture was, that so small a gesture could winnow away the years that cut between them.

WHAT THE
GROWNUPS DO

TWO THOUSAND MILES AWAY, BAT and ball connected. Home field advantage: the stadium roiled with sound and superstition. Fingers crossed, lips mouthed prayers and go-go-gos. Cups upended. Popcorn and beer. Peanuts. Cracker Jacks. Detroit, Michigan. Two of the Big Three had filed for Chapter Eleven the previous year. Unemployment was closing in on thirty percent and whole neighborhoods teetered toward foreclosure. If ever there was a city in need of a spectacular win.

Ground ball, right side.

The Homeplate held its breath.

The batter ran like hell for first.

Galarraga sprinted to cover the bag.

Seth couldn't hear it, but he knew from childhood the ball's leathery thwack as the pitcher caught it, the solid planting of a white shoe on first base. Out! A perfect game! The crowd erupted, sportscasters crowed, and teammates tensed to rush the field.

But baseball's a funny sport. Even Alison, raised on its easy pace and lyricism, would have to admit that much.

Because here came the official call. The first-base umpire raised his hands to his chest. He was a professional, impartial to the point

of anonymity. But not for long. In a second the world would know
his name. Jim Joyce's arms splayed out, unmistakably to the side.
Safe!

The call was flat-out wrong. Obvious as the top *E* of an eye test.
But this was baseball: no instant replays. No take-backs or appeals.
The rules were the rules. A funny sport indeed.

For a slow, muscular moment, Seth thought his jinx had bent the
universe and he shook off an unseasonal chill. The crowd's jubila-
tion downshifted. Sportscasters lamented through the replays. The
Homeplate deflated and diners began to make fussy *check, please*
gestures. "Wow," he heard a McCain say, elongating the word by
two syllables. His McCain-companion griped that in football they
could have changed the call. They used instant replay in hockey and
basketball; hell, they even used it in figure skating.

"It's the game," Seth said, because Ali would have said it had
she stayed. The league had a history older than Adah Chalk.

"Well, it sucks," said the McCain, using slang he was much too
old for.

Seth felt ancient himself. Ossified and done, too ground down
to connect, though connecting was why sports bars existed, why
sports did. "It's the game," he said again, and sat silent through
the postmortem. Jim Joyce wept openly and apologized. Galarraga
said he understood. He hugged the man. He said without bitterness,
"Nobody's perfect." He said this without the slightest ironic lilt, the
kind of man Seth knew that he was not, clear-eyed and accepting.
Rules were rules even when they did not serve you well. The past
was past and unreachable by wishing. Galarraga said, "I know that
I pitched a perfect game, I believe I got it." Seth thought, *Yes. It
happened. So what if they won't count it. It was real.* Galarraga
said, "I'm going to show my son. Maybe it's not in the book, but
I'm going to tell my son, 'One time I got a perfect game.'" Son.
Seth waited for the astringent pulse of envy. When it didn't come,
he got out his wallet. He thought of the U-Haul. One state of fifty or

another, randomly assigned. That preposterous bet. He had no clue
if he'd won or lost it. Galarraga had pitched a perfect game, and also
he hadn't. Seth didn't wait for the tab. He left a crumpled twenty.
The festival was still in full swing, which felt strange. More
time should have elapsed. He threaded through the crowd, gathering quotes as Lobel had directed. The couples he chatted with could
just as easily have been brother-sister as husband-wife. A breeze
started up without warning. Strings of paper lanterns bobbed. One
mariachi song bled into the next and the air felt battered and fried.
He passed a display of chili pepper wreaths, their colors tradition
reversed. A booth of purportedly authentic Navajo dream-catchers
whose dangling peacock feathers belied the claim. A floor of dancers who weren't much better at it than the kids back in Chettenford
and, beyond it, the mariachi-filled festival stage where in an hour
or so his wife would regale them with the mighty frontier deeds of
Adah Chalk. And there, beside the stage, in the sparse shade of a
cultivated palm, was the lady herself. Ali.

He was too far away to read her face, or even to make out its indi-
vidual components. He knew her by body type and by the clothes she
had worn in The Homeplate. Add a list of distinguishing features—
her appendectomy scar, the navel piercing she'd allowed to close up
years ago—and you had exactly what the police would note if she
simply vanished. What a terrible mind he had. Alison kicked off her
shoes. She rummaged through her bag for something. Her phone. His
rang a breath later. The anachronistic jangle his wife liked best, saying phones should sound like phones. She could be such a goddamn
snob. He answered, shrinking to the far side of the dance floor, knowing he could watch without her seeing him watching.

Ali asked, "Where are we on that amnesty?"

"What?"

"The amnesty thing. The game."

"You never took the bet."

"Pretend I did. Where are we?"

"It's hard to say." He knew what happened and Ali did not. His wife, who could rattle off the names of pitchers like they were the names of all the saints. This was what power felt like. Power, and also pettiness.

"It's simple, Seth. A game is either perfect or it's not."

But it wasn't. He explained, looking deliberately away. This was the intersection of history and baseball, absolutely the kind of thing she'd get off on. He didn't want to see how much more it meant to her than real life. All along Main Street, McCains drifted from one booth to the next. The Mrs. McCains did, too. Seth couldn't recall the name of the senator's wife.

His own said, "So. No amnesty then." She sounded less keyed up about the blown call than he'd expected. Seth checked. Alison wasn't even on her feet.

"I don't know," he said. "Does it become a perfect game in the moment he pitches it, or does it become one when the umpire says so?" They used to talk like this, debate; they used to actually talk.

Alison only said, "You should have studied philosophy." She stretched and did something fidgety in the neighborhood of her shin. Stockings in need of smoothing, maybe. She'd put on the whole getup for her big Adah speech.

"I don't know," Seth said. "Maybe. I'd probably have talked myself in circles."

"I guess we'll have to decide ourselves. About the game. The clean slate. All of it. Make up our own minds. That's what the grownups do."

"Or so I'm told. Okay, then. Amnesty." Who knew what he'd have said if he was close enough to read her face. Who knew what message she'd have spelled there.

"Don't say that yet."

"Huh?" A Mrs. McCain brushed past him toward the line for frybread.

Ali said, "I'm stalling. I have something to say. Full disclosure, before you make up your mind."

"Amnesty, Alison. Period." God knew Seth needed it. He'd come inches from hitting a man. He'd daydreamed of U-Hauls and harbored visions of her copulating with their boss.

"I've been fired," she said.

"What?" The dance floor couples kept dancing. He must not have been as loud as he thought.

"Let go. Laid off. Made redundant. Shit-canned. Just now, in Lobel's office."

"With the lead pipe."

"I'm not joking."

"Please. Hoagie loves you."

"Loved." She didn't shrug, but she used a shrugging sort of voice. Perhaps she would have shrugged if she'd known she was being observed. She didn't look like someone who'd been sacked. She was crisp and coiffed and didn't have the requisite cardboard box.

He said, "I call bullshit."

"Call it what you want."

It was possible that she hadn't taken anything with her. Her still, spare office hadn't had much in it. The orange on her desk. The overly bright stuff of still lifes. "Did you take the orange?"

"What?"

"The orange on your desk yesterday."

"That's what you ask me?

"Fine. I'll play. What happened?"

"Your intern spent the day at county records. Acting on some kind of tip he got at the HOA. Anyhow, he found the paperwork. Adah Chalk died two and a half years into her marriage." Alison sounded grim and pissed about it, like the woman had let her down. "Hoagie wasn't pleased."

Seth should be doing frantic math, tallying their savings and monthly expenses. Instead, he thought, *Good for Nicky.* The kid had chops after all.

Alison said, "I really fucked up." She stood then. The edge of her slip showed. Even at a distance he could see it, a frail, white strip of lace. He should tell her. Ali wasn't vain, exactly, but she liked to look put together in public.

"Seth. At least say something."

"Adah's got to be a pretty common name. Back then, anyway. So you made a mistake. Once Lobel has a chance to calm down—"

"I didn't make a mistake. I made it all up."

"You can't have. There were letters. You quoted from Susan B.—"

"Everything. The letters. The schools. The clinics. The lemon pie." Thank God for the square of dancers separating them. The hours she'd gone on about Adah. He could've slapped her. "The snakebite cure. The English lessons. The fight for women's suffrage." She made it sound like a game, like she was back in the café, naming pitchers.

"This is our *life*, Alison." A nearby McCain tightened his grip on his wife. A reasonable enough response, if he recognized Seth from the HOA mess.

"I said I was sorry."

"You didn't. You said you fucked up."

She sighed, breath blasting through speakers. "You should've been a lawyer."

"You don't get to make this funny. Fuck, Alison." The music had stopped. The band opened bottles of water. The books all said it was toxic to score-keep. Even so, the emotional calculus. His fist-fight. Her fraud. Stick it out and one of them was going to wind up with enough ammo to win all the fights, forever.

Ali said, "It's not—not a disaster."

"It's one whole income we're down."

"The contract was up in a few months anyhow. We knew that. Our rent's dirt cheap."

"You lied. You got up in front of everyone and lied."

"I—I couldn't write it the way it was. Adah Chalk." Her voice. She had more tenderness for the dead woman than she'd had for him in months. "She died in childbirth. Twenty years old and no doctor for miles. Stuck in this nothing with a husband who couldn't even write his own name. And that wasn't even her first child. There'd been a daughter the previous year. Breach. She didn't make it. I wanted to fix things."

"That's the stupidest thing I've ever heard."

"It wasn't fair. There isn't even a record of where she's buried."

"So? It was a hundred years ago. You suck it up and write it down and then you work on something else." Alison tensed at that; his voice—his actual voice, not his phone one—must have carried. Her hand rose to shade her eyes and when she spied him it rose again in an instinctive wave. She stood, stepping neatly back into her shoes.

"No. You stay where you are. Don't come any closer."

"I grew up with these three great, hulking brothers."

"So what? They don't have anything to do with this." The music struck up again. Slowly, the couples did, too.

"It means I'm crap at the talking thing. When something's wrong, you gut it out till it's fixed. You fake it if you have to. That first time Dad got sick? The four of us kept smiling these stupid pumpkin smiles." She meant Jack o' Lanterns, hollow and glowing for outward show. He knew the smile in question. These days it was the only one he knew. "And you know what?" Ali's voice thickened. "We came out fine. Great, even. Fantastic. I edged out Mattie Gibson for valedictorian that semester and Neil started to locate like you wouldn't believe."

"Well, good for Neil. He nabbed a sweet baseball scholarship. You got fired."

"That's not fair." She was at the edge of the dance floor now and crossing.

"I said not to come any closer."

"I'm sorry." She stopped. The crowd had thinned during the break. He had no excuse not to see her.

"Don't be sorry. Don't pretend. Talk."

"It's like—"

"That's pretending. Don't say what it's like. Say what it is."

"You wouldn't want to talk to you either. It's like—"

"I said, no metaphors."

"It's like living with a caged wildebeest. You lash out every which way and you never forgive anyone anything."

"It's a damn sight better than running away."

"That's not what I'm doing—"

"What do you clock on the mile again?"

"The book said—"

"The books said. The books said. You don't even let the books on the shelves."

"Not the books, the *book*. The pregnancy one." She said this last part at a whisper, like a child afraid of getting caught cursing. "You know," said Ali, "the one with the crazy foot."

Seth knew the book. A black-and-white photo on its cover. A great, waiting moon of a stomach, the small imprint of a foot pressing from within. The rest of the books—and they were the Colliers, so of course there had been many—had Madonna and child covers, rocking chairs, rattles, and the like. He said, "I didn't know you'd been reading them. Rereading them." He wondered where in the condo she had stashed them.

"Not now. God. But I looked through it, after. The first night home from the hospital." He wondered how the hell she'd stood it. Her body swollen and scraped out, her breasts gone Playboy with wasted sustenance. "I had to find this aside. You know, in one of those little boxes?" As a teacher, Alison ranted about the side-box approach.

Here, on the page, is real history. Here, in a sidebar blurb, is how it was if you weren't white or a man or well-off. Ali said, "I don't even know why I remembered it. One of those cute little did-you-knows. No, *didja*. They spelled it *didja*. Ninety percent of mothers retain fetal cells in their bloodstream for the rest of their lives." She drew a shaky breath and adjusted an earring. "So I run now. I eat right. I was nowhere near this fit when I played varsity softball."

"You could have said." He could have asked. The obvious retort. Ali didn't say it. A sign, maybe, that they still had a shot at something. Seth said it again, knowing it was bait, knowing she still could lash out and take it. "Alison. You could've said."

"What, that this is the only way I have to take care of him? If you could see yourself, Seth. You wouldn't want to share the hard stuff with you either. You crash through our life looking for ways to feel hurt, and you're fragile and manic and fuck, my heart." She gripped her chest where it was presumably beating. And hard. He thought he could see the pulse in her neck. "I wear earrings now," she said. "I do foundation and I wear the right kind of bra. I thought if I did a better job at all that girl stuff, then maybe next time—" She folded in on herself as if pained. As if fetal.

Seth was adrenal-awake, comprehension solidifying like a clot. The slimming down. The gussying up. It wasn't for Lobel or even for herself. It was for Timothy. The absurdness of it. The ice knife in the gut.

A shaky sound from Ali, and it registered. Next time. His wife had said next time and it wasn't the first thing he'd latched onto. That had to bode well for the two of them.

Alison righted herself. She'd been doubled over and no one had stopped their cha-cha to help. This place. This cold, selfish construct of a place.

"I can't do this on the phone," she said. "You know I can see you, right?" A hollow laugh. "C'mon. All these happy couples between us? It's like we're points in someone's bad term paper."

He could've said his newest, purest truth: He hated Arizona. Instead, "I miss the bad term papers."

"I miss a lot of things."

"Chettenford."

"Yeah, Chettenford."

Their bathroom had a freestanding tub. From October through March the pipes sounded like demonic possession. God, he missed it. The racket of a place well lived in, the chalk-dust seasonality of the school year, and the weekly tromp home from The Book Croft. "You know what gets me?" he asked. "We got the books from the same place. Both sets." The Book Croft. Nine months apart and three shelves over. How to bide your time while hoping and how to get over having hoped in the first place. "It's absurd," he said.

"Not really. We were in and out all the time. We worked right around the corner."

"Even so. That one little store can hold that range."

"I don't know." Their minds held it, their lives, every day they breathed through.

"Do you know what they named the new cat?"

"At the Croft? How would I know?"

"You keep in touch. You're the extrovert." She was their social curator. People were drawn to Alison and she held them fast. But not here. They had no one but each other in Arizona.

"You can't honestly expect me to know that. The cat, really?"

"I wondered, that's all."

"You're a strange one."

"I'm sorry about Adah," he said, like he was offering condolences on a recent loss.

"What are we going to do?" She didn't sound panicked. She sounded simply tired, like all the sleep she hadn't gotten since Timothy had caught up with her.

Seth knew it didn't say much about him that he had waited for this show of weakness before stepping toward her. "I can get you

your job back," he said. It sounded chauvinistic to his own ears. A
puffed-up shot at playing the hero. He said it anyhow. This small
slice of past he had a balm for.

"And a pony, too? I'd like a pony." She didn't stir, waiting for
him.

"It wouldn't fit in the condo. Besides, I'm serious. I can get Lobel
to change his mind." That headline. *Slow Sale of Rosko House Due
to Internal Error.* He'd quoted Lobel in the piece; he had the man
on the hook for the lies. He was an arm's-length from Ali now; she
zipped her phone into her purse. She reached for Seth's next and her
fingers grazed his cheek. She powered it down and slid it into his
back pocket. It had been so long that he couldn't tell if the touching
was deliberate. "He'll take you back," Seth said. "At least for the
length of the contract."

"I don't think so. He was really pissed. I think mostly because
he wasn't the one to figure it out. All those letters I quoted from a
man who couldn't write his name." A breathy snort. "Sorry, but it's
funny."

"You've got balls, I'll say that."

"Ovaries, please."

They let the word sit there, awkward in its potential.

Seth said, "I can be persistent. With Lobel."

"I know that, but no."

"I've got dirt."

"No." She didn't ask what and he was grateful. He didn't want
her knowing.

"Okay, then."

"We can't have kids here," said Alison, a hand waved to indicate the festival midway, the architectural fakery, the overcultivated
greens beyond.

"It's a weird place," he agreed.

"It's a freaky nowhere town, and I'd be thinking about Adah on
top of it all. How scared she had to be. All that blood and dirt."

Alison's skin had come alive with gooseflesh. He slung an arm around her. In Chettenford, he'd said, we have to leave. She was the one to say it this time. There were states with serious teacher shortages; she'd been doing her research. Western states, with serrated mountains and ferocious skies. States whose histories held real Adahs. She might even think about writing a book. In job interviews they could spin their stint in Arizona as a mistake; they had left the classroom only to discover it was their true calling. Alison said, think. They could live in a place with weeds and proper seasons again, find a snug house with a wood-burning stove. They'd buy in a good school district and hang a tire swing. Montana, she said. Wyoming. One of the Dakotas. We'll buy us a pair of matching cowboy hats. Seth listened, first to her words and then to that rhythm, to her repeated use of *we*. Now and then his synapses sparked with the collective nouns that went with the plans she was making. A disagreement of states. A quiz of teachers. A huddle of houses. A fascination of hats. He squeezed Alison's shoulder, said something about putting in a garden plot or maybe adopting a dog. For the first time in ages, he felt the full *wrongness* of the next collective noun that came to mind. The list he'd hung in his Chettenford classroom had its two reductive options: a multiply of husbands or a suffering of them.

THE THALESES OF
MILDEW STREET

BEN'S KITCHEN SPONGES SMELLED WET and dank. He'd been meaning to replace them a while now. He grabbed the biggest one and
attacked a nonexistent counter spot. He knew how Veronica's mind
worked. One whiff would mean a thousand capitulations. That she
was right and you had to wring out damp sponges for a full thirty
seconds. That on some level he missed their life together in which
she'd replaced the things before they grubbed apart at the corners.

The back of his ex-wife's calves were pink with faint sunburn.
The tips of her ears, too. It was evening now, time for a late dinner.
Cooking together was preferable to the courtship implicit in a meal
out, to the apathy of a pizza in. There was also a guaranteed course
of conversation, as Veronica didn't know where anything was. He
tasked her with peeling garlic. Ronnie seemed surprised he had a
head of the fresh stuff on hand. She separated skin from cloves by
smashing them with the flat of a knife.

Ben went to the pantry for olive oil. He didn't have the kind
that she liked, but you couldn't taste the difference. He laid a pair
of chicken breasts on the cutting board, glad he had the makings
of a full meal on hand; how's that for an aging bachelor? Black-
ened chicken, sliced thin. Pasta, a pack of that baby spinach, shaved
parmesan, and a dollop of cream to cut the heat. He wrapped the

chicken in plastic film, pounded it thin, and worked in a generous dose of Cajun rub. Veronica asked if the garlic was chopped finely enough. He nodded without really looking; she rinsed the knife. The recipe didn't actually call for garlic, but its scent would mask the sponges nicely.

The chicken went out to the grill; the pot on the stove came to a boil. Ronnie rattled the spaghetti in its box. "I don't know how much you need."

"Eyeball it." Ben was iffy at guesstimating, but she didn't have to know that. He always wound up with either a Tupperware of clammy noodles or an overabundance of sauce.

She shook the box again, testing its weight, then added its contents into the pot, brushing a few starchy splinters from the counter. "What? Why the look?"

"Don't you need to break them first?"

"Huh?"

"The noodles." He mimed snapping them along the middle.

Ronnie gave a great, merry, masculine bray. He'd always liked that. There was something about a pretty woman with an ugly laugh. "What?" he asked. "You always used to."

"Maybe back on Mildew Street, when we only had the one little pot." Her hands spanned the remembered circumference. Mildew Street was what they'd called their first place together, a sublet on *Mildred* Street, clean enough despite the moniker. They hadn't been married their first year in that apartment, just engaged, and at the time that had felt very daring.

"I guess I thought breaking them made it cook faster."

"That's salt, Benji. It raises the boiling temperature." She rifled through the cupboards to find some. Ben stood very still; with Ronnie in his kitchen the slightest movement could wind up fraught. Touching was impossible without the crowd to chaperone, the music to dictate for how long and in what way. Tonight's recipe called for onions, sliced lengthwise and seared on the grill, but it was probably best they skip them. Neither he nor Veronica should chop onions tonight. Neither of them could risk tears.

When they sat down to eat, Veronica said, "All in all, I quite like your girlfriend." She said this with an air of ceremony, a sommelier with a bottle of something especially fine.

"She's not my girlfriend." He couldn't chance a look out the window. What lights were on at Sadie's place were on without his knowing.

"If you say so. But I do like her. Surprise, surprise."

"She's a widow. Her husband passed last year."

"Yes. She said. And I'd have figured it was something like that. You're hardly the sort to *cuckold* someone." Veronica gave a dry, mirthless caw at the anachronistic word. She reached for her wine-glass, swirled the contents, and set it down without a sip.

Ben made a big show of drinking his. Deeply. Too deeply. He sputtered.

And then Ronnie was laughing, really laughing, the length of her neck alive with it.

"What?"

"I don't know what's funnier, that that girl ran you over—"

"It was a minor collision."

"Or that you're sweet on someone who's an actual grandmother."

"Stephen and Anjali might—"

"Someday, yeah, but that'll be a baby. Sadie had to be what when she had that kid's mom, twelve?"

"Lily's dad, actually."

"That's not the point and you know it."

The point was, Veronica was jealous. A proprietary thrum filled his chest. "I'll tell Sadie you think she looks as young as all that." It never got old, that adolescent thrill of hearing your girl praised.

"You'll do no such thing," Veronica drew her arms close to her sides. The contrary woman he'd spent his life with. Everyone else he knew flailed about when mad, or stood, chests puffed and hands on hips, making themselves bigger, as if for some evolutionary advantage. "She'll think I'm ridiculous."

"She won't think—"

"I *am* ridiculous. Coming down here like this. I don't know what I was thinking." The pasta was soft enough to cut with the side of a fork. The chicken, he'd chopped bite-sized. Veronica still went to town with the knife.

"Ronnie. You're not ridiculous. It was a—it was a kind thing to do. Coming here. You and I—we haven't always been kind."

"No. We haven't." She set the knife across her plate like she was waiting for a waiter to clear it. Forget kind. They'd been vicious bourgeois brutes, toxic when they should have been tender. That was a hell of a thing to know about yourself. Whatever was budding with Sadie he probably didn't deserve.

He said, "I looked crazy. I did. I'll give you that much."

Veronica raised a hand to her mouth to cover what had to be a smirk. "Cunt." The word was pensive, soft, divorced from connotation. "When I first met you, you couldn't even say *goddammit*." She shook her head. "The small-town boy who blushed. God. I stayed awake nights thinking about how to make you do that."

They'd met at twenty. She'd been haunting in autumnal light. He remembered the clean slope of her forehead bowed low over textbooks. The cottony flash of a worn summer dress. He did the math to stop himself from saying something soppy. They were forty-eight years times three hundred sixty-five nights from the time Veronica had lain awake. He said, "I wanted the story to blow up. Bigger even than it did. I thought our girl might be out there somewhere. That she'd see it."

"Oh, Benji."

"I know."

"You're an imbecile." She said the word like it meant something else. My love. You remain my love.

"I didn't exactly think it through."

"I'll say. What exactly about that showing would make her want to come home?"

"Like I said, I didn't think it through."

Veronica sighed.

He said, "You've given up on Tara, haven't you?"

"Not on your life. I'd never. But—you could've died in the ICU."

Ben would've said *Chicago*. *You could have been killed in Chicago.* It was either a symptom or a disease that they no longer had the same shorthand. If something terrible befell the Thaleses of Mildew Street, they would've held a common stock of words with which to speak of it.

Ben said, "I think maybe we've both given up." He felt his heart hammer. He'd felt it that night under the Chicago footbridge, too, in the second before the thud of boot to chest.

Veronica scowled. "I'm still in the house." One woman, four bedrooms, three and a half baths. Ninety dollars a week to their housekeeper, and all on the impossible chance of a late-night knock.

"Yeah. You are. And I'll never be sorry for making an ass of myself all over the Internet. Even so. I don't think either of us really thinks she's coming home."

Veronica shunted a curl of pasta from one side of her plate to the other. "If you'd died, I don't think I'd have forgiven either of you."

God did he ever miss Veronica. Day to day, he missed her more than Tara. That was the biggest truth in his life, and also the least forgivable. Instead of voicing it, he asked, "Do you think we'd still be together if she'd stayed?"

She shrugged. One of her infuriating, imperious gestures.

"Answer the damn question."

"I don't know. Sometimes I think she saved us from splitting over something stupid. This is really good." She meant the pasta. It would've been better with the onions.

"I'll send you the recipe." He'd type it up the way they'd made it tonight. Ronnie would figure out the onion thing anyhow. She added them to everything. She'd invented this insane sandwich: peanut butter, dried figs, and caramelized onions. Vile sounding but actually tasty. Stephen refused to ever try it; Ben didn't remember Tara's take on the matter. He topped off their wineglasses. He supposed he should ask about people in Portland. Last he knew, the Gilmans next door had put their house on the market. The couple he'd sold his practice to was converting the neighboring property into a doggie daycare. A colleague's kid was back from a semester in Peru and trying to scare up capital for a lunch cart. Ronnie set her glass down too fast. It clinked against the silverware like she wanted to propose a toast. He and she had no small talk left. Pretending they did would take more from him than tackling what actually lay between them. "I've given up, too," he said.

"Sure you have. Cunt. Cunt!" Ronnie was an adroit mimic. She nailed the mean turn of his mouth.

"That wasn't rational. You know how it goes." If Ben wanted to be cruel, he could pantomime Veronica at the jeweler's stall, the way her breath had caught at the glint of gemlike green. Folks who waxed on about the essence of hope had never had that essence slap them across the face. But all that was pure feeling. He was talking about the stuff he could actually help. "I knew—my brain knew anyhow—that she wasn't coming back when we gave Stephen her college money." They had saved for both kids from the day they were born. Undergrad for each would be neatly covered. But then Stephen waffled about where to go for law school. BU came with one hell of a price tag, Case Western with a significant scholarship. The discussion with Ronnie clocked in at less than an hour, and a part of Ben that he loathed thought *serves the little brat right for leaving* when they cut his son the check.

Veronica said, "He'd never have met Anjali at Case." She glowed at the mention of her daughter-in-law. At the thought of their happy son.

"No. He wouldn't have." You couldn't frame it as a trade. Not if you wanted your lungs to keep doing their thing. Still, he thought of

Anjali, whom they both adored. Of the bedroom she'd taken the trouble to paint summer blue, though the kids were renting and would be
moving on in a matter of years. It's our home right now, she'd said. If
the landlord gives us trouble, well, why else did Stephen and I bother
with law school? Stephen had brought her home for the first time midway through his 2L year. Thanksgiving. The table looked right again
with four people around it. Anjali and Stephen were all ambition and
subtle touches. The space between them crackled. When they held
hands for the one prayer Ben spoke aloud each year, they had seemed
connected by live wire. It wasn't about sex, at least not sex alone. It
was the pure rightness of possibility. Their fingers stayed twined after
the amen. There was nothing like that between him and Veronica.
The wire that linked them was down, and down was worse than dis-
connected. Touch it wrong and you'd fry.

Veronica helped herself to a last bite of chicken. She pinched it
right off the platter like she would've at home.

"What are we going to do?" he asked.

"You and me?"

"Yeah." The bulk of his life lay with this woman. Nothing would
ever tip that balance.

"Oh, I don't know." She sounded casual and exasperated both,
like she was standing before the mirror in their bedroom, debat-
ing between two blouses. "I should probably let the house go. Buy
something manageable."

"You could come down here. I've got a neighbor looking to
relocate."

"So I hear." Veronica stood, cleared her plate, and looked out on
the twilit cul-de-sac.

"It's not the stupidest idea ever. Just because it turns out we
can't live together doesn't mean we can't—"

"Golf."

"Sure. Or play tennis."

"Do yoga."

"It'd make things easier on Stephen, for holiday visits. And we'd be right there for each other in case—"

"It sounds like a sitcom. The ex next door."

"Always popping round to borrow a cup of sugar." That sounded more licentious than he'd intended.

"I could take up bridge." She turned back from the window, her expression brimming with fun. "Chaperone you and Sadie."

"She's a good neighbor."

"I'm sure she is."

He pushed his chair back and went to stand beside her, swept up in the lovely improbability. "The Rosko place is priced to move. You'd get it for a song."

"Bad bargain," said Veronica, pointing. Her finger tapped the glass. "Looks like your woman's Lily never got the message. See? Smoke."

ANY FUTURE
SELF-SORTING

THEY BOUGHT GLITTERY PINWHEELS.

Gnarled little gnomes.

Even some actual pink flamingos.

TP-ing the Hacienda Central was the best terrible idea Lily could come up with at short notice. Gran hadn't even asked what the initials stood for, just smiled and said they should invest in enough supplies to *really* piss off the Flamingo Police. She hadn't called it stupid and she hadn't called it juvenile, and in the absence of those adjectives Lily felt how true they were. They loaded the car. Gran had a good eye for spatial relations. She could have been an architect or a Tetris grand master. The garage was much too hot, like standing inside a horrible mouth. Gran pointed to the boxes on a low shelf, labeled with Grandpa's deliberate hand: *xmas, vtines, hween, mischols.* "We should use those."

"Gran. You'll want them later."

Gran lifted *hween*, turning it so Lily could see the seam of unbroken packing tape. "We haven't opened them since the move." Her voice went singsong. "Blame the HOA."

I'll want them, Lily thought. But what was she going to do? Be that creepy girl at Wesleyan/Brown/Oberlin/Smith with a plastic leprechaun and full-scale scarecrow in her dorm?

"I live here now, Lily," Gran said. She raised the box higher and Lily could see the definition of her biceps. "I'm building a life."

Maybe if she were supremely confident, Lily could make the scarecrow her big ironic thing.

"I'm never going to use them," Gran said.

"You might move. Somewhere else. You never know."

"Even so. Gary had fun with it. On my own . . ." She gave a hapless shrug. There it was. The quick, treacherous bite of guilt. When Gran and Grandpa said they were moving away, Lily had been sad, of course. But she'd also been in middle school. There'd been an undeniable bloom of relief. No one at Day would ever find out she was affiliated with the big old house in Ladue that got dorked out for every holiday. Gran said, "It wouldn't ever be the same. It's foolish to pretend." So Lily shunted the box to the car. Gran said to rotate it. Ease it into the slot behind the passenger seat. There. Look at all the space saved.

They waited till dark and they waited for the festival to close. Nights got chilly, so Gran channeled her inner responsible adult long enough to insist on long sleeves. She grabbed a cashmere cardigan, black, with a sheer appliqué of gray umbrellas. "I guess I look like a widow after all."

"You look like a ninja." Lily gave a fake karate chop. Gran reminded her to buckle up and they backed down the drive. The pervet and *Die Exfrau* were visible through lit windows.

"I still think she has duck neck," Lily said.

Gran gave her a look. She could've said something, too, something pat and knowing and *uber*Gran. Instead she picked up speed. Lily was glad. Their night would tumble down on itself if Gran returned to wisewoman mode. The lights of other houses slipped by. They came to The Commons' palm-flanked entrance. Gran parked and fed a fat fistful of quarters to the meter, never mind that they were gearing up for some amateur vandalism. Only Gran.

They began with the flamingos, which were banded neck to neck. One pair wouldn't separate so Lily arranged them like they were fully fornicating. Gran unloaded the holiday boxes. She lined them up in calendar order and opened them one by one. Their corrugated scent overpowered the cut grass, briefly, then was gone. Lily realized that they'd forgotten the toilet paper, which completely cracked up Gran. She uncoiled the string of Chinese lanterns her grandparents always used for New Year's, wound it around the waist of a schoolmarmish Easter bunny, then threaded it slalom-style through the knee-high ranks of a gingerbread army. Gran balanced a Speedo-clad gnome at the fountain's edge as if ready to dive, then lifted a chubby cupid. Lily tugged at the antlers of a wire reindeer. There was bunting to unfurl, a caroling family of snowmen to pose, a squat brigade of pumpkins, and a scarecrow waiting in the back-seat. Gran said to hurry. They didn't want to be caught.

Lily stacked the pumpkins totem style.

Gran tucked a pinwheel behind the scarecrow's ear. The breeze picked up and it spun. She threw her head back. "Look. Stars."

"Yeah."

"Sit a minute. We're almost done."

Lily sat.

Gran flopped on the grass beside her. "This was ridiculous. Thank you."

Gran didn't look any older, lying there starlit, but even so, Lily swallowed panic: Gran would die someday, and what if it happened before Lily got a chance to sort herself out? "You're welcome," she said.

"What is it?" Clearly, Gran could tell she was thinking *something*. Step one of any future self-sorting: acquire poker face. "Conscience got you?"

"No conscience. I'm a delinquent, remember?"

"A terrible influence on young and old alike."

"They'll send me off to Aunt Manda's next."

"Nah. I think I'll keep you."

The cool night went vivid with the hope of it. She'd stay here. She'd never have to face down Sierra or the drama-minions she was bound to be recruiting. She'd never have to see Rocky or Jennifer Vogler again. "You'd have to move," she said, thinking of Ty. She wondered if Mom and Dad had put down a deposit for her next year at Day.

Gran rolled over on her stomach, ankles crossed. Sierra's standard posture for studying, but Sierra'd never studied Lily with any kind of intensity. "Lily—" Sierra's voice had never been so tentative and kind.

Of course. Lily wouldn't be staying on. Gran was joking. Lily made her smile expansive. "Too bad I've already knocked off the summer reading." An outright lie. The paperbacks lay, spines unbroken, in the inner pocket of her suitcase. *Daisy Miller. The Things They Carried.* In Addition AP Students Should Come to Class Prepared to Report on a Title That Pertains to Our Theme of Americans Abroad.

Gran flopped down again and that smarted. Just because Lily wasn't a source of constant joy didn't mean she had to go limp with relief that she wasn't expected to keep her. Still. It was Gran's paper reverse-iversary. Give the woman a pass. "You like it here," Lily said.

"I do."

"I'll tell Dad. Aunt Manda, too, I guess. Because they worry."

"Good. Tell them. I'm happy. Or mostly happy. Or I'm going to be." Gran plucked a blade of grass and drew it to her lips. She blew and a bleating whistle carried.

"Shhh! Gran! They'll hear us."

Gran giggled.

"I won't tell them about Ben. When I'm home. Not if you don't want me to."

"It's not—well, it's not anything, and it's not a secret. And if it were it'd be a hell of a thing to ask you to keep."

"I would."

"A hell of a thing. No."

"He's nicer than he seems. Isn't he?" He'd have to be. Gran's feet pointed, then flexed.

"Sorry. That was rude."

"I'm thinking. I'm trying to see how he'd seem if you didn't know him."

"He doesn't—it's not my business—"

"Motorboat."

"Huh?"

"Motorboat. Remember? Your grandpa used to say that when he knew a 'but' was coming. But, but, but." She made the words sound like a motor sputtering to life.

"Sorry."

"No. It was rude of me to interrupt."

"I was going to say, he doesn't seem very much like Grandpa." Grandpa, who she never once heard say that motorboat thing, probably because he knew what the Rocky-boys meant when *they* said it.

"I don't know. Maybe. Ben's a whole person already. I'd known Gary for years by the time we were your age." She paused. "We grew up together. It'd be greedy to think we'd grow old together, too." She propped herself up on her elbows. "What a self-indulgent, sentimental thing to say."

They'd *made* each other. Grandpa and Gran. From the shapeless putty of childhood. Everything Lily thought was an infantile variation of it's not fair.

"I was twelve when I met him. Ice skating with my girlfriend. Joyce Maddox. Her parents gave us those silver napkin rings for our wedding. You used them for pirate treasure, remember?"

Lily didn't, but in a moment like this you couldn't say you mean another cousin, Gran.

"He stole Joyce's hat. Glided on over and took it. He could *skate*. I went after him. Joyce was the clumsiest thing." Gran stood and surveyed their work, the baffled scarecrow, the jumble of holidays, the pinwheels, the garish plastic flock. She swayed to and fro, pumping her arms like a skater. "The thing is, I don't remember it. It's a story they told. Gary. Joyce. My whole life changed in a moment that I didn't get to keep. By the time I knew Gary *mattered* he was already a—I don't know—a fixture. I wish I'd known he was going to be *Gary*. It would've been nice to pay attention." Her arms froze midswing at the distant sound of a car door slamming. Lily stood, prepared to vacate the scene of their crime. No one came, and Gran said, quieter now, "I like Ben. I like Ben a lot, but there are days I'd trade away knowing him to remember the color of that hat."

"Maybe Joyce would know." Sierras of the universe, take note: Neglect thou not thy best friend. You never know when she's been paying attention.

"Joyce Maddox." Gran shook her head. "For the longest time I thought it was her Gary was after. Maybe because it was *her* hat."

"My best friend's completely paranoid now that she has a boyfriend." Best friend. It just came out that way. Something for Lily to work on.

"Paranoid how?" asked Gran.

"Paranoid sneaky. Paranoid mean. She'll do anything to keep him." Lily blushed, hearing her words bridge the generations, knowing Gran probably thought she meant sex. "Not—well, anyway, I think it's stupid."

"Maybe," said Gran, but there was nostalgia in that *maybe*. "For the longest time I had this mania about skating. As if I'd somehow *won* him by skating fast. I practiced all winter, all my free time, like that would mean I could keep him; I don't know what I was thinking. I got *good*, too. If I hadn't predated Title Nine . . ." She gave a sneakered approximation of a skater tensed for the starting gun.

"But that was Grandpa." Rocky wasn't worth a lap around a roller rink.

"But I didn't *know* that. It's life. You don't get sneak previews."

"Sierra used me to humiliate this other girl. With my blog. You know. Because she thought maybe Rocky liked her instead. And now I'm the one everybody's mad at." It sounded so petty in the face of what Gran was trying to say.

"Maybe you should talk to her."

Points for trying, sure, but that was guidance counselor advice. Lily thought of Joyce Maddox, wobbly at the ankles and hating Gran a little as she sped away silver on her blades. "*Sierra's* the one who dropped *me*. The second he showed interest. And the guy's a doofbutt."

"That sounds like a kind of bird. The greater crested doofbutt."

"Gran. Please. The *lesser* crested doofbutt."

"Probably her loss then."

"Probably?"

"Like I said. There's no sneak peeks."

As if Rocky would be Sierra's *Gary.* "Your friend. Joyce. What happened to her?" Lily crossed her cheeseball fingers. Let Joyce have gone to Ghana with the Peace Corps. Let her have been instrumental in establishing Australia as a major wine exporter or shortlisted for one of the lesser known Nobels.

"I don't think I've heard a word about her since the napkin rings. People drift." Gran made it sound as inexorable as the tides, governed by something cold and distant as the moon. She made it sound like no big deal. And maybe that was better than any cheese-abiding thing her grandmother could have said. Whatever dogs—puppies really; they went to a progressive prep school in the year 2010—of war Sierra let cry, someday she would be someone whose hats Lily no longer remembered. Her hand shot out for her grandmother's and the older woman's palm was dry against her own.

The next morning, the semester's grades would post to the website of the Forest Park Day School. Lily's cumulative GPA would rise a decimal or so. Mom and Dad would phone their congratulations and fix the date, three weeks distant, for her return to St. Louis. She'd pack her bags. Autumn would come, another school year would pass, and then another summer. Senior year and she'd be itching to step into the October blue of a college view book, where the trees wove a red-gold brocade and the students all looked like they'd been ordered from a catalogue.

She would sit with her application packet—early decision to Smith, huge cliché, sure, but one she hugely wanted. *Evaluate a significant experience, achievement, risk you have taken, or ethical dilemma you have faced and its impact on you.*

No duh she should choose *Lipstick* or Mona. How I Built and Lost My Blog but Learned Valuable Lessons about Being a Better Person. How I Wanted to Help but Got in My Own Damn Way. Both subjects cast her just right. Accomplished, then humbled, left eager for the tools that would help her go forth and do righteous things. But instead she'd fix upon this moment. The cool, cultivated scent of green. The bright plastic riot of flamingos. The eclectic array of her grandfather's collection and the childish dream of all the holidays come at once. Fastidious Gran producing Kleenex to wipe the work from their hands and how, for an instant, the world had the unwavering grace of an equation.

SAFE AS HOUSES

BEN SHOT OUT INTO THE street; there was smoke, most definitely. The bite of it in the air. How much was hard to say in the gathering dark. Veronica followed, calling his name. From inside the Rosko house, a shriek pitched higher than sirens. Some other neighbor had the stereo on, something plaintive involving dulcimers. Another shrill from Mona's courtyard. The sky turned glancing bright, and then dim again. Ben's eyes smarted. His lungs gummed up with all the smoke he'd ever breathed. Childhood bonfires. Out camping with kids of his own. Warming his hands in squats out looking for Tara. They had cast strange light, those fires, and the smell stayed with you. Needful smoke. There was something of that in the air tonight.

Bile rose. His throat clenched too tight to release it.

He'd been beaten in late summer. His bruises yellowed with the leaves. In Hyde Park no fires had yet been lit. The scents, until the blood and the wet leaked out of him, had been remarkably clean. Even so, the air now brought it back. Everything inside him coiled for another cascade of blows, but he was on the Rosko steps now, sprinting up to the door. If he didn't run to, he'd run from and he wouldn't be able to stop. His blood knew this, his marrow and breath.

The house was not illuminated. Ben called in to his neighbor.

Veronica, huffing, called him back from the street.

It was a still night, that quick desert cool he still hadn't gotten used to. Mona's front door was open, welcoming the air. A latched screen door kept the gnats away. The smoke smell was stronger now, the interior of her home dim, and Ben could feel the air thicken around him. No response when he called their names. No help for it then; he put his foot through the screen. The mesh peeled away like the skin of a blister and he ducked inside, pulling his shirt collar over his nose and mouth.

A light switched on. Ben threw an instinctive arm up to shield his eyes. From fist or flame he honestly couldn't have said.

"What the hell?" Mona Rosko stood beside the light switch. She wore a yellow robe. Her legs beneath it were solid and bare. She held a cut glass vase aloft as if to parody the Statue of Liberty. A bang carried in from the courtyard and footsteps ran pell-mell down the hall. The child appeared. He wrapped his arms around Mona's waist and peeked out from behind her hips.

"I smelled smoke," Ben said. The words came out choked, like he'd been breathing it in by the lungful. He smoothed his shirt. He must look like a bandit from some old Western film.

"Oh, for Pete's sake." Mona lowered the vase and drew the edges of her robe together.

"I'm sorry." Where there's smoke, there's fire, or so the adage went. He was sixty-eight though. Entirely too old set his life by such things.

"My husband will pay for your door." Veronica peered at them through the battered screen. Her fingers wriggled in a cheery wave. Two thoughts twisted into one. She shouldn't have followed him here. She shouldn't be saying husband. Good Lord was he ever tired.

"Get out. Get." Mona hefted the vase again, her free hand gathering terrycloth across her chest. The raised arm cast a shadow on her grandson's face. "This is still my home. I've still got my thirty days."

"I smelled smoke," he said again. He backed away, hands up, absurdly, as if in formal surrender.

"So call the Flamingo Police."

Sadie called them that. He'd thought she was the only one.

"I said get. And you'd best wipe away that smirk."

"It's a good turn of phrase, that's all. Flamingo Police." As for the smirk, it was the natural shape of his smile. Fond. Sadie would know that. Veronica did, too, but she did not come to his defense.

"Get out."

"We really are very sorry," Veronica said. She stood outside the useless door. He'd only really wrecked the bottom bit. The top part hung intact, pixelating her face.

"This is Veronica. My ex."

"Fantastic," said Mona. "It's lovely to meet you."

"Ben," said Veronica. "Let's go."

"Okay, okay." He retreated. On an entry table, Mona had placed a lacquered bowl for change and keys. One of her lamps looked like one his mother had owned. They'd been neighbors for more than two years. They'd never been inside each other's homes. Veronica held the door open. The burning smell hung heavy all around. "There really was smoke. I'm only trying to be neighborly. Don't you smell that?"

"I swear to God, when I get back on my feet my next neighbors are going to be ten miles away in all directions. I got an offer on this elephant. So, fireworks. Had to use them up anyhow. Ty and I'll be long gone by the Fourth."

"An offer? That's wonderful."

"Cash on the barrel. Not much of it, mind. And he wants us out ASAP. Nevertheless." Mona shrugged and the robe gapped a bit. You could tell she was a woman given to emphatic gesture. The vase in her hand bobbed about like a conductor's baton. Down the hall, Ben could make out the sturdy brown of boxes. In the living room, the built-ins were mostly bare. And the lacquered bowl was empty. He'd only guessed at the keys, the change, the everyday artifacts that belonged there. He closed the screen gently, like gentleness still mattered. Now it was Mona Rosko who seemed televised, an amalgamation of colored points. "I worried," he said. "Veronica saw it across the way. It's a fair bit of smoke."

"So call the fire department. I've got every other kind of do-gooder waltzing through. Social workers and all these neighbors who up and decide to bring food."

The boy said, "Miss Annie let me use her markers."

You could tell Miss Annie was the social worker from the barbed thing Mona did with her mouth. "This, though. This is beyond." She kicked a bare foot at the battered screen. "I should call the cops."

Tyson's eyes saucered. "Are they going to jail?"

"You people," said Mona.

"Come on out and I'll show you. The scent really carries."

"I should've brained you with this thing."

Veronica said, "I'm sorry. I don't know what he was thinking."

"You're the one who mentioned burning the place. You're the one who put the thought there."

Tyson asked if the police were really coming. Mona's grip on the vase tightened. She kicked furiously at the broken door. Her robe fell open. Beneath it she wore drawstring shorts and a T-shirt with the faded logo of a hardware store. "That girl's a real piece of work. Lily. Telling a child like that. She's not right. A girl like that, who knows what she'd do? I was up all night thinking she'd burn us out."

Tyson said, "My mom is in prison. That's the same as jail."

"That's private, Ty. We talked about that."

Ben said, "If *you* thought a fire was possible, you can see how *I*—"

"I should've called nine-one-one the instant I saw you. Look. I'm setting off firecrackers and burning some old *Bon Appétites*. If I let you check, will you go away?" She held the door wide. The raw edge of the screen snagged on the carpet. "Come right on in. Take a picture. Turn it over to Sadie. That'll get the word out."

"The Sadie who lives there?" Veronica pointed at the wrong house, but Mona nodded.

"Neighborhood busybody. And that granddaughter—well, like they say. Every pot has its lid."

"I'm sorry," Ben asked, "you're burning *Bon Appétite?*" Veronica had a subscription, too. Every month, she clipped recipes and tucked them away in the binder that she'd organized by course. Ben estimated maybe five percent of those recipes had ever been attempted.

"We're not going to have a whole lot of space. And maybe *you* haven't noticed, but they gouge you on trash services."

Fifty bucks a month and they separated the recycling for you. It hadn't seemed unreasonable. He didn't remember anymore what the cost had been in Portland.

"I told Ben he'd get screwed buying here," his ex-wife said.

Mona agreed. "And how."

Somehow, allegiances were shifting. He'd always been a bit dense when it came to the social stuff but Ben was pretty sure he got it this time around: Veronica liked that crack Mona made about Sadie. Tyson asked if he could please do another sparkler.

"In a minute. Once our guests leave. How about you pick one out and wait?" The boy trotted off. Nothing about Mona changed, but the sum of her seemed harsher without the child to counterbalance. She set down the vase and wheeled on Ben. "I don't let him play with matches. I supervise. Be sure to tell Sadie that. Her granddaughter, too. I look after my grandson. Safe as"—she paused and Ben could see how the phrase got caught in her throat. Safe as houses. The older you got, the less apt those old sayings were. "I *do* for him," Mona said. "I never stop doing."

"He's a lovely child," said Veronica.

"There's a lot of his mother in him."

Veronica smiled like she knew the mother in question. "Little boys." She shook her head. "They're almost prettier than little girls because you know in a few years they'll be these galumphing creatures. With girls, there's a chance they'll hang on to some of that—" she stopped.

"Delicacy," Mona Rosko offered. The same word had been on Ben's lips. He was thinking of Veronica though, not Tara. And of Mona, too, unexpectedly. The play of lamplight on skin no longer young.

"That's it," said Veronica. "Delicacy."

"My Carrie—she looked young when I visited, not hard like I'd thought she'd be. They don't allow makeup."

Prison. Rand Danovic routinely checked records for *Thales, Tara R.* in correctional facilities across the fifty states. Ben wondered how it would feel to learn she was actually in one. He asked Mona, "When does Carrie get home?"

An assessing stare. "Out. Most people say out."

"Sorry. Out. When does she—"

"Ty'll be in grade school."

"What—" Veronica started to ask.

"I don't talk about that." Mona drew the robe back around her. "Good night."

"Grade, I was going to ask. In school? I wouldn't ask the other."

"Third, maybe second. With funding cuts and good behavior— it's more fluid than you'd think." She shot a dark look toward Sadie's windows. "Carrie didn't want Ty to know. That delicacy you mentioned? That's where it is. That's how I see my girl's still my girl."

"Our daughter ran off when she was sixteen years old," said Veronica. "No sign of her since. Vanished." Hearing it like that made him think of those nutjobs going on about Roswell. Tara on some violet planet, lit by a dozen glowing moons, tracking the complicated tides.

"Huh. At least I know where Carrie is."

"She was a junkie." The unstinting ugliness of the word shocked him every time and Veronica knew it. She used it even so. And she was right, they had to face facts, he got that much, but still, that word. Its emphasis on junk. The child they'd made reduced to litter.

"Carrie's been going to meetings inside, and her cellmate—
Cellmate. I can't believe that's even a part of my vocabulary."

The women shared a bitter laugh.

For all her graces, Ben knew that Sadie would never be able to
have this conversation.

And he knew this, too: There was a rich vein of weakness in
him. That Sadie couldn't have this conversation was one of the reasons he liked her.

"Where are you heading?" he asked, if only for the sake of
changing the subject.

"My husband's sister's kid did up her basement as an apartment.
Up in Eloy?"

Ronnie nodded like she knew the geography.

"She's putting us up till I find—who am I kidding? She's putting
us up for the foreseeable. Half what she'd normally ask for rent. She
was always a twit." The insult sounded graceful and extraordinary,
like something keen and lithe slinking through the trees.

"Nice of her."

Ronnie glowered. As if he hadn't realized how sickeningly
pious that sounded.

"I'm losing my home." Mona Rosko's tone was frank. "Gary
loved this place. He'd worked hard all his life. He wanted to *play*.
I'm glad he never saw—" For a confused moment, Ben thought the
woman meant Sadie's Gary. The two dead husbands must have had
the same first name. He wanted to tell Mona. Look. Everyone in the
universe has some slight thing in common.

Veronica said, "I'm sorry."

Mona's arm twitched like she was considering a handshake.
"You aren't one of those women who never does sweets, are you?
All the guilty neighbors have been baking. Going to rot that kid's
teeth and leave me with the dentist bills. More pie than I'll eat in my
life. Let me get you one."

She retreated. The torn screen hung limp. Veronica nudged it with her foot. "I hope she overcharges you for that. You're a disaster."

"What?"

"We were fine at the house. Comfortable, talking, and then you run off to—Jesus Christ." Veronica bent and fingered the broken place.

"You're the one who called smoke."

"It was a joke. A little puff, a little joke, and you ran off screaming. That's not normal."

"I wasn't screaming."

"Here." Mona was back, extending a tin topped with a sudsy billow. "I think it's lemon under there. You mind? Citrus makes Ty blotchy."

"Lemon's great," Veronica said. "Thanks."

From the courtyard Tyson whined for his grandmother to hurry up. Mona looked the two of them over. She sniffed. The smell of smoke was everywhere. "You don't have to share with him," she said, and she closed and locked the door.

Veronica shook her head.

A high shrill sounded, and then a percussive crackle. Tyson with a firecracker.

Ben said, "Credit where credit's due. I hardly know the woman and I was willing to run into a burning—"

"You actually thought it was burning. Firecrackers, Ben. It breaks my heart."

An eruption of sparks. The timbre of the boy's laugh. Buyer wants us out ASAP, Mona had said. It was possible he'd never see her again.

"Are you this afraid all the time?" Ronnie asked.

"I wasn't. I'm not."

"Ben."

"I'm fine. This week—it's been a weird one."

"But there's no telling when it's going to be weird. You could have fifty-two weird ones in a row."

Not here, he almost said, and he saw it like Veronica would. The daily perimeter walk. The easy pattern of sport and sociability. She'd have another name for all this peace and she would not be entirely wrong. Instead, he said, "Weird can be good."

"Not for you. You look wrecked."

"Okay. Yes. Maybe weird throws me more than it should."

"You think?" Another round of ricocheting light. He made sure not to flinch at the pops. Veronica studied him. "There's tense and then there's—"

"Point taken, Ronnie."

"If there's really a fire, you don't run into it. You call the—" She paused. "And of course you don't have your phone. You're a mess."

"I'll get it tomorrow. My phone."

"That was blind panic back there. It wasn't pretty."

"Look. What time's your flight?"

"It's a problem, Ben. It's not going away because you offload me. You can't possibly—"

"What time?"

"Eleven. Ish."

"Okay. So I need to stop by the hospital and get my phone anyhow. You come with me, you see me make an appointment to talk to someone, you go home happy."

She had something to say. Ronnie always had something to say. She worked the words over in her mouth like a cherry pit.

"I'll go," he said. "Scout's honor. I'll go for a run of—let's say—four appointments."

"Eight."

"Ronnie."

"Can't help it."

"Four. But I'll have them take my picture. Right in the guy's office. With the day's *Times*, like a hostage."

"Now you're making fun."

"A little. But if it helps you feel better." At his age you had to be able to look at yourself unflinchingly. And with *that* eye he could see that he was past due for some help. He'd been getting by, yeah. He'd had a lovely, predictable idyll. Golf twice a week, tennis twice a week, a daily long-distance brain twister. It was nice. It was safe. It was passing time though, not living.

Veronica said, "It's not my place to feel better."

"Come off it. Will it help?"

"Yeah. It would."

"One condition."

"Shoot."

He made a swipe at the tottering meringue. She shrieked; the sound carried and then was matched by another Rosko firecracker. He lunged. She dodged. He knew what it must look like. *Pie.* He knew the connotations. Veronica was jogging now, the tin held awkwardly before her. The air in the street was acrid, and Ben drew in a deep breath of smoke. Veronica turned and walked toward him. He inhaled once more and remembered how his lungs had burned during her last month at business school. They'd bought a case of cigars because she was going to learn to like them, damn it. The men all did, those titans in their hushed, upholstered rooms. She was going to join them, breathe it all in till the world was hers. How he loved her then, how he loved her still. But the look she gave him. You never looked that way at a husband. It was an expression he'd seen before, soft, lit with pride, tempered with a startling bloom of sorrow. She'd worn it as their children, backs slim and squared, rode away from them for the first time, wobbly on their bikes.

STATES TO THE NORTH

ALISON BROUGHT THEIR FLATTENED MOVING boxes in from storage and the lunch-bag smell of cardboard filled the condo. She said she'd skip her morning run, restoring box after box to its original shape. The condo wasn't spacious; the efficient thing would be to fill one box at a time as needed. But Ali had it right. Nearly twenty stood empty at the ready by the time Seth headed out to tender his resignation. The sight hit him, giddy in the chest.

They were on their way.

The grounds were a mess, the too-earnest façade of the Hacienda Central presiding over the drunken remnants of a Hallmark convention. A wire Christmas deer lay on its side, as if the adjacent cupid had brought it down. A peevish plastic leprechaun had lassoed an Easter bunny with a string of colored lights. A turkey, its plumage thicker and more vibrant than anything actually farmed for meat, sat atop a foppish scarecrow, and a flock of fake flamingos stood interspersed. Seth took it in a minute, then went to track down Lobel.

It didn't take long. The holiday junk was still *in situ* when he left the Hacienda. He phoned Ali. "Done," he said. "Two weeks' notice."

"Wow. Terrifying."

"Yeah."

A groundskeeper began to clear away the chaos. He hoisted the cupid under one arm and Seth realized: The whole setup was so bizarre that the statue hadn't even registered as a baby.

"Was Lobel surprised?" Ali asked. "He couldn't have been."

Odd. For all their troubles, Seth must have seemed, during their tenure here, the sort of man who made the love of his wife his life's rudder. He'd taken a swing—a physical swing—at a septuagenarian who'd looked at her funny. He'd allowed himself to curdle professionally. He felt buoyant. It was no small thing to be thought of as such a man. "You know Hoagie," he said. "He took it like a cowboy. And get this: He's going to give us both references."

"No."

"Hand to God."

"Huh. You really did have something on him."

"I reminded him of what he said. Remember? When we interviewed? He wanted history where there's really none." The way he'd phrased it in Lobel's office was *Alison was giving you what you wanted and she's not the only one on the books with a slippery grip on the truth. Your IT guys take care of that Rosko glitch?* Seth had been glad to be sitting when he said it. He felt like he was reading lines from a play. Lobel seemed more amused than intimidated, but he went along with it, and Seth had felt an unanticipated fondness for the CEO.

Alison laughed. Actually laughed. "He *did* say that. You remember everything, don't you?"

"I've got an ear for it. Things like the periodic table though . . ."

"Well, who needs the elements?"

"They only make the whole world."

Seth watched the groundskeeper go for the leprechaun. He tugged but the thing held fast. He set the cupid down and used both arms. The leprechaun wiggled and came free, thin metal stakes coming up with it from the ground. The groundskeeper hauled it toward the edge of the grass, where a pickup waited, The Commons' logo on its door. He'd have to make upward of a dozen trips, though he'd be done in minutes if he were allowed to park closer. But this was The Commons. The grass, if nothing else, was sacrosanct.

Seth would be jobless in two weeks. He was thirty-two, a husband, and a father of sorts. He began to gather up flamingos; he needed to move, needed to be anywhere but back at his desk. The groundskeeper gave him a funny look but did not interfere. They worked quickly and the truck filled. When the lawn was clear, the other man extended a hand as if to shake, then seemed to change his mind. He gave the pickup an assertive thump and swung up into the driver's seat. The truck pulled away and Seth wished he'd thought to snap a picture of all those crazy lawn ornaments for Alison. That or snagged a pair of flamingos to bring home like a triumphant hunter, dangling fat birds by their feet.

He and Ali would travel on. They'd be a pair of blue dots in another red state. Arizona would make the news in the coming years. The Colliers' inboxes would fill with outrage and grassroots requests for monetary support. Arizona's definition of marriage. Arizona's definition of life. Arizona's vigilantes and Arizona's anti-immigration measures. They'd make PayPal donations—small ones; after all, they had quit two jobs each in the space of one year—and sign petitions online. They would track, in horror, the breaking news of gunfire in a grocery store parking lot. And Seth would think that it only went to show how crazy they both had been. Half a year in the Grand Canyon State and an oddball display of holiday decor was the nuttiest thing he'd allowed himself to see.

Veronica spent the morning on the phone with friends and friends of friends, gathering recommendations and securing him an appointment. Next Wednesday, two P.M. The doctor was called Jordan Cable and Ben didn't know if he should expect a man or a woman. Veronica had him swear up and down that if he didn't click with Dr. Cable, he would get a referral for someone else. She found an old Bible and made him raise his right hand. That was, they both knew, pushing things a bit too far, but that was how things stood now. There was a new kind of space between them, a space best filled in with bold strokes.

Ben drove Veronica to the airport. His ex inched the passenger seat forward, her knees folding up like a mantis'. He'd forgotten the way she got jittery with too much space before the dash. The radio saved them from more conversation. Callers argued about a blown call at some baseball game last night. Veronica yawned.

"Sleepy?"

"Under-caffeinated."

"We could probably track down a Starbucks." He gestured at the GPS.

Veronica scrunched her mouth in playful distaste.

"Next time call ahead. We'll find the most potent sludge from here to Nogales."

"Or you can teach me to use that crazy machine of yours."

They were probably both wondering if there ever would ever *be* a next time. He said, "We'll track down that *Gone with the Wind* dirt too." If she never came, he'd find it himself and send some her way. She could swap it for the sand in her Zen desk garden, comb it with a miniature rake whenever her mind needed quieting. They arrived at the airport. He pulled up to the curb and helped Veronica with her bag. His ex disappeared through the revolving door. Ben thought, as he suspected everyone did now at airports, of the towers and the day they fell. He really was getting old. Old and pickled and ungenerous. Three thousand people died in those attacks and here he was, grateful that he could just go home, that security measures spared him the departure gate question of whether to accompany Veronica in.

From five states to the North an official proclamation came: *I, Jennifer M. Granholm, Governor of the State of Michigan, do hereby declare Armando Galarraga to have pitched a perfect game.* Ali's voice filled the condo that had never seemed properly full before. She was on the phone with one of her brothers, squabbling full tilt. No, Alison was saying, Galarraga should under no circumstances make the record books. Nope, not even with an asterisk. "No. I don't *care* what they do in hockey. Instant replay's for wimps." The condo was a whirl of to-do lists. She had drawn a neat, open square beside each task to be ticked off in the days to come. He kissed the knob at the base of her neck. She said, "C'mon, Ryan. Would you feed that line to the guys you coach?" Pause. Her brother's reply was unintelligible from where Seth stood. "Please," Ali said. "The emperor of Chihuahua can proclaim that I'm a parking meter, but that doesn't make it true. No—No—Listen, Seth's here, I've got to go, thanks." This last ran together almost as a single word. She hung up. She told him that she'd had the exact same fight with her brother Neil and again with her brother Brendan. She told him she considered him proof that not all males were gibbering idiots, but that he'd better not think of taking their side. She said that Ryan thought they were nuts to up and leave without a plan but had offered to store some of their stuff in his basement while they found their footing wherever it was they were going to find their footing. They could ship a bunch of boxes media rate. They could Craigslist their heavy furniture. Maybe swap for some quality camping gear.

Then Ali broke out maps, stacks of them, annotated all over. They had nowhere to be and so could travel slowly; make a big-time road trip of it: Santa Fe, the O'Keeffe museum, the Grand Canyon, Arches, a Shakespeare festival in southern Utah. She'd written that paper on Shylock—remember?—but had never seen *Merchant* performed. They could hike the Narrows and Angels Landing, see the Tetons and Old Faithful, maybe do some rafting on the Snake. Come August, they could meet up with her brother in Helena. He'd be going up against the AAA Brewers. They'd score tickets on the first-base line.

And so they packed. Seth started with the books. When they first moved in together, marrying his library to Alison's had felt like a bigger commitment than picking out a ring could ever be. He checked an empty box for damp and slotted the first book in. Alcott, Louisa May. He worked along the alphabetized shelf. Unless Ali made a big thing of it, he'd jettison the volumes under the sink. She was all zeal and sudden energy; they both were. He wanted to ride that, indefinitely, and the sink books would say it was not to be trusted. The box was full by Bambara, Toni Cade. He tore a strip of packing tape and without warning was lit with a feeling so pure he couldn't say where it had originated. Despite it all, they were young. They were American. They wouldn't really be in trouble till they ran out of West.

Five A.M. Two hours till Lily's ridiculous crack-of-dawn flight home. *Home.* The word was a glutinous mass in her stomach. School started up in another month. Sierra'd had a whole summer courting people to her side; Lily would have to be strategic. Forest Park Day had a tradition: Upperclassmen never wore uniforms on their first day, and she was a junior now. People would be watching. *Lipstick*'s ex-chickadees. Headmistress Brecken. Sierra. Jennifer Vogler, in all probability. She had bitched about the uniforms for years but now she got them. She was still hard at work forming herself. It was patently unfair to expect a visual display of the person she meant to be. Maybe she would wear the uniform. Melt their collective minds, signal that Sierra was the interloper and *she* was the one who belonged. Lily could work the whole Cathy Coed thing. Saddle shoes. Knee socks. Yes.

She toweled off and pulled a striped sundress over her head. Cotton, because she was a paranoid little freaknugget. Organic fibers were best for air travel, the logic being that if the plane went down, synthetic ones would melt into your skin.

In the kitchen, Gran made toast. Lily's hair was still damp and her blow dryer was zipped away in her suitcase. She grabbed a rubber band from her carry-on. She worked her fingers through her hair and twisted it into a pony. She heard Gran say, "Huh. Here comes Benjamin."

Lily looked out the window. Benjamin Thales, sure enough.

Gran said, "I was teasing him about that giant espresso machine. He said he'd bring some round, start you home with a proper send-off. Good grief, at this hour."

Lily smoothed her ponytail and went to the door. She had been thinking about what to say the first time she ran into any of the zillion people who were ticked at her back home. It had to be polite because she didn't want to make things worse. It had to be savvier than social autopilot because what if she said something like *wow, nice to see you* when obviously it wasn't. She was pretty sure she had a line that worked, and here was Gran's would-be *whatever* to practice on. Lily opened the door. She said, "Mr. Thales, what a surprise."

He held out a trio of travel mugs. Even though it was dead early, Lily had managed lipstick and blush, eye shadow, liner, and a quick coat of mascara. She still felt impossibly bare. It was, of course, the ponytail. Her thing about ponies wasn't just that they were lazy. It was that they made it impossible to hide your flaws. Oval faces turned full-on equine; rounder ones chubbed out. Without tendrils to smooth its angles, Lily knew that her face looked sloped and sharp. Well. It was only the per-vet, and she was almost sixteen. About time she learned to carry herself exactly as she was. Besides, even a pony couldn't screw up her eyes. She had read once that they were the only part of you that stayed the same, their size and shape unchanged from the moment they opened to the day—distant, distant, please distant—they shut for good.

No one in The Commons noticed when the deed of ownership for 16 Daylily Crescent officially passed from M. Rosko to H. Lobel. County Records recorded it, as it had centuries of transactions and transitions, the land claim of Garner Chalk, the ordinary death of his ordinary wife. No one reported on it. The *Crier* had been reimagined as an e-calendar and weekly newsletter and the Rosko story had nothing approaching national legs. No one was left to ask Lobel: Nicky Tullbeck wasn't digging, not now that the course catalogue for Rice had arrived. And the Colliers were in a grocery store, stocking a cooler with beer; they would cross into Utah tomorrow, camp for a bit around Moab, and Utah was the land of 3.2 percent alcohol by volume. Still, it would have been nice to know. Did Lobel's checkbook open out of kindness? Paranoia? A circling of wagons, or a true belief in what he'd built? Maybe he'd use it in promotional materials. The Commons: so fan-damn-tastic even the founder bought in.

Picnic season, the worst of the heat finally waning: Ben packed the last of the donut peaches and the first of the Honeycrisp apples. Crackers remembered at the last minute and soft, herb studded, spreadable cheese. Sugar cookies sliced from a refrigerated tube and baked at three hundred fifty degrees for fifteen minutes. These, he'd rolled in a mixture of cinnamon and sugar before popping them in the oven. A domestic trick of Veronica's, her failsafe in case of last-minute bake sales, and he pondered the ethics of using it for an excursion with Sadie. It probably wasn't the thing to do, but his life was here now and he had to get on with that life.

Sadie stood at her door, watching him cross the street. He liked that he seldom had to knock. That would have brought back too much of his youth: Ben, as a boy, sauntering up the nervous walk in a shirt that his mother had ironed. No. This with Sadie was something different. For one thing, he did his own ironing now.

"Ready?" Sadie had on funny sunglasses, green and lilting up.

"Yup. I packed a knife and napkins, the whole shebang. Can't have you thinking I'm in this because I can't take care of myself."

"Oh, who the hell can take care of themselves?"

They took Sadie's car. She was one of those people who actually
enjoyed driving. They'd been meaning to have this picnic a long while,
but he'd had a hard time pinpointing exactly where they were supposed to go. He hadn't kept the damn *Crier* article, and it was harder
than he'd anticipated to track the directions down. Follow the belt route
to the northern edge of The Commons. You'll find a shallow box canyon. Park and hike in. In about half a mile, you'll find a stump. Back
when it was a tree, it marked the boundary of Garner Chalk's holdings.

They stopped. Sadie's sunglasses gave her an inadvertently
coquettish look. I'm out of practice as a flirt, she'd told him once. I
met Gary at twelve and never really learned how. I'm fond of you,
Ben, but not enough to learn at this late date. Ben liked that about
her, that study in contrasts, because she looked the part to string you
along. He spread the blanket on the ground. Pendleton wool, itchy
and from another life. The blanket unfolding was ripping and intimate and couldn't help but call to mind a bed. When they sat, they
kept their spines straighter than they otherwise might have.

Ben scooped up a handful of dust and let it run out between his
fingers. "The red earth of Tara," he said.

"I've never seen the movie all the way through," Sadie admitted. "I get snippets on TV now and again. Aside from the costumes,
I don't really get the fuss." She opened a bottle of water. He hadn't
remembered cups, so they took turns drinking. They caught each
other's eyes. The shared gaze was self-conscious, and how could
it help but be? They were old enough to know this was the sort of
scene they showed in movie previews or used to promote a new
brand of antibacterial soap. What a funny thing. The moment was
cheaper for that awareness, but sweeter, too.

If they'd been looking—and they weren't—they might have
noticed a slight disturbance of earth, a few paces south of the stump.
Or they mightn't have at all. It was subtle, a mound of fist-sized
sandstones leaning one against the other. But before Ben or Sadie
was born, before their parents were, or their parents before them,

that stump was a tree and its branches fanned out, casting its shadow a gracious cool. Garner Chalk had stood there, sweating, its shade the only possible place for the work at hand. He wiped filthy palms against his thighs, then fashioned a wood marker, binding its short planks tight with twine. Sandstones secured its base. The rocks were smaller than the rancher would've liked, but the ground was hard and dry and his strength largely spent from digging. The cross was decades gone now, but the rocks endured, and beneath them, in what weathered scraps of calico remained her, lay the bones of Adah Chalk and her unnamed son, cradled quiet in earth that in truth never dressed the set of *Gone with the Wind*.

It was dusk when the Colliers passed into Montana. Alison had her feet up on the dash and thumped a drumroll with bare heels. It was true what the license plates said. Big sky country. A thousand blues melded one into the next. Here were clouds, rolling in a thunderous herd. Here were fields burnished by the day's last light. Seth thought *here*. This might be a place for us, its dome big enough for the things we feel.

They found a motel off Highway 15, an off-brand, shingled barn of a place with a politically incorrect totem pole visible all the way from the off-ramp. The room was warm and when the AC kicked on Seth smelled dust. The sheets were clean though and the bed made up with hospital corners. They coupled on that bed, and Alison laughed at the creaking springs that would give them away to anyone who cared to listen. His hands tightened at her hips; she shifted beneath him, then stilled, eyes crinkling at the corners with every breath. In time, with luck and patience, those crinkles would deepen into lines and Seth would learn to love them.

But that would be then. For now he held his wife. For now the sweat began to bead. Together, they held the knowledge, tender and taught, utterly daunting. She'd tossed her last clamshell of pills with their final move-out trash run. The foil accordion of Trojans lay unopened in their suitcase. The thought of it was nearly enough to collapse him unspent. Shift his hips this way and it was one baby; if she bucked to meet him in the moment, they might spark another entirely. And then there was this: Perhaps you were only ever whole for an instant. That cellular moment of fusion: each nucleotide reaching out to find its counterpart, two single helixes spiraling into double. One cell, briefly, then mitosis. One into two, two into four, eight, sixteen. Ali moaned, flushed on her cheeks and on her chest. Amazing. Amazing that you could call life beautiful—and it was—when it was relentless separation upon separation upon separation.